Shadows Falling

Book II of The Lost Trilogy

By Melyssa Williams

Red Team Ink
DBA of Zealot Solutions, Idaho LLC
5447 Kendall St.
Boise, ID 83706
Copyright © 2016 by Red Team Ink

For permission requests or information about discounts for special bulk purchases please contact: redteamink@gmail.com. Substantial discounts on bulk orders are available to corporations, professional associations, and small businesses.

Printed in The United States of America

Library of Congress Control Number: 2017930052
ISBN: 978-0-9982349-9-1

Title: Shadows Falling
Description: First Edition

Prologue:

From the diary of Rose Gray

Death came to me in a cornflower blue dress.

Chapter 1

The diary came to me in 1931 after most of the patients at Bethlem Royal Hospital had been transferred. It had been tucked behind a crumbling bit of stone in one of the bedrooms, and there was nothing but the plain red ribbon bookmarker trailing out. The bookmark was like a saucy child's tongue stuck in the wall, teasing me. My supervisor, Miss Helmes, would be along shortly to berate me for dawdling, so I thumbed through it rather quickly. I saw entries made in pencil and scrawled in uneven, childlike handwriting. There were no dates to place the journal, although the papers inside the red binding were yellowed with age. I was nearly afraid to handle it, and only the name on front helped indicate who the author might be. I had never heard of the woman, Rose Gray. My curiosity of the diary could not be denied, as I have always been a woefully curious girl, and I quickly pocketed it in my apron.

Would that I had not.

The nurses say, and so does Luke, that it is good for my mind to journal my thoughts. They say to write pretty pieces of poetry and nursery stories as a good little girl ought to do. Plus, my mind seems to be going and they think this will help. They are foolish and speak of things they do not know. I hate the writing, and I have no interest in penning my memoir, yet the boredom in this place makes one do things they promised themselves not to. Take old Louis, who is belting out raunchy rhymes in a terribly bad operatic voice as he wanders the halls in his ship captain's tri-cornered hat. I certainly think if he paused to think in his saner days, he would have declared his loud belting to never be.

Ah, love and hate and sleep and tedium, they make us do the strangest things. Eventually, even the strange becomes mundane in this place.

And I suppose my life has been interesting enough. More interesting than most.

Just the first few lines she's penned draw me in like a moth to a flame. And like a moth, I feel like I may not know what I'm getting myself into.

Will I look back someday, years and years from now, and say, "Had I known then what I know now, I would have returned the diary to its place in the wall, or perhaps burned it?" Once opened, will it become a Pandora's box to a teenage nursing student with too much time on her hands and too much inquisitiveness to spare? I am being dramatic as usual.

The scrawling penmanship is at odds with the sophisticated wording, and I cannot keep myself from reading further about this strange woman. Why had she been at Bethlem Royal Hospital, more commonly known as Bedlam? I wondered. How long ago did she roam these halls? Was she among the patients transferred to the countryside during this very transition or had she been a patient here long, long ago?

My apron pocket holds Rose and her secrets for the time being as I clean, tidy, and collect necessities from the asylum. There are many things to distract me as I move from room to room, and as usual I move quickly not wanting to linger in these rooms of madness and death. Though I am extremely interested in the things of the medical world, insanity is not particularly an area in which I feel compelled to study further. Although I hate to admit such a curiosity, I possess the common and vulgar nosiness that we all feel in such subjects. I think the mad to be quite sad and sorrowful, but I do not entertain any lofty thoughts of rescuing them from their demons. That is beyond my capabilities as someone with knowledge of herbs, tinctures, and remedies with the occasional setting of a broken limb or the delivery of a babe. The brain is an area of which I have very little knowledge, and I am more engrossed in the rest of our physical parts.

Usually being at Bedlam is a direct order from a supervisor, as it is a low position that no one important in the medical world would stoop to. One that a mere girl my age, an orphan with an insatiable desire for medical education would jump at. My supervisor is something of a legend among my peers. Not that there are many peers in my field, mostly just men young and old. I will admit that I ensure to do whatever my supervisor asks of me. Quite frankly, this packing and moving is last on my list, and in my schoolgirl fantasies, my supervisor would ask me to be his personal assistant. Or perhaps he'd need my help in a difficult surgery, but sadly for me all he desires is my grunt work, which any errand boy of eleven could easily do. In fact, this hospital would run more smoothly had we more errand boys, which probably explains why I am treated as such.

So, I collect the instruments he needs for the relocation of Bedlam. There are the tiny, delicate things that look like something that would be in a mother's sewing basket. I speak of things I do not know, since I never had a mother. There is also a frighteningly larger thing that could only be compared to a saw, and other dull things like notes, medicines, and drugs. I gather mostly things that were left behind as they deserted this building, nothing particularly interesting in the grand scheme of things. There are still a few patients here mostly the particularly frail and old. There is a lady expecting a baby soon, and a couple which is supposed to be collected by their family as they are deemed "cured." I know them all by name, but I know no Rose Gray.

There is nothing overly appealing here except the diary, and so I keep it. It feels heavy in my apron as I move about, the same way my red lipstick feels heavy on my lips. The lipstick was a gift from my girlfriend, Mina, and I am still getting used to the feel of it on my lips. I reapply the thick, matte stuff every couple of hours when I know Miss Helmes isn't peering at me with her eagle eyes. The woman is a master spy if you ask me, and I wouldn't be surprised to hear her start speaking with a suspicious accent and begin flying the wrong flag from her considerable bosom.

"Put those back immediately!" Miss Helmes' high pitched voice breaks through my thoughts like a scythe through soft wheat. Speak of the devil herself.

I sigh and plop a stack of documents I had been idly rifling through back onto the dusty desk where I had found them.

"They looked important, Miss," I argue halfheartedly. I've no mind to lug them back down the endless flights of stairs of Bedlam anyway. "Don't you think the doctor might want them? For his records, I mean?"

Miss Helmes snatches them out of my hands and nearly snaps my wrist in the process. Gentleness is not this spinster's specialty.

"You're here for other reasons, Lizzie, and it's not for smartin' off with me and forgettin' your place. Don't touch anything you weren't told to, girl. Why must I always be telling you that? Off with you now." Miss Helmes is gone as quickly as she had appeared, the rotten apparition that she is.

Of all the hospital staff, Miss Helmes is the worst. She looks like an eagle, with an unfortunate beaked nose. She is as skinny as a rail except for her rather well endowed bosom, which I know I mentioned before. Really, she has the figure of a Gibson Girl with the personality of the Wicked Witch of the West, a recent book I am rather fond of. Well, not recent exactly, but finding books after war time and especially when you're an orphan, leaves you pathetically behind the times when it comes to modern culture.

Had I chosen my birth I would have picked someplace glamorous like New York City. My mother would wear the finest perfume and heels, and my father would work in a fabulous bank and come home each night to embrace his daughter. We'd eat steak and cake and sip cocktails like everyone in the magazines do. When I'd find my Mr. Right, Father would shake his hand and sternly tell him to take care of the love of his life. Also, I'd have one of those fabulous bobs all the American girls are sporting, and I'd wear long strands of necklaces. Once again I continue with the drama.

Sadly, I was born to parents who didn't love me enough to survive the war, and thus I was left here in desolate London. A place as nearly gray and dreary as Dickens painted it to be with his depressing pen. Of course, not all is bad. I have Mina, my health, and Miss Helmes.

Lord help me.

Eventually my hands are full, and my arms are performing an

insubstantial acrobatic dance of ridiculous proportions as I wield my loot towards the stairs. A stack of precariously placed surgical instruments with dull edges nearly fall and with terror for my feet and toes. I yelp and stagger back, and down they go. They clatter with an ungodly crash below, and the echoes seem ludicrous in their volume. I expect Miss Helmes to come rounding the bed at any second shouting at me to behave and to act like a lady, but all is silent, eerily so. I pick up the rascally instruments and shiver allowing my imagination to run wild again. I picture them being used, their dull edges requiring excessive force to slice through any type of skin and bone. I quickly blink and order my thoughts to behave.

I feel the diary in my pocket, and some premonition of tragedy causes my skin to prickle.

"Goosebumps," said an old beggar woman to me once. "Someone's just walked on your grave, little girl. On your grave."

I rub my arms briskly as I reach the bottom of the stairs, and find I am not so eager to shake Miss Helmes' presence after all. I locate her quickly, and she is taken aback at my relief when I do so. The look on her pinched face would have seemed comical at a different time, but I am too relieved to laugh and we finish our work in our usual silence. The rest of the afternoon passes uneventfully, and when I am finally curled up in my bed at my own little flat, I am so weary, and hungry that I fall asleep. My pitiful supper of toast and milk didn't suffice tonight and in my exhaustion, I forget the diary entirely.

*   *   *

The morning dawns as dark and lackluster as one might expect from an April morning in England My internal clock has always awoken me promptly at six a.m. and even though I am tempted to pull my thin sheet over my head and deny the time, I know I cannot linger in bed like an invalid. I have never been a sickly girl and my small body has always been as strong as a horse.

When other girls got sickly at the orphanage, I was usually instructed to tend them, seeing as how my constitution was so virile and healthy.

Maybe that's where and when my interest in medicine arose from smoothing back those fevered brows and coaxing broth between parched lips.

In any case, I had to choose some sort of way to support myself when I was too old to be adopted by some wealthy, non-existent patron. The orphanage superior kicked me out on my ear at the ripe old age of sixteen. I've been on my own now for over a year and though the silence bothers me sometimes, I'd say I've made a go of it. Oh, I'm no sophisticated city girl, but I do all right. I save my coins and get along well enough. I have my feline companion, Hamlet, to keep me company during long nights. Hamlet is more of the communal, neighborhood cat, but I am fairly certain he prefers me to anyone else. I have purchased his affection with fish and make sure to frequently remind him where his loyalties lie.

As is my custom, I braid my hair in two plaits that reach nearly to my waist. I am old enough to properly pin up my hair like a lady or get it cut and curled in a more stylish fashion, but I find I can never quite fit the part. For some reason, the braids are a part of my missing childhood that I loathe to leave behind. Perhaps I think the second I abandon them, my last chance for a carefree childhood will be gone forever. As long as I have them I am still a little girl, at least in my head, and in my soul as well.

My nurse's kerchief is next, and it makes me feel a bit more grown up. It means next to nothing really, besides giving a free pass to a doctor to order me around like a slave. I sigh, but walk briskly to work. I am not looking forward to another day at Bedlam. Lord, how large that building is. It will be a month of Sundays before I am done running errands in that place. I'm sure it will be nearly a hundred years before Miss Helmes is satisfied and has every last needle and file and cotton swab where she wants them. At which point I can finally become my eternal reward, a withered old spinster wearing braids.

I am still laughing a bit at the thought, when I bump into Mina.

"You shouldn't be wandering around scaring people," she admonishes, her eyes big and hazel. She squeezes my hand good-naturedly. "You'll give someone a heart attack in this melancholy place."

Mina is beautiful, smart, and very privileged. In truth, I shouldn't like her. She should be far above my station: snobby, petty, spoiled, and mean. But in reality, she is a bit of an angel. Her family is one of the richest in the city and though she could have everything any girl could want, she is down to earth, eager, hard working, and humble. I tried to dislike her, as a penniless orphan should, but she is simply impossible to hate. She is gentle with everyone and keeps volunteering here at Bedlam even after her wealthy father informed her that she was free to move on to another charitable work. She told me that she's found her calling and though I can't imagine choosing to be in such surroundings, she shows up faithfully and cheerfully at least three times a week. There's no accounting for taste, Miss Helmes says.

"Who will I give a heart attack? The ghosts? I'm beginning to think everyone here is already dead, Mina. Didn't you know?" I lower my voice and try to sound spooky.

She shudders and eyes me strangely. "That's a terrible thought, isn't it?"

"Is it? I suppose, although it's probably nice to be a ghost. Tiptoeing wherever you like, knocking things about and eating whatever you please without fear of gaining an ounce…" I wink so she knows I am joking. One thing Mina is a bit short on is a sense of humor. She tries, the dear thing, but she never seems to fully appreciate a joke. Maybe it's a side effect of the well-to-do. I have yet to meet a jolly, rich person. "Can't you picture Mr. Limpet strolling around, disappearing through walls, shouting at you for biscuits, reappearing under the table? Boo and poof and all that nonsense?"

"You're silly," Mina rolls her eyes. "There is no such thing, and if there were ghosts here, they'd be thinking of more important things than pounds and biscuits and eavesdropping."

"If you say so," I consider telling her about the diary of Rose Gray, but something stops me when I open my mouth. It's as though an inner voice sternly instructs me to be quiet and keep this little secret. So instead I find myself making small talk and keeping busy as we move about the hospital. The little red diary seems to burn a hole in my apron pocket until my lunch break arrives and I can break away into the garden on my own.

Chapter 2

I am so incredibly sick of this place. It pulls me in constantly, like a perverted tide. I am tossed about and end up here again and again and again. I dread opening my eyes. I know the smell even before anything in my vision accosts me. The cursed stench of insanity.

I want to sleep forever.

Either that, or I want to be awake forever.

Which is it? Choose, Rose. Sometimes I hardly know myself.

Sometimes I hardly know myself.

Sometimes I hardly know myself.

"Well, she certainly was confused," I think to myself as I munch on a piece of stale bread. I dip it in my tea to make it more palatable, but it only sogs, and a chunk drops off in one fell swoop. I groan as if a loved one has died; I had been greatly looking forward to that last bite. There are weeks in my life where nothing is more exciting than that last bite of perfectly despicable bread.

No small wonder the poor thing was confined here though. Rose sounds crazier than a loon, and I am only a smidge into her story. I find one last crust of bread tucked beneath the curve of my saucer, and though it's terrible and tasteless, my stomach growls and wants another. I had forgotten to pack my own lunch again, and the extras from the kitchen make a poor substitute. The inmates, excuse me, patients rather, don't generally care what they're eating, so I can't say that our cook is world class. She isn't even London class. I don't think she's even village class. I pour more tea and keep reading.

The only comfort I have is that I am not alone any longer. He is with me here and with me there and with me everywhere. His loyalty brings me happiness where once there was none. Now I know what it means to care about another, and with that knowledge comes a sort of peace. Though...

Do I want peace?

I never have before, not really. Anarchy is more my specialty, and truth be told, disorder brings a peace to me all its' own. I'm not good with happiness. Not good with love. It makes me nervous.

I fear him and what he means to me.

Just a bit. I've always been alone; even when I wasn't, I was. It's how I exist best. But this is so much better.

See? Just the thought of Luke distracts me again. I was writing about my hatred of this blasted place, and suddenly I am spouting sonnets of love? I think the traveling messes up the workings of my brain, either that, or being in love does. Something isn't right. Like a yo-yo, I am yanked back to these walls and manacled to them, either figuratively or literally. I am more a prisoner here than anyone else. More than anyone!

Luke, on the other hand, is too good at the ways of the theater, curse him. He passes for anyone sane whenever he comes back. A visitor, a guest, a servant, a relative, a doctor even. He fools everyone, every time.

No matter how hard I try, I don't fool anybody. Not for long.

They all know I belong here, and that belonging is my downfall and my sorrow. I look in the mirror and I don't see what they see. I see a girl trying to fit in, that's all.

Just a girl.

Harmless, really.

For some reason, I don't quite believe the words and it is with a shiver that I turn another page. Was she harmless? She'd hardly have been here if she was completely harmless. And apparently, she'd been here more than once she had said with her own pen. I mean, we certainly do get a few patients who aren't really crazy. Often they are recovering from a traumatic event or have something physically wrong with them. They aren't certifiably insane and usually don't stay long, and by no means do they stay against their will. However, maybe back when Rose Gray wrote this, things were different. After all, Bedlam isn't famous for its humanity. We now strive very hard to change that reputation. Naturally, keeping people who are sane is on our list of things we try not to do.

I think back to my last time here in London, not here in the hospital, but here in this city. I cannot figure what went wrong. Every time I think of it, I am so angered again, and then I can't organize my thinking. I let that dark haired demon girl get away, and all my work was nearly for nothing. I say 'nearly' because at least someone near to her is dead, and all because of my handiwork. So, that's something. Something to keep me warm at night.

Harmless indeed, I think, sipping tea and frowning. A murderess then? I have seen one or two of those in my time here, and I haven't even been here that long. We have a woman named Ann who poisoned her husband with herbs she carefully cultivated in her garden. Rumor has it, we have an old man who killed his whole family and buried them under his floorboards. I'm a bit skeptical of that one though, as it was so many years ago, and the facts are greatly exaggerated. He probably killed his hamster and buried it under the floorboards. I suppose that sin wouldn't get you life in an insane asylum though.

It isn't good enough though, not for all the trouble I went to. My life's work, really. I never even got to confront my father and I barely got to say the things I wanted to say to my sister because I kept getting distracted and forgetting why I was there. She nearly killed my Luke, and by the time I discovered what she'd done, she was gone. It's been a year.

A year of nothing but rumors and speculation. It's as though she dissolved into the mist somehow.

She is mist, and I am ocean. She drifts by, carelessly, willy-nilly, and I am tossed up on the shores of Bedlam yet again as though I am to be punished.

I don't deserve to be punished like this.

I hate her.

Poor sister. No small wonder she disappeared. Mentally, I wish her God-speed.

"Lizzie? Is it you? Or is it…?" Miss Helmes' voice cuts through my pleasant, solitary picnic.

I mentally groan, but outwardly manage a polite and professional smile at my superior. "It is me, ma'am. Did you need something? I have ten more minutes, I think."

She approaches my seat in the middle of the overhang of the tree and bats away a bee impatiently. Miss Helmes has no time for bees. I'm always surprised they dare to fly anywhere near her. I certainly wouldn't, were I a bee.

"Tea again, is it?" Miss Helmes peers into my cup, and I detect a bit of patronizing in her voice.

"It is customary for most people, yes, especially at this time of day." I have to resolve myself from rolling my eyes. Miss Helmes must be the only British woman in the history of the world who does not like tea. "But I'm nearly finished now. Did you need me somewhere?"

"I need you to stop wandering off," she snaps. "I don't have time to constantly be wondering where you are and if you've gotten yourself into mischief. Lord, girl, I do have other things to do. You aren't the only person around here. So, if you're done with your little picnic..." She trails off, and taps her pointy shoe, impatiently.

"Back to work, yes, ma'am," I stifle my groan and leave my little teacup behind in the garden. I should have picked it up and returned it to the kitchen, but Miss Helmes' intolerance of me gives me angel wings, and I cannot stop my momentum.

My chore again is to scrub off a disturbing stain from the wall. I wish more eleven-year-old boys would sign up for it, so that I can be free to do more interesting things.

Mina is wheeling a very elderly man, our Mr. Limpet, through the ballroom when next I see her. He barks at me as they pass by me.

"See you there!" Mr. Limpet's voice is raspy like a seal when he's finished with his three little words. He waves at me cheerily. He is forever bossing people around, and no one ever knows what he's talking about.

"Sure, Mr. Limpet. I'll see you there," I agree, and smile politely.

"We'll all have a nice time, won't we?" He looks at me intently, waiting for my response. Mina shrugs at me as she has no idea what he's referring to, either.

"Of course," I pat him on the arm, comfortingly. It must be difficult for him to be moved from his home, though he's been here so long I doubt he remembers his real home anyway. I'm pretty sure he's a lifer.

"And we'll have parties again?" he whispers, conspiratorially. "And dance?"

Though the thought gives me the willies, I force myself to nod and smile some more. He's harmless, but occasionally spooky.

"Sure, Mr. Limpet, I'll try to save a dance for you."

"Oh, that's nice. That's sweet. You won't forget now?" He leans out of his chair, and peers fretfully back at me as Mina begins to wheel him away again.

"I won't forget," I speak loudly for the sake of his old ears, and go back to my scrubbing of the wall as he disappears around the corner.

"I like your braids!" I hear him shout back at me, and then cough again in his barking way. "Nice girls wear braids!"

I chortle as I continue scrubbing, and I hear the heavy solid doors of Bedlam slam shut. Whatever this wretched stain is, it seems to have seeped into every last stupid crack. "I should be helping with surgeries and medicines," I grumble to myself, "not slaving as a scullery maid." I'm so preoccupied with feeling sorry for myself and my raw knuckles that I don't hear someone near me until they clear their throat.

I nearly jump out of my skin.

"Blast it! Don't go sneaking up on people like that!" I scowl and drop my brush into my bucket of slimy cold water, where it splashes at me in revenge. I bite back my next retort as I look up at my frightener. He is, quite frankly, the most handsome man I have ever seen. Man or boy, I cannot decide and maybe that's half his appeal. Not too much older than I, but enough to make a world of difference. Several worlds of differences. He is tall and lanky with dark blonde hair and sparkling eyes that seem to be laughing at me. They're hiding under the type of expensive hat that I usually only see in the movies.

"Beg your pardon, Miss," he tips his hat at me and transfers his gaze to the stain on the wall. "And what happened here?"

I shrug. "Who knows? I just know I am the lucky girl to clean it up."

"It looks like blood. Did someone get hurt?" He actually looks concerned, and for a brief, indulgent moment I pretend it's for my safety and well-being. How nice it would be to have a gentleman concerned for my circumstances. Then again, he probably has a loved one as a patient here and is concerned that this could be their grisly remains splattered on the wall.

"Oh, I don't think so. Most of the patients are already gone. Are you looking for someone?" I tuck back some stray hair behind my ears, and as I do I get a whiff of my hands. It may just be his suggestion, but they do smell like blood, coppery and foul. I hadn't noticed that before. I kind of thought someone had hurled a bowl of stew across the room and it had shattered and dripped down the wall. I like my scenario a bit better, I must admit. I much prefer dinner to murder, and not just because I skipped lunch, but because I always prefer dinner.

"Oh, I'm always looking for someone," he smiles, and as he does he is even more handsome. His eyes positively sparkle. I hadn't known that was possible before now. I thought it was merely an artistic expression like, *a babbling brook,* or *a broken heart.* "Is everyone mostly gone then?"

"No, well, that is, yes, most are, but there are still a few. It takes a while to transfer when you need to go one or two at a time. Can't exactly pack them all in one car, can we? Riots and jealousy and claustrophobia and all that," I hope I'm not being crass, but it's simply the truth. Paranoid people don't do well in crowds.

"I see. Do you want some help? Is there anything I can help you with?" He actually looks as though he means it.

"Of course not." His helpful demeanor makes me nervous as I've never had a real gentleman offer to do anything for me, and I practically stammer in my surprise. "Miss Helmes can help you locate your person. If you like, I'll fetch her for you."

Then, as is inevitable, Miss Helmes manifests herself immediately during the mention of her name. She slinks into the room like a skinny cat that smells a mouse. My teacup dangles from her long fingers, as though it is distasteful. I imagine her knocking me over the head with it.

"Ah, Mr. Connelly, did you find—" Miss Helmes' voice cuts off when she sees me there, standing directly beside the man, and she frowns. "Oh. I see."

"Mr. Connelly here was looking for someone," I go back to my scrubbing.

"Yes, I know. Mr. Connelly, a word?" She exits as quickly and as silently as she arrived. I let out the breath, that for some absurd reason, I had been holding.

I feel a soft tug on my braid and look up, surprised. The man smiles and gives me a slight wink.

"Good luck with that." He tips his hat, and then, suddenly, he is gone too.

The day concludes with that meeting being the most interesting part. Indeed, it's the most interesting part of my whole last year, sadly enough.

I tumble into my bed that night with a snack of cookies and milk and the little red diary.

I think back to last year and wonder where I went wrong. Perhaps Luke complicated things and muddled too much for me to properly concentrate on my task. Perhaps I should leave him.

I think sometimes he will leave me.

But, it's depressing to dwell on such things. The medication they give me makes me morbid and melancholy. I tried telling that to the doctor, but he said morbid and melancholy is better than violent and murderous. Then he snorted so loudly I was convinced he nearly consumed his own substantial nose. What an amusing sense of humor the new doctor has. I think he has never dealt with someone like me. I shall have to indoctrinate him in the ways of Rose. I doubt he'll laugh so easily then.

My odious nurse and jail keeper forced me to wash down the wall and attempt to get rid of the bloodstains in the dining room. No amount of

I feel a distinct chill as I realize my hands have scrubbed the same stain
that Rose's did, and now I know for sure that it was blood, not soup, like I
had imagined. I find myself wishing I had not saved this diary for such a
late night reading, and also that I had some hot water and good soap to
scrub up again. The water on my nightstand will be cold and frigid and
won't help wash off the, now imagined, smell of blood.

I start to close the diary, but of course I cannot. Right after Mr. Connelly,
this diary is the most interesting thing to have happened to me in ages. I
feel a bit of guilt that I may have misjudged whether the doctors would
have wanted to read this narrative. On reflection, the diary of a patient
and the inner workings of her brain and thoughts would most likely be
quite helpful in their research.

The main frustration in caring and curing our patients is not being able to
understand them. This little journal could go a long way towards that end,
and a little nursing girl is the one who keeps it. I should probably feel
even guiltier than I do. But really, it could give me quite the edge, and
perhaps I won't be scrubbing walls much longer when someone realizes
how much knowledge I can bring to the table. That's what I tell myself as
I turn another page. Also, there's the fact that Rose's words are proving to
be quite addictive, and I'd like to know her whole story before I relinquish
her diary.

*I wish to start my crusade again, but I find large chunks of my memory
and thoughts gone. I think Luke is right, traveling too much and too
frequently hurts my brain. I come back each time to bloody old Bedlam,
more confused than the last. I had best rest a bit here and regain my
purpose before I live up to my mad reputation.*

Mad.

What a silly word.

I am not mad. I am driven! There is a difference. For all their medical knowledge and social proprieties, they cannot see the difference. What a bunch of loons, I say. I have purpose. I have goals. I know what I want.

On the other hand, home is home, and home is where I am for now. It will do me good to rest. Luke visits and sleeps here with me more often than not. I promise and promise not to go anywhere without him, but he does not promise the same for me, I just realized. Why is that, I wonder? Does he sleep on the grounds somewhere when he is not in my bed? He does not possess the power I do to control his traveling, no matter how many times I have patiently tried to teach him. And if he leaves me... ah well, I suppose I would have to find him again and teach him a lesson in faithfulness. Silly boy.

He is the only friend I have ever had, really. I can count my friends on one finger:

Luke.

I had an imaginary friend as a little girl. I had not yet learned of my abilities, and I was lonely in the village. Old Babba ignored me mightily with a steadfastness that shocked even me. I had to invent my playmates as no flesh and blood children would come near me. Their parents said my family had abandoned me, and left me to my evil ways. I was ashamed and refused to admit they must have fled somewhere. Like an unwanted changeling baby, I was left behind in the care of an old woman who despised me.

My favorite make-believe friend loved me all the same. She knew all my darkness and cared not a farthing. She was quite non-judgmental. I have not had such good luck with friends since that time.

But my thoughts ramble again. This is supposed to be a memoir, and I hardly have anything else to do with my time. My fingers are cramped from writing, but I will continue.

I was seven when Old Babba finally died. Couldn't have come at a better time really, as she was beginning to anger me quite constantly that year. I can admit that my temper was frightful, and sometimes she would lock me out of her dreadful house. I was as skinny as a string bean from her feeding me barely enough to keep me alive. Her and I were always doing this ridiculous dance around each other as we each tried to out-ignore the other. Only God knows why she was scared to death of me, and I didn't exactly trust her either. Both of us used to feed bites of our food to the dog to make sure it wasn't poisoned. It was only a matter of time before one of us succeeded in doing in the other.

In the end, even I was hardly equipped for murder at the ripe old age of seven, and Old Babba kicked the bucket naturally enough. Hardly surprising, as the hag must have been at least a million years old. I made a great show of burying her, which included dragging her body out of the house. This was no small feat for a little girl, and I cheerfully rolled her corpse into my homemade grave. Tossing in the dirt after her was great fun too, and I hadn't enjoyed myself so much in years. I even made invitations for the villagers, inviting them to the funeral, but no one came. Can't blame them. She really was an old witch. I sang snatches of a few hymns I had heard at one point or another. I then moved onto nursery rhymes and anything else I could put to song. I even danced a bit.

The night I buried her was the first night I traveled. It must have been my light heart that made me sleep so well.

Chapter 3

I am groggy and listless the next day. I hadn't slept well. I dreamt of wicked old ladies, poisoned dogs, and starving little girls. I feel oddly consumed by thoughts of Rose Gray and her story. Her handwriting had become so bad by the end of last night's reading that I had to set it aside and rest my aching eyes. By the way she writes, I wonder, could she still be alive? Either way, past or present, she pens like a child, alternating between large and small letters. They are harshly drawn with her ink almost tearing through the paper. Then there are her lightly scratched, tiny, loopy letters that are nearly unreadable. It's as if several people took turns writing. Several six year olds, to be precise.

I cannot stop thinking of her through my breakfast of egg and toast. I cannot stop thinking of her through the plaiting of my hair. I simply cannot stop thinking of her at all.

When I realize I could easily find out what happened to her through the files of patients I am privy to, I want to smack myself in the head for being so daft. "Really, Lizzie," I mutter to myself as I hurriedly tie my nurse's kerchief on my head and shove the diary in my pocket. "You'd think you haven't a brain in your skull."

Snooping in other people's business should probably go against the grain of a lady, but I can't say I was brought up to be a lady anyhow. Rose said it herself anyway, that boredom makes you do strange things. As interesting as I hope my medical career will be someday, at the moment it's as dull as watching paint peel, and any divertissements are welcome. Besides, I have justified to any objecting thoughts, that it's part of my medical research.

I find myself nearly merry as I greet Miss Helmes. I ask her cagily enough if she has anything in particular for me to do, or shall I start to begin work in the former doctor's office room? Since the former doctor was a bit of a messy hoarder, no one has been especially anxious to begin clearing out his space. So, as I knew she would, she only hesitates a moment before giving me her permission.

"There is nothing in there of any interest, Lizzie," she warns. "You'll find it dull. Are you sure you won't stay out here with me and help polish these spoons? The time would be better spent."

"A tantalizing offer, thank you, ma'am, but no. I must be of service to the hospital, and I'm sure some of those papers will be invaluable." I keep my voice breezy.

"I doubt it," she snaps. Oops, too much breeziness annoys her. "Run along then." She goes back to her spoon with a vigorous attention to detail.

"Oh," I say as though I had just remembered something. In truth, my pause is rehearsed. I place my hand on the doorframe and do my best to look casual, not that she is looking my way anyway. She is peering intently into her spoon. I expect it to spontaneously explode any second now. "Did Mr. Connelly find his missing person?"

Miss Helmes turns her intense stare towards me now. "I expect he did. Why do you care? Run along."

Run I do. Partly because of my renewed energy at the prospect of finding out more about Rose, and partly because I have to pass a wing of the hospital that I have always been frightened of. It's a deserted place now. Even when the rooms were all full of patients and they were free to roam about the place, no one ventured this way, so I'm told.

The rooms have a haunted feel, and a neglected whispering mood that murmurs of the not so distant past. They are tiny medical examining rooms that once were pristine and sterile, or perhaps not so sterile. There's the occasional one with just a lone operating table or an overturned chair. One with a tattered white jacket that lies forgotten in the doorway. The air teems with other's memories that are just beyond my mind's reach. I know they're there though. I feel these reminiscences of tragic illness, and they float unbidden through the tainted, stuffy air.

It's always hotter, darker, and stuffier here. It feels as though there are too many people in one place, even though it is only me here. The air has weight to it. Weight that could bury you alive if you let it. I cannot imagine being held a prisoner in this place. It makes my skin crawl.

I am through the hated wing soon enough, and when I enter the old doctor's room, I let out the breath I had been holding. His old office is not nearly as bad as the hallway, though it's already full of cobwebs and dust. There is nothing left in the office besides stacks of papers, and an ancient heavy desk that I don't blame them for not moving. It must weigh a ton, even when emptied.

Bookshelves are here too, even though at least half the shelves are empty. The other half is full of dusty books that are too outdated for anyone to want, and the stacks of papers look aged as well. Regardless of the chill in this room, I opt to crack open a window for the breeze and the tie it gives me to the outside world. Though I'd like to hang my head out the window for a bit and gulp in some freshness and admire the view, this isn't a room I'd fancy turning my back on.

I begin my search and very quickly find my enthusiasm dwindling. The doctor needed a secretary and badly. His form of filing was archaic, senseless, and utterly useless.

After a couple hours of searching and finding nothing on Rose Gray or anyone who might fit her description, I nearly miss the hypnotic comfort that only polishing spoons can give.

I woke and found myself in a very crowded market place. People were colorful and dressed in strange garb, and no one seemed to be speaking English or German. These were the only two languages I spoke at home with Old Babba and the villagers. The people were darker skinned than I, though not as dark as some. They were maybe the same shade as the man in the village that used to sell peaches. He was from India.

I was under a table, and I only awoke because someone had kicked me. You'd think I would have been scared, not of being kicked as I'd had worse from Old Babba, but of finding myself some other place other than where I fell asleep. Some place other than where I had grudgingly called home for seven years. That's what you would think, but no. No, I was delighted! I had been rescued! Like a fairy princess in a fairy story, I had been set free. My captor was gone, dead as a doornail, and my true life was about to begin. It was as though someone had opened my book, my story, and began to read right then and there. Once upon a time...

My life had truly started then. No more spiteful looks from Old Babba and no more cold nights. No more loneliness and emptiness, no more hungry belly, and no more dirty clothes.

I scrambled out from under the table and blissfully joined the throng of shoppers. I was certainly eyed a bit strangely but that didn't faze me. I was quite used to the stares of people, and they didn't bother me or put a damper on my happiness. I had never much cared what people thought of me. I ran around merrily for most of the day. Since no one spoke my language and I didn't speak theirs, we all got along beautifully. I'm sure when concerned adults did speak to me that day, they were trying to deduce where my parents were. I just smiled innocently and managed to convey that nothing was wrong; nothing was out of the ordinary. I found myself even saying things like, "my mother is over there, buying cinnamon, do you see her there? Over there? See?" though no one could understand me and I would wave and smile some more. They would shade their eyes from the sun and look intently. Of course, there was no one there to find, and no one who looked anything like me. There was no woman with yellow hair and blue eyes. I would wave at my imaginary mother anyway, and sometimes when I was playacting at my very finest moments, I would nearly see my mother wave back.

Yes, sometimes I was quite certain I could see her.

Goodness, Rose, try to blend in a bit better, I think. Her story has become fantastical. Though the glimpse into her strange little mind was disturbing, it was also addicting.

My feet are propped up on the old mahogany desk, and I am reclining in
the worn chair in quite an unladylike fashion. I have given up entirely on
finding any records of Rose, so I have removed her diary from my pocket
and am reading once again. Her handwriting is better in this part for
some reason, and I can speed through quickly.

I have no idea why she thinks she has moved countries in the night, but
since not much has made sense before now anyway, I don't bother trying
to find the logic in the story. So, I read on.

*I spent a happy day at the market. When night fell, my stomach was at
last full for the first time since I could remember. When the tides turned
with my exotic looks, and my blonde hair didn't get me free samples,
then I simply snatched them. I had my fill of apricots, strange rice balls,
spicy breads, nuts, and cookies that tasted like tea.*

*I tried to join in a game with a group of children, but they were
unfriendly towards me. The ball they were kicking came hurtling at me,
and I ran to fetch it and throw it back to them, but they angrily took it
from me. They wouldn't let me in their silly game, and I tried not to let it
bother me. The knowledge that my fairy tale peers were as cruel as my
former village peers was disheartening, but I rubbed the tears away
very quickly and admonished myself for being a weak ninny. I was sad,
but only for a moment.*

*I have always been very, very good at turning sorrow into anger, where
it can be properly trained and taught basic survival skills.*

*Those first few weeks I slept in the market place. I was a little thing and
at seven years of age, I could easily have passed for a child of five, whilst
I was also quite sneaky. The two attributes served me well. It was an
easy enough matter to remain undetected and it became a game for me,
like a sort of cat and mouse. I even made up scenarios of fake guards,
and soldiers who would march through the square determined to find
the little orphan urchin. Their ineptness would result in hilarious
adventures. I would drift off to sleep quite content and happy with my*

stories to keep me warm. In truth, no one was chasing me because no one was looking for me.

I suppose the idea of a small child living on her own that way would seem strange to those who do not know me, but I am special. The times in that year and in that place, were among the best times of my life. I learned eventually that it was India and the year was nearly one hundred years ahead of where I had spent my first seven.

Whatever was she going on about? One hundred years from her village? India? She really was mad.

Poor, dear, wretched girl. Had her family truly abandoned her then? Left her to an old lady who was abusive to her? Much less has been known to turn a person insane, I suppose. Nothing bad has ever happened to Mr. Limpet, and he's as crazy as they come.

When the rainy season came, I knew I had to find different shelter than my beloved market place. I hated to leave it, but I knew that it was time to move along.

A strange group of traveling performers came through and they took me in. A girl with yellow hair and light eyes was good for business. They were experts in magic, illusion, and sleight of hand. They made a living swindling people out of their wages, and the people were all too willing to hand over those wages. They sold worthless trinkets for pennies on the dollar and bottles of tonic that promised to cure everything from wasting diseases to hair loss to infertility to death. The cure for death in a bottle. Some people will believe anything. Idiots.

And I? I could sell anything with a wink and a smile. I'd wear a fluffy pink skirt and sparkles in my hair, I was their golden girl.

My once upon a time had come. Could it be that my happily ever after had already arrived as well? It seemed for a time that it had. My days were spent doing whatever I liked which included, wandering, picking up the language, eating, pretending, and turning cartwheels in the grass. My evenings were spent selling broken promises and dreams. We traveled quickly to avoid angry customers who may return for a refund. That was key to our success, and so we were never in the same place twice.

It was a lovely life while it lasted.

I gnaw on the end of the pipe I had found in the drawer of the desk. I chew on it contentedly and enjoy the stale smell of the cherry tobacco that drifts up to my nose as I nibble on the pipe. If I could have, I would have lit it just for the wickedness of it. When someone walks in unannounced, I nearly fall off the chair and the pipe clatters to the floor with a telltale clank. My wickedness is purely speculative.

"Ah, there you are," says Mr. Connelly. He tips his hat at me and leans against the doorframe, crossing one foot over the other in a casual manner. I hurriedly remove my feet from the desk and tug my skirt down modestly.

"Oh. I was taking a break from cleaning. This isn't what it looks like, well, that is," I give up excuses and try a smile instead. "It is what it looks like, I suppose. I'm bored stiff and was relaxing."

"Can't blame you there. Though I have it on excellent authority from cutting edge medicine, that tobacco is quite bad for you. Blackens your lungs, I believe," he crosses the room in three long strides and picks up the pipe from the floor. He hands it to me with long fingers. "Your grandchildren will agree with me someday."

I wave away his words and drop the pipe back in the drawer where I had first found it. "That's silly. Anyway, did you need something?"

"You," he drawls out the word casually, making it sound almost tantalizing. I feel either nervous, or scandalized; I'm not sure which since I'm unfamiliar with both emotions. At my blank look, he speaks again. "Miss Helmes asked me to fetch you. It's time to move along to hospital."

"Hospital?" I know I sound ridiculous, but it's as though I've lost my train of thought altogether around him. I shake myself out of my stupor and nearly glare at him in my attempt to show him how he does not affect me.

Which, of course, he does. "Yes. I'm nearly ready. Am I to accompany the last of the patients then?" It is our last day here. It's a monumental day in history really, and I've been wasting it by chewing on a pipe and reading a story. I can't really think of Rose's missive as non-fiction, even though she evidently believed it to be autobiographical.

"Yes, I believe there is a Mrs. Ness and a young girl they call Marie. The very last now of the patients and then we can stay away from this place forever. Such an end of an era, isn't it?" He appears especially thoughtful all at once, and it's almost as though I am not in the room with him at all.

What an odd thing to say, I think. What an odd man. Barely beyond boyhood, and yet there is something strangely old about him. An old soul, some would say. An odd soul, I would say. In my limited and parentless childhood, odd is something not to be trifled with. I dislike odd intently.

"There's nothing here worth taking." I say, stepping away from the desk and stepping near Mr. Connelly. "I'm ready if you are. You are to accompany us, then?"

"Yes, I thought I might. That is if you have no objection. I believe I will find what I am looking for at the country hospital. As you can imagine, the patients and staff can be quite lost in the shuffle during this move."

"Yes, I *can* imagine." My voice sounds tart. "Since I've been working so hard to get there myself. It's been very colossal, this relocation." Actually, it's been quite boring, but he doesn't need to know that.

"I hope you haven't been overworked, my dear?"

And now he speaks to me as if I am a small child in need of his petting and soothing? My attraction to him is quickly dwindling into a sort of irritation at his meddling. Perhaps I am just not used to the attention, or perhaps the coddling is distasteful to me. Perhaps I do not want this old soul to treat me like a delicate little girl when I want him to look at me as a capable woman.

Perhaps I analyze myself too much.

"I enjoy my work, sir," I pass him as he lounges in the door frame and turn to smile back at him. "There is no place I'd rather be than in Bedlam." Well, there are some words that have never been spoken before in history, and most likely never will be again.

Chapter 4

I realize I'm stuck between that stage of not quite asleep, and not fully awake, that I have lost the diary. I realize it with a pang of dread, and a sense of loss that hits me so deeply that I jerk myself back to awareness with a start. I had come to my bed so fully exhausted from my day of work that I had fallen into my typical pattern. I tuck myself in tightly, warm my feet deliciously with my hot water bottle, and plump up my pillow. I hadn't even thought of the diary until it appeared unbidden in my mind's eye. Without any warning at all, I felt as though I heard the word "Rose" whispered in my ear. I jerked myself upright knocking the hot water bottle to the floor, and grabbing my blanket tight around my chest.

I had left it at Bedlam. Not Bedlam now, but Bedlam before. There was no one there now in the abandoned building. Everyone was gone, and whomever they'd sold it to would presumably destroy any rubbish left behind. I had declared that room, hadn't I? With the big old desk, and the pipe that now for some reason I desperately wanted as well. Now Rose's diary was there locked up tight, where I'll never see it again. I'll never open its red cover and never make sense of its garbled, sometimes nearly unreadable print.

I need to hear the end of Rose's story, like I need to know my own.

Frantically, I try to think of a reason for Miss Helmes' to allow me to go back. Something I'd forgotten, perhaps? An instrument? A book? A novel of medicinal importance that could not be left behind as they start their hospital in their new location?

Try as I do, I come up with nothing. Lying has never been my strong suite. I become fidgety with the first hint of suspicion. I begin to twirl the ends of my braid and look about as casual and nonchalant as your basic, run-of-the-mill axe murderer. I have no gift for it. Also, truth be told, I'm a bit scared of Miss Helmes and her eagle eyes. If not scared exactly, then certainly respectful. She could fire me without so much as a by-your-leave, and then where would I be? On the streets, that's where. I've been there and am not terribly fond of them.

Two things I'm not scared of though, are the dark and the hospital. Well there is that one shady wing, but I can hold my breath and pray my way through it. Though I've not come to any personal conclusions about God, it really doesn't do to hedge your bets when you need Him.

My flat is tiny and infested with vermin that keep Hamlet busy. It's also not far from Bethlem Royal Hospital. Well, the giant building that was Bethlem Royal Hospital for hundreds of years, I mean. Today it is simply another building with tales to tell that are perhaps more sensational and titillating than most, but a building just the same.

Nothing to be nervous about.

Simple breaking and entering really.

A child could do it.

Determined, I shake off the last of my sleep and with it the last of my doubts. How hard could it be, really? I know the place like the back of my hand even in the dark, and I'm sure I'll find my way. Besides, I have a trusty torch that is not only excellent for seeing in the dark, but also for clubbing any accosting marauders I might meet. This midnight adventure will be a story I can tell my grandchildren! They'll find me so spunky and brave.

April in London in the dead of night isn't the cheeriest, and my feet carry me swiftly through the dark alleyways and around the shadows. I see no one in the short walk to the hospital. When I am in sight of the place itself, it looms like a misshapen monster out of a fairy story or a sea monster that's biding its time while sitting still like an island. That is, sitting still until I tread upon its scales of brick and stone, and it awakens with a roar to devour me.

I feel quite devoured actually when I jimmy a window and find myself inside. "In the belly of the beast, dear girl," I mutter. "As long as you're here and no one's home you might as well steal an old, unwanted diary."

The silence is overwhelming, and I miss the sounds Bedlam had during the daylight hours. Even a familiar shriek or the rantings of the criminally insane would make me feel better. The quiet is quite oppressive and heavy. I pass by the stain on the dining hall wall and as if I have no control over my own limbs, my hand reaches out and touches the red. My torch hadn't even picked up the stain even though its yellow glow was trained straight in front of me. Yet somehow I knew instinctively where to find it. I don't find that knowledge nor the compulsion comforting, and neither is the sight of my pale ghostly hand against the dark red. Ghostly. What a wonderful word to pop, unbidden, into my head as I'm locked in an abandoned insane asylum. "Wonderful, Lizzie. Really wonderful. You do come up with the loveliest ideas before dawn. You should write a book, *101 Things to Do in a Mental Hospital for Fun and Profit*. Or perhaps, *How to Scare Yourself to Death for No Good Reason*. Suddenly, my reasoning for coming in the dead of night seems ridiculous. It would have been easy enough to simply ask Miss Helmes. She isn't Lucifer himself. She surely would have let me come back to retrieve my shawl or my spectacles. Granted, I don't wear spectacles, but I doubt she'd know or even care.

I make my way on cautious feet, and then in a burst of the rebellion I feel towards the old place I thump my way along defiantly to my rapidly beating heart. Let the ghosts and the spirits and the darkness hear me coming. I'm not afraid.

Slightly nervous maybe, perhaps a touch concerned for my life, but not afraid.

The wing that I hate has all its doors open, which is somewhat creepier than having them shut. Instead of seeing nothing in their depths, I see partial things. It is worse than seeing nothing because there are shadows and shapes that my imagination is only too happy to provide bodies for. I move along quickly with my torch as a beacon in the night. The full moon that shines through the windows at me is a friendly, winking pal guiding me through the halls. I fixate on it with a ridiculous fear that the moon will go out like a torch. Perhaps it will flicker and leave me in the ebony darkness of the asylum.

I've forgotten his name now, but the old doctor's office is just as I've left it. He's only been gone but a month or two from this place and though I try not to, I exhale a breath of relief at having reached my destination all in one piece. No goblins or bogey men or stray, forgotten inmates have ground my bones for bread or flossed their teeth with my hair. Success, Lizzie!

My success continues as I find the red journal exactly where I had left it on the desk during my surprise visit from the mysterious and enigmatic Mr. Connelly. Had he not jostled my thoughts so, I would never have left it behind. Bloody man. This is definitely his fault. If I make it through my adventure unscathed, then I am going to give him a piece of my mind. I'll knock the sparkle right out of those beautiful eyes.

I pick the diary up quickly and am startled by the sound of a soft breath just to my left. It's so close I nearly feel my hair lift with the whoosh of air the sound made. An exhale of sorts, like the one I just let out myself seconds before, but it can't be from me, for I am holding my breath yet again. I stiffen and though some people's resolve and instinct may be to whirl around, in such a situation, I do not. I stand very still and very quiet. I do not breathe. I have had practice at the orphanage faking sleep and sneaking out. I wish now for our old warden of the orphanage, Mrs. Temple. I had never welcomed her presence in the middle of the night before, but I do now. I feel as though my heart does not even beat. My blood is frozen and still in my veins, so silent am I. The only thing that moves along at a furious pace is my thoughts.

What did I hear?

Is it still here, in this room with me?

What do I do?

I cannot stay motionless and breathless for the rest of my life. My first entrance into the land of the living is a swallow. It seems loud in the stillness. Without moving my feet, I turn my body and search the spot where my torch cuts through the blackness. I do not see anything, but I feel something as real, warm, and alive as my own body. I feel something there with me that searches me as I search it.

I do feel afraid, but not yet terrified. How strange that I should so suddenly know the difference.

However, my alarm is heightened when I feel the diary torn from my hands. With a force that makes me cry out, this time in terror, it is dashed against the wall and knocks over a statue of a horseman there. The statue topples to the floor near the diary.

My heart is racing, and it is the loudest sound in the room. No longer can I control my fear, and yet I do not dart away. Whatever is in this room with me is supernatural and therefore cannot be outrun. My logical mind says this is so, even though it may be an odd contradiction to think of logic and the supernatural in the same breath. So, I stand and I wait.

I wait for what seems like ages. The place is quiet. No one breathes in a disconcerting fashion against my neck again. I do not feel the same presence I felt before, even though my suspicion and fear block what may be left of my reasoning skills.

“Are you finished then, ghoul of Bedlam? May I go now?” I speak and my voice sounds unbearably quiet and small. But it’s the best I can do under the circumstances. Circumstances of course, being utterly ridiculous and ludicrous.

No one answers me, and I order my feet to take me to the diary. I pick it up, where it is sprawled like a wounded bird, and open it. I flip through the pages quickly and see all the strange, yet fascinating handwriting still present and accounted for. I feel vaguely relieved somehow. I had had an odd premonition that it would be completely empty and my journey with Rose would be over, but the diary was still full and waiting for me.

I pocket it, and where I had felt no persuasion to run before, I do now. I run back the way I had come, past the dreaded rooms that always gave me unpleasant feelings. Now I would associate those feelings with Dr. Whatshisname's office for the rest of time. I thunder down the stairs with a lack of grace that would appall Miss Helmes, and trip towards the open window. The only thing that slows me down is that damnable stain on the wall. Again, I am pulled there as if by unseen forces. Desperately not wanting to be drawn, but also not able to stop myself. I halt and shine my torch, which flickers now in a sad death march of low batteries, upon the burgundy colored bit of stone.

Of course, the stain is still there and still ugly, and still not stew.

Something else is there as well. A single word, written in familiar, childlike script.

ROSE.

Chapter 5

During my stay with the gypsy sideshow I wore a pink skirt, and ribboned ballet shoes that criss-crossed up my legs. I had golden sparkles on my skin, and wore a crown of ivy leaves. It made me appear even younger than my eight years and like a pixie child. Mothers cooed over me and fathers smiled fondly while little girls tried to befriend me. This newly acquired popularity had come too late as I had no interest in friends any longer, and children bored me. They were too easily frightened and too dull. My senses were more advanced than theirs, and their babyish games only served to annoy me. Adults weren't much better in my book, the book of Rose, but at least they didn't bother me.

The adults in the show were mostly gypsies who were a crew of odd and mismatched puzzle pieces. They were put together in a fashion so that their edges stuck out and nothing quite fit. There were ten of us, if I recall everyone correctly, and we were extreme opposites of one another. There was Bertha, who was as large as three men put together and wore huge patchwork skirts. I used to steal her extra one off the line on washing day to play circus tent with it.

The opposite of her was Dell, who was skinny as a pole and with the same personality of one. He was the only pale skinned person, besides me, and wore a top hat. Dell had the appearance of an undertaker, if you could pigeonhole an undertaker's appearance. His face was stretched tight over his bones so you could visualize his skeleton quite easily. Indeed, he looked more like a skeleton or a corpse than he did a living, breathing person. He was not fearsome though in character, only in his bony exterior. They billed themselves as Jack Sprat and His Wife even though they were not married in real life.

Another two-some that drew the crowds were Gertie and Lulu, our Siamese twins that were conjoined at the shoulders. Gertie was nice and even-tempered and Lulu was snappish and persnickety. They weren't real gypsies at least not by blood, but they laid out in the sun all the time achieving darker skin that tanned like leather, and dyed their blonde hair black.

They had been with circuses before, but were tired of all the "politicing," they said. They liked the traveling gypsy life better. Every time I smell tobacco smoke now, I still think of those two. Solomon said Gertie was a parasitic twin, and she was only nice because she wasn't entirely capable of being any other way. She didn't talk, but she sometimes smiled in a lopsided fashion or made a strange noise that we all took for laughter. She was just an extra head and arm for Lulu.

Solomon was our doctor. He was not a real doctor, of course, but a con man. He was a charlatan, a wolf in sheep's clothing and he had the voice of an angel. He'd call those crowds in to us mesmerizing his prey with his pretty words, and his beautiful brown eyes and long lashes. He had all the moral fortitude of the devil himself. He'd take candy from a babe, the last coin from a widow, morsels of food from a starving man. He didn't apologize for it either. Instead he'd laugh and say, "Stupid is as stupid does." We got along fine, we did. His name was Solomon, and a better father I never had.

That does explain some lack of...what did she call it? 'moral fortitude' in Rose's personality. Raised by a pack of thieves and left to our own devices, would we all be nothing but the devil's minions?

Then again, I never had a father either, and I don't go pinning ladies' hands to the wall with scissors, not even in my very worst mood.

"Judge not, lest ye be judged," Miss Helmes' voice rings through my head, and I obligingly banish my unkind thoughts.

Solomon was an expert at all things devious and shifty, and it was from him that I discovered how to be two-faced in order to get something I wanted. Though at first, I only learned from afar by watching. I had never tried to be someone I wasn't, so this playacting with this façade was new to me. He was one way with one customer, even adopting a different accent to go with his different personalities, and then entirely different with another. The outcome was always the same, and this was the prize! People handed over their money to him as if under his spell, and I watched in my little pink tutu as he manipulated them, left and right. I didn't know Solomon's true personality myself, no one did, and his moods changed as quickly as the weather. After a few weeks of my eyes on him, he noticed my interest, and my training began in earnest.

I wasn't lured by the thought of getting rich the way he was. No, it was the illusions and the lives he created for himself. And, of course, the manipulations of people I found so fascinating. That was his trick I longed to study. The power he had over them and that spell he cast. That was what I was after. His world was the strangest place in the universe, and I was happy to be a part of it while I could.

While I could.

The damning prologue and epilogue of my whole life. Everything has its seasons, but mine are always unfairly shorter than others. I knew now what I was, at least in part, and I knew some morning I would wake to a new place and new people. One morning there'd be no Solomon, no gypsy wagon, no sideshow crowds, and no crown of ivy leaves twisted in my yellow hair. The knowledge gave me more intensity to learn from Solomon as quickly as I could, before I would be forced to leave him forever. He called me his "odd little goose," then "little goose," then just "Goose."

"Goose," he'd say. "People are like sheep. And you and me? We're the big, bad wolves. And that's nothing to be ashamed of, now is it?"

I'd shake my head obediently. My ivy drooped into my eyes and I pushed it back onto my head. I needed a mother to properly pin my hair, but I had no mother. Bertha wouldn't come near me, and Gertie had no gift for beautifying anyone. Solomon was no help as he was just an overgrown boy.

"Cuz some people have to be the sheep, and some have to be the wolves, and Goose, wouldn't you rather be the one who has all the power? I

know I would. I would indeed."

"I would indeed, too," I answered. *"Anyway, I like wolves better."*

Even though I felt like a fool for doing so, I ran home last night, pell-mell, through the darkness. Sure, I could not explain the diary suddenly leaving my hands and hurling through the air nor could I explain the message left on the wall, but my analytical and scientific mind simply could not process what I had experienced this night. I was not ready to believe in ghosts, and more to the point, I was not eager to prove myself wrong. I only knew I would never tell a soul what went on there that night, or they might lock me up too.

I try not to think of it at all, and lose myself in Rose's accounts of her strange, and very sad life. I am not prepared to believe every fantastic word she writes, since a mind as disturbed as hers cannot be trusted. It is certainly addictive reading at its finest, especially when the only other book I have is a medical dictionary. Which is not riveting midnight reading even to a nurse like me. So, even though my gooseflesh has not yet dissipated, I read on and am shocked when the sunlight streams through my window. I have only read but a few pages! Had my nighttime adventure taken so long that I have missed sleep altogether?

This is shockingly bad news for me, as I have a huge load of work for me at the new hospital.

I really am a nitwit.

*   *   *

My work day dawns as full of doom as I thought it might. I am completely exhausted. Really I am dead to the world, and my limbs feel like week-old porridge. I yawn constantly and don't even bother to hide it. Miss Helmes simply stares at me with her pursed lips and frowns, as though I am a great burden, her Christian cross to bear.

The new hospital is grand and everything inside it shines. Naturally it does, as the inmates, or the patients rather, haven't had the time to mess it all up. There is new staff as well, and they are just as shiny and polished. I can't help rolling my eyes at their naiveté. "Wait till the first one vomits on you or grabs you by your hair," I think. "You won't be so chipper then."

Mina is there with her cheeks flushed, eyes bright, and full of energy. Well, of course she is. After all, she didn't go traipsing through London at midnight breaking into buildings, and having odd supernatural adventures. She probably went to bed at a decent hour and slept like a baby all night long. I really must try to be more like Mina, ladylike and dear and wonderful. I wonder what she would do with the diary? Most likely she'd hand it over to Miss Helmes, I suppose. I'm quite sure she'd never feel the compulsion to read it. I don't *want* to read it either. Well, not exactly, but I feel I must.

Mr. Limpet is very excited to see me again and he goes on and on about dancing and parties. The poor man has been here off and on for many, many years. Just when his family thinks he's doing well at home, wham bam, here comes another bout of what they like to call his "spells," and he's back wandering the halls in his creaky wheelchair. This has been going on for most of his sorry life, I've gathered. He eats a biscuit slowly while he talks to me, the crumbs and spittle fall into his lap. So, I try to keep my eyes on the task of changing the bed sheets in all the rooms, like a maid. Oh, how I long for a good, gory surgery or a broken bone or some suturing!

"And during the war we didn't have no sugar," he went on, and I hear him chewing behind me. He passes to swallow noisily. "Remember when everyone threw the pie at each other because it tasted so awful? Do you remember, girl?"

"No, Mr. Limpet, I wasn't alive during the war. I'm not yet eighteen," I sigh, but then I feel bad for being so peevish and I turn to smile gently at him.

"Oh." His face falls. "Oh."

"But that sounds like a lovely memory. What kind of pie was it?"

"It was berry," he mumbles and I hear his chair creak as he turns to leave me at last. "It was a berry pie. Tart them berries were. Needed sugar." His voice begins to fade as he turns the corner. "They didn't put no sugar in our pie. Don't know why you don't remember. Hard to forget a pie like that." The last thing I hear from him is his barking laugh echoing down the hall and then mercifully, he is gone.

I tuck in the last corner as tight as possible and flip the thin blanket up in the air. Orphanage living taught me excellent bed making skills and you could bounce a coin off my smooth beds. The sheets go up in the air and billow down, then up in the air again, and *crack* go my wrists as I yank it down and it settles perfectly into place.

At the end of that year, we grew into something more than a magic show, potion peddlers, and freak exhibits. We began to advertise ourselves as something of a circus sideshow, albeit the world's smallest. Not enough to draw large crowds and not enough to make plenty of money, but we still honed our skills as bizarre and stupendous and miraculous and not to be missed. Our tent would go up with a flick of our wrists on our tiny stage. Then suddenly we weren't just a strange band of misfits, but a professional group of entertainers. We had no name, we had no reputation, we had no expectations, and therefore, we had freedom.

Solomon stuck to his potions and gimmicks, and I stuck to Solomon. The others could do their tricks, their performances, their silly shows, their oddities of bodies, but we… we were the ones not to be missed on those hot summer nights.

I did not know the exact date back then, and I do not know it now. Looking back, I didn't care. What did it matter anyway?

Time meant little to me then, and it means even less to me now. A ridiculous institution it is, time. It's beneath me.

Solomon began to take an interest in me finally. He taught me to distract an audience and how to turn their eyes towards something unimportant, so that I could slip jewelry from their necks or money from their pockets. I could palm a lady's hairpiece and put it away in an instant. She'd be never the wiser until she returned home and took up her brush before bed. I could lift a pocket watch easily and so quickly that the gentleman would never even miss it for hours.

Of course, all of this was petty thievery. But it was a good way to make a living and better than most.

Somewhere along the way, we had acquired a bear. A silly thing that was as mild mannered as old Methuselah. He was a reject from some circus where he had once ridden unicycles in all his glory or some such idiotic contradiction. His claws were long and black, and I remember the smell of his fur. All in all, he was frail and not fearsome. Still, he was a bear and some odd perversion of nature requires mankind to revere, love, and finally dominate a wild thing. It knew stupid tricks and performed for fish. I had no respect for him, even though the tiny crowds we drew loved him and indeed, so did the others in our troupe.

Gertie and Lulu were a draw too, naturally. They had a reputation and their names alone went ahead of us in the night. If we traveled by train, which was a rare treat, then the names of the twins went bobbing along beside like a beacon in the night. If we traveled by foot, then their reputation rushed ahead of us paving our way for a bit of success. They'd usher in a bit of promise, the delight of a full belly, the joy of a happy crowd. Lulu and Gertie were our bread and butter, and that dumb animal was the jam.

I began to learn more tricks.

Solomon could throw knives at people's heads like a magician, but with the skill of a marksman, and the grace of a dancer. He began his show with a request for a volunteer. People being people, therefore complete and utter wastes of skin, would consistently endanger his skill. No matter the brave farm boy, the savvy city girl, the mustached gentleman, and so on and so forth, they would consistently ruin his show. Flinching was the best he could hope for, but utter panic, ducking and screaming were the norm. It annoyed him mightily, although he smiled and pretended to be sympathetic. Really, he wanted to show his skills, and it was difficult to do that when your assistant was running off. So, I became his girl, his never flinching, brave girl. At the age of nine I could do what most soldiers could not. I stood fierce and calm as he threw razor sharp knives at my body.

Our routine was this:

I would stand flat against a painted back drop of canvas. It was painted bright white, and red was used to paint a huge target that completely engulfed me. I stood straight as an arrow and twice as still with the first throw. It would always go a little off.

On purpose, of course.

It would barely even hit the canvas winging madly off the side and clinging only just to the very edge, and then it would wobble and throb in the peripheral of my vision.

The second would be nearly as bad.

The crowd would begin to jeer a bit.

"No wonder she was your willing participate, sir!" they'd laugh. "Why, I'll be up there next if that's the best your aim can do!"

The third shot would wildly veer off and pin my skirt to the canvas. The crowd would gasp a bit, though it was mostly the women and children. They realized I could not easily go anywhere should a shot go awry, since the knife held me fast.

The fourth would whiz by my ear, my stoic and never flinching ear. It would land so close to me that a lady would inevitably shriek.

The fifth would pin my hair to the board, and still through it all I never moved.

The sixth would land square between the third and second fingers of my left hand. Of course, it was just like we had practiced. If I lifted my thumb and forefinger, I could nearly caress the metal blade and I was always tempted to, but I held still. The crowd would now be utterly silent, but I could normally hear a murmured prayer or two.

The seventh would bind my skirt more tightly to the canvas bull's eye, and the eighth would miss my boot by the tiniest hair's breath.

The ninth would graze my hair again, and I would feel the ivy crown tremor with the weight of the blade as it settled through the leaf. At least half the crowd would now be telling Solomon to stop.

The tenth and final knife would be thrown with such force that I would have been knocked backwards without the heavy canvas backdrop behind for support. It would pin me to it like a girl's embroidery caught in its hoop. I was stretched tight, and a quick escape would have been nearly impossible.

The knife would just miss my throat, but only by a hair.

The audience members would swoon and others would curse. A few would shake Solomon's hand merrily while others would rush to help me, and they all would pay their admission in relief.

The time came when I was weary of being the prey of Solomon's knives. I wasn't frightened but I was bored and he grudgingly let me practice my own throwing skills. At first I was dreadful. I had no depth perception, no knowledge of the mechanics of force, gravity, or flight. I had no premonition of where my wayward tosses would land, but I loved the feel of the handle in my palm, and the way it fit perfectly in my tiny fingers. I loved they way the cheap silver glinted in the sun, as it somersaulted and flipped its way to its target. I felt at home and secure with the knives.

Wonderful, I think nervously. Give a mentally ill girl a set of knives. A fabulous idea, Solomon, old boy. Remind me to thank you.

I find myself dreading the next few pages, but of course I'm caught like a ram in a thicket. Escape for me is impossible now, and I must rely on my instincts or my rescuer for liberation. So, I read on as my duties go unperformed, and my mind cries out for sleep. My rescuer is absent, and my instincts are asking for more of the same.

Naturally at first, no one would stand still for me, not even Solomon. I used an outline on the old canvas target that I chalked in that was a bit like the murder victim's outline that would be used decades and decades later. I digress.

Odd, I think.

I practiced and practiced, until I knew the weight of every individual knife. Of course, they were a set and they should have been equals, indistinguishable and identical. They were not. They had their own personalities, their own quirks. One was just a hair lighter, while one flew inexplicably faster. One was chipped only the tiniest bit on the tip, and one was not quite right in the handle. Different somehow, but only in ways that were minuscule to the everyday human. But to a knife thrower?

Wholly dissimilar.

And the best part was the element of danger that even I, as the artist and the magician, could not predict.

I relished it. I loved it.

I became quicker and faster, until my throws were a blur. Partly because it was the act, and partly because I liked the thrill of not knowing which knife I had chosen until it had fled from my fingers. If I slowed down I could easily adjust for the knife's idiosyncrasies. Not adjusting was simply more exhilarating.

Where would they land? I mused as one went wildly awry. Where would they land, indeed?

After I became skilled enough with the knives, Solomon let me use the bear. It roared at me as it was lashed to the canvas. Had it any sense at all and knew it was a bear, it could have untied its ropes easily. This never occurred to the bear, as it was a captive from birth, and captives are helpless if they don't learn early on to free themselves. In vain he struggled pathetically against his ropes, complaining that his food bowl was left too far from his reach. The knives that whizzed by his fur didn't faze him much at all, and I was disappointed by his lack of terror.

By my tenth birthday we had traveled for what felt like the length of the globe and back. I did not know how long my time with Solomon and the gypsies would last, and I felt the pull of some strange gravity tugging at me. It was like the ticking of a clock.

Tick tock, it mocked.

Hurry up, girl.

Hurry up girl, indeed, I think hastily, as I shove the diary back in my apron and make a show of bustling out of the room. Footsteps are coming my way, and I don't need Miss Helmes' iron glare at my laziness to condemn me. I make a show of smiling brightly at her as we pass in the hallway, me with my bucket of cleaning supplies and her with her disapproving looks. She stands straight and watches me like a hawk with her long, skinny neck, and without a word as I turn down the hallway. I feel like running, but I am far too tired to do more than shuffle quickly.

A shiny, cheerful new member of Bethlem's staff stops me as I nearly plow into him. My bucket of supplies clatter to the floor, and my duster rolls away merrily. The boy steadies me with his hands at my elbows. A boy he certainly is, as he can't be older than myself, and I would wager a year or so younger.

"All right then, miss?" he inquires politely. He has the stocky build of a farmboy, and an unfortunate shade of red hair.

"Quite all right, thank you, but I seem to have lost my duster under the settee there."

"Ah." He looks the way my finger is pointing. "I expect a gentleman would go after it, wouldn't he?"

"I expect so, but I've never met one in this sodding place. Anyway, my arms are thinner than yours, so I'll find it, thanks. Hold my bucket?" I hold it out expectantly.

"Of course." He does so, but his manner suggests he'd rather not. He holds it out to his side gingerly as if he's afraid of the bleach, vinegar, and scrub brushes.

"I'm Lizzie, by the way," I say as I crawl as far beneath the settee as the space allows "And you are?"

"Mack. Just Mack."

"Well, Just Mack," I stand again with my feather duster in hand and retrieve my bucket. "I do hope you like it here. It's always an adventure, isn't it?"

"Quite."

"Helmes got you cleaning cracks in the flooring yet? Or stripping blood off walls?" I can't help myself, since he's so impressionable looking. Still has his mother's apron's strings attached, I'd bet. I reach out and pat his back as I turn to go.

"Blood on walls? Really? Where?" To my surprise, he seems intrigued.

Maybe there is more man to him than I'd realized.

"The other place. Never mind. My point is, you'll be doing a lot fewer medical things here at Bedlam than you will be doing laundry and kitchen duty."

"Well, we all start somewhere, eh? And me, I've been told to start in the operating room today. Assisting a lobotomy." He puffs out his chest boastfully. "My first, you know."

Lucky sod.

Chapter 6

About an hour later I come across Mr. Connelly, him of the impeccable clothing and ludicrous good looks. There is on other word of what he is doing besides *lounging* in a chair in the waiting room. His polished shoes are propping up with his feet and legs on Miss Helmes' cherry wood end table. His hat is down over his eyes and the reason, it seems, is that he is sleeping.

Sleeping in a mental institution.I can't help feeling bemused. What a relaxed man is our Mr. Connelly. Most visitors are jumpy and anxious when they're here. He seems quite at home.

I give in to a childish impulse that can only be blamed on orphanage living and kick his feet out from under him. He slides wildly to the floor in a heap of clothes, legs, and arms. He glares up at me and rights his hat.

"Oh dear, I'm dreadfully sorry," I deadpan. "I thought you were dead, or perhaps a victim of one of our dear inmates. Some are dangerous, don't you know?"

"Yes, I met the most dangerous one not a few moments ago. A Mr. Limpet, I believe. Asked me to dance. Tried to take me in his arms. Afraid I had to decline. My girl wouldn't like it. You got my pants creased." He looks cross.

"Dreadfully sorry," I repeat. To myself I think, *he's got a girl?* Well, good, she can press his pants. "Did you ever find who you were looking for?"

"No, not exactly. I was hoping you could help me with that actually. You've been here a bit longer than some of the others. The last boy that ran through here, eager to help me, had been here about ten minutes, I think. *I* had to tell *him* where to find the toilet."

"Sounds like Mack. Evidently, he is one of our best surgeons, and yes, before you ask, I'm a bit bitter about that. Anyway, who are you looking to find?"

"Small girl, young, about your age, I suppose. Blonde. She's been here—," he pauses and reflects for a moment. "Oh, I don't even know. Not long. A fortnight, perhaps? Or longer? At least, I think she's here. She should be here." His voice trails off a bit, and I can't quite catch the next part. "She's always here," is what I think I hear.

"We have a few under the age of twenty, yes, but a name would probably expedite our search, Mr. Connelly."

"Oh, I thought I'd said that." He pulls the brim of his hat a bit lower and averts his eyes from me. "It's Gray. Rose Gray?"

* * *

I feel like I've been punched in the guts, but I recover quickly. Here I'd thought I was reading the diary of a girl long gone and yet the ink had hardly dried. My age then. Now. Here in my hospital, to boot? Unexpected, and not quite the pleasure I would have thought it to be.

I had caught my breath when he had said the name of our mutual acquaintance, and now I let it out and allow my eyes to find his face again. He is looking at me quizzically.

"Do you know her then?" He looks at me like he can read me like a book. He is positively scanning my very soul with those eyes.

"No, no I don't know her, but I have heard of her," I falter.

He smiles ruefully. "Yes, our Rose's reputation always precedes her, I'm afraid. What has she done this time?"

"Oh. Oh, well, I believe she stabbed someone through the hand with sewing scissors." No point in lying to the poor chap. After all, he'd find out eventually.

Mr. Connelly surprises me by laughing outright. "Ah, that's my girl," he says, fondly. "I do apologize on her behalf, of course. The staff should know by now not to let her near weapons though. If I've warned them once, I've warned them a thousand times. Actually, I *have* warned them a thousand times." His rueful smile is back, and though I've not the foggiest notion what he's talking about really, I can't help but smile, too. "Where is she then? Do you know that? Miss Helmes seems vague on that particular detail."

"I'm afraid I don't know either. Not exactly. I don't know her personally or by sight. I do know…" I take a deep breath, but feel as though I cannot go on with the divulging of my secret. It would be sharing her, sharing Rose, and though I've no love for her, I do not want the diary confiscated until I can finish it.

"Yes?" Mr. Connelly prompts.

"I do know her words, that is, her handwriting. That is, I have this. It belongs to her." I reach in my apron and bring out the small, red journal. He takes it from me and turns it over in his hand and flips through the pages. Though they aren't terribly old, I know now, I'm still worried for them.

"It seemed older at first," I interject. "I thought she was a patient a long time ago. I had no idea she was still here."

"She's always here," he muses. He had said that just a few minutes before, hadn't he? "But yes, yes, it seems old because it is old."

"I don't understand."

"I know," he looks at me quite sorrowfully. "One of these days though, my girl, I'm afraid you might."

"Whatever does that mean?" I am taken aback.

"Nothing. Nothing at all. I was only hoping you'd know her, know my

Rose. But you don't, do you?" His eyes search me again, but this time, he is the one to pull away first. "It doesn't matter. Will this tell me where to find her then?" he looks again at the diary, this time with more interest than before.

"I don't know," I pause. "I haven't made it all the way through yet. I am still learning about her."

"And what have you learned?"

"Well, your Rose seems a bit…" I pause, once again, but this time because I am choosing my words carefully. "A bit confused and lost."

"Ah. You've hit the nail on the head. She was indeed. And are you reading of her childhood then?"

"Yes, I'm up to the part where she thinks she's traveling with a sideshow. Ring any bells?"

"Mmm. India perhaps, or the gypsies?"

"Gypsies, yes. They've taken her in, and they are traveling while she chucks knives at wildlife."

Mr. Connelly laughs. "Yes, she told me about that. And then? Where did she go from there?"

"I don't know yet. Perhaps you could tell me once you read it?"

"Me, read it?" In surprise, he looks down at the diary as though he'd forgotten he held it. He hands it back to me. "No, I think you're doing splendidly on your own. I already know the past. Only the future interests me. If you find a clue to that, Miss, would you let me know?" He tips his hat. "And don't worry, she'll turn up."

After the bear died of old age a few weeks after he became my partner in the knife throwing, Solomon stepped in. Of course, it made him seem terribly brave or terribly stupid, but really it was all a question of skill and mathematics and science and practice. I would never go too quickly with Solomon against my target as I was quite fond of him. I wouldn't have relished a life in that era without him. The twins were strange and odd and didn't care for me, not even sweeter tempered Gertie, and neither did anyone else. They only tolerated me at all because I brought in more of a crowd with my tiny, angel-like appearance and because any misgivings they may have had about my personality were stifled by Solomon's watchful eye and quick tongue. I was used to people not liking me, so it hardly bothered me, but that didn't mean I wanted no company at all.

One night in late October, a party came to see us. We already had a crowd, and their group of ten or so, mostly blathering young girls, made it the largest I had ever performed for. We did coin tricks, sold bottles of potions, collected tickets to see the twins in their dark and separate tent, and told fortunes by the light of the gypsy wagon. The group of girls were rich, their frocks the whitest whites with huge bows and boots that laced up tightly. They all had gloves of lace with pearl buttons, and I found myself desiring a pair myself. I eyed them longingly as I took their tickets.

One, a girl of perhaps twelve, was the ring leader (it was her birthday party) and saw me looking. She tucked her glorious locks of ebony hair behind her ear and tapped me on the nose.

"Would you like gloves like mine, little gypsy urchin? Look, girls, how she stares at us!"

The others tittered.

"As if we are the odd ones here!" another whispered loudly.

"Why are you so yellow haired, gypsy girl? Did they steal you away?" The first girl leaned towards me, as if voicing a conspiracy. "Were you a nice girl like us, with a family, and the dirty gypsies came and stole you away?"

"Or perhaps she has an English father somewhere, with a taste for gypsy women?" said the second girl, and they all laughed uproariously.

"Here, little child," The first girl unbuttoned her glove dramatically. "Take mine. Never let it be said I don't know how to give to charity. That should shut Mother Louisa up this week." She slapped them against my cheek with wicked force that stung and would leave a red mark behind to remember her by for days after, and they left to get their fortunes told.

I'm sure it seems quite obvious that I hated them very much. Any girl would at that point, but I am not just any girl.

When they came to my tent I wore the white gloves. I threw every knife perfectly, narrowly missing my dear Solomon, who pretended alarm at the last throw, just for the audience's sake. Everyone in my crowd applauded loudly, but not that group of girls. They only looked at me with contempt.

So I asked for a volunteer.

Here the diary has such terrible handwriting that I peer at the book in earnest. My heart is thumping, and my mind is jumping to violent conclusions about Rose Gray and her set of knives. I read on, haltingly, fragments working themselves out into sentences again as though her pen has steadied.

Of course, the girl who gave me the gloves—her lily white hands bare now, bare and lovely and graceful, not tanned and with bitten nails and knife scars like mine—volunteered, the way I knew she would. This one wouldn't back down from a challenge. She wasn't easily frightened or intimidated. She knew how to get places and what to do, and say, and act, once she got there. She was ruthless and arrogant. I very nearly liked her, if only she hadn't turned her contempt towards me. Perhaps we could have been friends?

Solomon watched me warily, and with concern, as if he knew I wasn't feeling well. For the first time ever, my hands shook ever so slightly as I picked up my first blade. I steadied them immediately. I stared at her, with her black shiny locks of hair artfully arranged around her shoulders, as she stood against the canvas backdrop. Her pointy little boots stuck out to the side in a ballerina's stance, and her hands were clasped in a dainty fashion in front of her stomach. Every man and every boy couldn't pull their eyes off her, and every girl and every woman wanted to be her. I motioned to her to put her arms to her side and spread her fingers. She did so without hesitation or qualm. The only movement she gave me as the first knife found its mark in the bull's eye was a bored little yawn.

"She's never worn gloves before," Solomon explained to the police later when they arrived. "They made her hands slippery. She's only a child. It was a tragic mistake."

"Whether or not the victim lives, we'll have to shut you down," the police told him. "Pack up, but don't go anywhere until this is sorted out."

"Yes, sir."

"And you, girl. No more playing with knives, do you hear?"

I didn't want to talk to him, but Solomon nodded at me, urging me to. "Yes, sir." I muttered.

"We wouldn't want more accidents. Play the piano; take up painting. But for God's sake, don't play with knives. Tragedy happens when you miss what you're aiming for. Could have happened to anyone now." He looked at me with sympathy. "Could have happened to anyone, child. Anyone can miss."

When he leaves, I run to Solomon, and he ruffles my hair and calls me Goose.

"I didn't miss," I say into his chest.

Chapter 7

We did not stay put as the police instructed. Solomon knew what I had done and knew I wouldn't feel the need to lie about it either, so he spirited me away that night cloaked in blackness, me in a dress of black with my black boots, he in a black cape that he took from Lulu's peg above her wagon, the one she used it to cover her twin when she didn't want attention. He swung me up on Vlad, the largest horse in our caravan, and we left the gypsies forever.

It was the closest I think I've ever come to crying out of sentimentality. Though they did not love me, I felt at home with them and did not relish the severing of our ties. Also, I worried and fretted that Solomon was angry with me, for they were his home too, and now he could never go back. Solomon was all I had; I couldn't bear it if he was angry with me.

I was his progeny, and I loved him so.

Thoughts of Rose and her madness plague me all the next day. I can't seem to escape from her, but ironically I am so busy at the hospital that I never have a chance to crack open the diary again and catch up on my reading. I am also becoming a bit concerned at the little red volume; I have a superstitious dislike of flipping to the last page, but it seems to me that when I picked it up off the floor that time when it had hurled itself across the room, the last good bit of the manuscript was blank. It had lain on the floor with its spine open before I had mustered up the courage to pick it back up, and blank white pages had stared up at me, hadn't they? I am now preoccupied with worries that it will end abruptly and I'll never get any answers to my questions. I want a nice tidy ending of some sort. I feel she owes me that after haunting me the way she is.

Haunting. What a peculiar word to drop unbidden into my thoughts. It fits though. Rose is stuck like a burr to my thoughts.

It's after the sun goes down and I am back at my flat that I finally find time to read. I make tea and tuck my hot water bottle deep inside my covers where it can warm my chilled feet. I am weary to the bone from scrubbing and fetching and washing and fluffing and pushing wheelchairs and all the other tedious chores and errands Miss Helmes had me running, and I need a hearty meal and a hot bath, but nothing will keep me from discovering where Rose and Solomon hid themselves.

The handwriting is wretched once again. I sigh and take a bracing sip of strong hot tea before I squint and force myself to concentrate. Slowly the chicken scratch becomes letters, the letters words, the words sentences, the sentences a hypnotic story.

We took refuge in the oddest of places, a place called The Bodleian Library. We lucked into it really, by chance, that very next night. We had sold Vlad for a tidy sum as soon as we made it to the city, and on foot, we stared up in awe at the massive library. Do you know how sometimes a moment freezes and you know you'll remember it forever? Standing there in the twilight, with Solomon holding my little hand in the shadow of the library, was like that. As if summoned by God himself, a man suddenly approached us and mistook us for the new librarian, a man who had been expected the morning before and who was supposedly coming with his small daughter.

Solomon never batted an eye, never raised a brow, never faltered in his speech.

We had been delayed on the road, he explained. A minor accident. Became turned around in this lovely, but large, place. How nice to have arrived, and were our rooms ready? Somehow the proof of our identity was talked about, nearly produced, almost exposed, yet, not quite. Solomon would turn the tide, he would artfully change the subject, becoming the likable but firm business man he assumed a librarian of that caliber would be. The man would very nearly hesitate, in some sort of alarm or suspicion, and Solomon would be soothing his worries with gracefully spun stories and explanations.

I stayed silent, marveling at Solomon's complete lack of honesty, and nearly believed him myself. Perhaps I really was his daughter? Were we really expected with bedrooms made ready and a respectable profession? I found myself momentarily as confused as the man who inadvertently hired us. The man called me Amanda, and he called Solomon Mr. Benning. Was I Amanda? I felt confused.

We were ushered into the sprawling building, and I brushed my fingertips against the spines of the books we passed. I was lost before we ever arrived at our rooms, but I was already devising maps in my head. The exploring in this place would take me years!

But of course, I didn't have years, did I?

So, to make up for the time I wouldn't have later, I ate, drank, breathed the library. Ironically, all the information we needed to run the library came from the depths of the building itself. Its other names were Bodley, or The Bod, or The Tower of the Five Orders, the latter being my favorite. It sounded mysterious and dark, which appealed to me and my nature.

I worried about leaving my new haven, so I slept only when I had to, which was infrequently. I did not want to wake someplace new, someplace without Solomon. Solomon read to me when he discovered I did not possess the talent myself: The Woman in White, A Cricket on the Hearth, Jane Eyre, Wuthering Heights, Othello, Hamlet, then onto works of nonfiction, biographies, histories. He read at a breakneck pace, quizzing me along the way. He expected me to learn how to do it myself, but I was stubborn. I didn't want to admit it, but the lines and curves of the letters made nearly no sense to me. It was a puzzle, and I had no gift for puzzles.

"You speak four languages and yet you cannot read even one!" he bellowed at me one night. "That is nonsense! You aren't trying!"

"I am," I cried, for he had never yelled at me before. "I am trying, I am!" I hurled Pilgrim's Progress at his head. He didn't even give me the satisfaction of ducking, and it hit him squarely where I had aimed, his sharply beaked nose. He wiped away the stream of blood and said not a

word. I stared, hypnotized, at the sight of the blood. Like a river running down his face it ran, and it reminded me of the smirking girl back at the side show. I cocked my head, remembering.

Though he kept reading to me as though nothing had happened, he refused to read the last page of any story or novel from that point on. "If you want to know what happens, read it yourself," he'd say, and snap shut the book with finality. I'd growl with disappointment at the unfinished tale (unless it was some frivolous frippery like Austen where I could invent a better ending anyway). But the ending of A Thousand and One Nights preoccupied me, and when my wheedling and pleading had no avail, I began to pay attention to Solomon's fingers as they traced the letters on the pages.

Eventually, I learned the twists and turns of the letters, and I was glad of the knowledge. I escaped into worlds of enchantment, treachery, love, suspense, murder, laughter, deception. I became a student of these characters. I studied The Artful Dodger's techniques of thievery, Cathy's wildness, Mr. Rochester's descent into denial and lies, Ivanhoe's goodness and purity. I took what I respected from all of them and left the rest. Austen I had no use for, nor Bronte much, but Shakespeare was a treat, and I especially found the tragedies intriguing. The comedies, however, were a waste of my time and a waste of the great bard's talent.

Naturally, the real librarian and his real daughter came by one day not a month after we had settled there. They had fallen ill and delayed their trip. Somehow, fate I suppose, had lost their letter of explanation and their request to hold the position, and Solomon turned them away with a cunning hand. They left quickly. I laughed at them, and they heard me. Though they turned and looked for the source of the laughter, I was hidden behind a shelf of books and they couldn't see me. It must have seemed to them that I was a ghost.

So the ghost of the library I became.

Ours days melted into one another. Since I didn't sleep and the library was dark at all hours, it seemed even more so. Visitors were few and far *between, and most ignored me. Most were there for some dull bit of research, and they wanted to be left alone with their genealogy or their philosophy or whatever. Children never came, and sometimes days would pass without a single solitary visitor, at least in my area of the library. I was becoming rather weak and frail from the lack of sleep, so I didn't move around much.*

Solomon was a surprisingly good librarian for a fake, and no one seemed to notice when he didn't have an answer, so self assured was he with his answers and his hand motions and his excuses. He could distract them by a tall tale of something else, and they'd leave so amused they'd never even realize they hadn't gotten what they'd come for. Or he'd ask leading questions so that they really gave him their own answers to begin with, and he'd accept their praise with a humble smile.

When we grew tired of books, we practiced magic tricks and illusions. I could palm anything by now, and I was excellent at distraction. Cards were becoming easier to manipulate. I could write my name on the Queen of Hearts and tear it into tiny pieces, blow them from my cupped hands, then make those pieces reappear after the dust had settled, nestled in the tallest bookshelf, peeking out from a volume of Dante. The books and stories I was reading were feeding my imagination, so I could come up with elaborate tricks, some with levitation and death defying impossibilities (not all were realized, of course). Each of my tricks and designs and ideas I wrote down, in my new found script, and shared them with Solomon, who indulged me sometimes and asked me grave questions other times when I had genuinely peaked his magicians interest. I came up with plans to levitate a dueling pair of swordsmen— so preoccupied with their fight they would be, that they would not notice their floating until they bumped against the ceiling—and I designed a trick using mirrors that would make it appear to the audience that I had sawed off my own feet in a magical box. My imagination was fostered, and I thought I was the better for it. I thought we were the better for it.

A year passed.

I was eleven years old when Solomon left one morning and didn't come back.

All that year I had slept a fraction of what normal people spent in sleep. I was desperate to stay, determined to live all my life with him and our library; so focused was I on my task that it never occurred to me that he would be the one to leave.

My book of plans, ideas, designs, sketches and words and plottings and drawings, all gone with him. The space by Dante's Inferno where I kept all my treasures was barren. The space in my chest where I kept my heart was barren.

I pause and grieve silently for the little girl whose only father figure was a strange con man. Why had he left? Had she become too wild and strange for him to handle? Had some accident befallen him on his way to market one day, or had he left with intention and purpose in his abandonment? The disappearance of her writings seemed to suggest so.

And what would his desertion mean for fragile, yet terrifyingly capable, Rose?

Was it even possible for her to slip further in the shadows of madness? How deep did those shadows go?

The questions fire in my brain like they were catapulted there by a well-trained assassin, but a larger problem loomed. It was as I feared: I flipped the page, and without warning I had come to the last of the writing. The following pages were clean and bare and blank. The rest of the diary was empty.

* * *

I tell Mr. Connelly of the abrupt ending of the diary when I see him next, several days later. I had mused and contemplated and hashed out whether or not to speak to him of her at all, but I found my relief at seeing him stride through the door at Bedlam so great that I nearly tripped over my words in a rush to get them out.

He listened to my tale with a grave (or was it simply a tolerant?) expression. "I see," was his response when I ended with Rose's abandonment at the Bodleian Library. "And this leaves us where exactly?"

"I don't know," I stammer, then find enough pluck to meet his eyes. "But since you seem to have misplaced her, I thought her past might shed some light on her whereabouts."

He regards me with something like amusement in his beautiful eyes. "I misplaced her, did I?" he echoes, with a chuckle. "And here I thought the hospital might have kept a more careful eye on her. Allow your patients to go wandering about, do we? Check themselves out and join society whenever they feel the need, do they? Step out for some air and not come back in, hmm? Happen often, does it?"

"No, of course not!" I feel a chill as I realize the implication in his words. Had Bedlam lost her? There would be a scandal.

"Don't fret." His mouth turns up in a smile, and I realize he is only teasing. "Rose goes where she likes, and she's free to do so. She'll be back."

I think back to the night with the tossing of the diary and the writing on the wall. To me, words come unbidden in my head:

Or maybe she's never left.

Could she be hiding in the old asylum?

Chapter 8

I worry about the scandal a lost patient could cause for us. Not the least
Miss Helmes and me, but for the great doctor, the great doctor who I am
hoping to impress eventually with my skills as a nurse, if he would just
glance my way with something other than the desire for the fetching of
sandwiches. While no one fetches sandwiches like I fetch sandwiches, I
really hope to turn his head with something decidedly less pathetic. I
decide to ask Miss Helmes point blank about Rose Gray. If we've
misplaced a patient during the move, I should know about it.

She seems less than alarmed about the whole thing. "I remember Rose,
yes. Little thing. Precocious. Violent."

"And was she released? How long ago?" I persist.

"I'm hardly the file keeper, am I?" she retorts, mildly. "I'm only the
glorified house keeper."

"But why don't I know her? I know all the patients."

"I don't know why you don't know her," she minces her words, slowly, as
though I'm an imbecile. Her pinched nostrils flare with the effort it takes
to not reach out and throttle me. "Everybody else does."

"Mr. Connelly says she's here, or that she'll be back, or something along
those lines! He's rather cryptic." I frown, trying to remember just what he
had said.

"Mr. Connelly says a lot of things," she retorts, sharply. "Now, are we
done here? I've patients who actually want my help in their wretched little
lives." She crosses her arms with such fervency that I'm surprised I don't
hear her elbows snap. Of course, she has the cushioning of her colossal
chest to soften the blow.

"Yes, ma'am."

It's only later that I realize I didn't mention my worry that Rose could be holing up in the old hospital, and she never really told me anything about Rose being released. She didn't really tell me anything at all.

* * *

"And so you want to go to the library? On a harebrained scheme? To find Rose? What is she to you?" Mr. Connelly speaks out of the side of his mouth, through his cigarette. He removes it lazily and blows smoke in my direction, in more ways than one, it seems sometimes.

I wave my hand in front of my face and cough, annoyed. "I thought you said that stuff would kill you."

"We'll all die of something, my little one. Didn't you know?"

"Don't call me that." I feel insulted, or patronized. I'm not sure which is worse. "Aren't you concerned for her?"

"My questions first."

I sigh and try to remember them. "Yes, it isn't harebrained. Yes, I don't know. But if she's wandering around, that might be somewhere she'd like to go in her freedom." I'm still loath to admit our other option is the original Bedlam. I'm in no hurry to go back there, and besides, if she isn't locked in, why in the world would she stay? I certainly wouldn't.

"Fair enough." The corners of his lips turn up around the cigarette. "And you expect help, is that it?"

"I expect a ride. I can't exactly walk to Oxford, and I hate trains. I don't know why you aren't more anxious to find her."

"And I don't know why you are."

"Fair enough," I echo. "We'll agree to be mystified by one another. I'll have to ask Miss Helmes for some time away."

"Leave Miss Helmes to me. Shall we leave now?" He removes his hat long enough to run his fingers through his light colored hair, then puts it back on, a bit crooked. I fight the impulse to straighten it and cross my arms in a hurry.

"Now? Right this moment now?" I am taken aback.

"Why not? I am a wealthy, idle, young man. I have nothing else to do besides play bridge, woo women, drink gin, and gamble."

I ignore that. "You don't think we'll find her there, do you?" I ask, curiously.

"No." There is something like sadness in his eyes as he answers. "But I suppose I would like to walk in the steps she did, so long ago. It'd be nice to have something to do until she comes back."

"How long ago? Her steps, I mean." I falter a bit, but I don't know why. Something about my question unsettles me, and I am almost afraid to hear the answer.

"Lifetimes, little one. Lifetimes ago."

I'm getting a bit weary of the cryptic comments.

*　*　*

Mr. Connelly's car's passenger seat is the most luxurious thing I've ever sat upon, and that includes Mina's grandmother's embroidered Windsor chair.

"It purrs like a kitten, but is sleek like a lion!" I exclaim, without even thinking.

Mr. Connelly throws back his head and laughs. "Oh, you do remind me of someone I used to know!" He tosses the butt of his cigarette out the window of the car. "Girls and cars," he chuckles. "Some things never change.”

I ignore him and indulge myself with a daydream of being a fine lady, and him my muscular, eager to please chauffeur.

“What’s it called?” I ask, dreamily.

“A Rolls-Royce Phantom.”

“It must be the most lovely car in the world.”

“At the moment, yes. I suppose so.”

“And fast?” I sit up straighter, and I guess there must a gleam in my eye, for he laughs again.

“Not particularly.”

“Can I drive?”

“No. Now shut up so I can remember which road will get us there.”

“Great. You’re cryptic *and* bossy. Two of my favorite qualities in men.”

“Pout later. Open the glove box and get me a map, would you?” It takes me a moment of fiddling with the latch before I swing it open. Besides the proverbial pair of gloves, it’s empty. “Hey, Sherlock, where else would you have put your map?”

“I haven’t the foggiest. What I wouldn’t give for a GPS in this bloody century.”

“I would think you would organize this lovely car better. I know I would if it were mine,” I point out, only a little bit smugly, I’m sure.

“Perhaps it doesn’t belong to me either. Perhaps I stole it.” He turns his eyes back to me, and waggles his brows suggestively.

I roll my own eyes and hope the road signs to Oxford aren't few and far between. The next few minutes pass in silence, but since I've never been a girl who knew when to shut up, it isn't long before I am talking again.

"What's a ghee-pee-esque?" I inquire.

"What?"

"You said you wanted a ghee-pee-esque in this bloody century."

"Oh. It's a handy device for navigation. Very cutting edge."

"Do sailors use it?"

"I suppose they do. Are you going to talk all the way to Oxford?"

"I suppose I am. How do you know Rose? Is she your..." I want to say lover, but at the last second I am too cowardly. "Your sister?"

"No. Not my sister, but very dear to me."

"I'm sorry she's so troubled. Has the hospital helped much?"

He laughs shortly and, I think, bitterly. "Bedlam has hurt her more than helped her, I'm afraid. But it's better now. Better than it was before, I mean."

"In the olden days, you mean? Yes, it must have been awful for the patients then. Today we're so medically advanced! Really, she's lucky to be with us. I mean, to **have** been with us. In this enlightened scientific time. And we prefer Bethlem, you know, as opposed to Bedlam." Never mind that I typically call it that myself, and usually worse.

I can't be sure, but it seems as though it's Mr. Connelly's turn to roll his eyes. "If you say so. Medically advanced, my right foot," he mutters.

"And there you go with the cryptic comments again. You're an odd man,

Mr. Connelly."

"I've been called worse," he replies, mildly. "Now why don't you get some sleep and give my ears a rest? They're beginning to bleed from all the chatter. I'll wake you when we get to Bodley."

I quiet down and close my eyes, but I cannot sleep.

He called the library Bodley.

But he said he had never read the diary. How did he know its nickname?

"Silly girl," I chide myself after my heart stops racing. He's an educated man. I suppose everyone in all of England knows the names of libraries—everyone but silly orphan sandwich fetchers.

I tell myself to relax, but it's no good. I'm on edge, and I'm beginning to feel there might be something sinister about my new comrade that I didn't see before. Was I foolish to get in the car with him? My reputation isn't something I ever cared a fig for, so driving off with a man without a proper chaperon doesn't matter to me, but I hadn't thought things through to an unsavory or dangerous element. I was so on fire to get to the last place I knew meant something to Rose.

Who was this Mr. Connelly, really? Was I foolish to trust him so? I wish I had been more specific in informing Miss Helmes of our destination, and I pick tiny flecks of red lipstick off my lips with my fingernails in a distracted fashion the rest of the car ride.

Chapter 9

The library is so beautiful, and grand. More grand than anything I have ever seen, though to be fair, I haven't seen much in my time. I was even too embarrassed to admit to Mr. Connelly that I had never been to Oxford, a mere 60 miles from London. I wish to be more world traveled; I wish to see America especially: the land of Hollywood and glamour. I would take my pigtails down and hobnob with all the actresses and cowboys. In America, I could be anybody; I just know it, and someday I will find my way there.

Then again, their architecture would not be so fine as this, here at Bodley. The proprietor is a chubby man with outdated mutton chops on his face (he makes me think of someone straight out of A Christmas Carol) and a habit of turning every conversation into a history lesson, even our introductions. I confess to feigning interest while my thoughts run away with myself.

I am picturing a young girl, a young, frail blonde girl, amongst the books. She would be daring and light on her feet and very quick. You might think you saw something, a shadow perhaps, over your shoulder or near your knee, but in the split second it would take your eyes to adjust, it would be gone. Light as a feather and twice as shifty, the ghost of what you thought you saw would be gone forever. The ghost of the library, she called herself, and it seemed to me that I could imagine her as such without any trouble at all.

I touch the spine of a volume of Shakespeare and recall what she wrote about The Bard; she was a lover of the tragedies and found the comedies a waste of his talent. What a twisted mind our Rose had. Has. Did I expect to find her here, among her treasures and the dusty memories of her childhood? Why would I think she would come back to the spot of her abandonment by Solomon, the cruel pretender? Would I, in such a spot? No, but I may have left a clue, and that is what I am wishing for.

"Do you have photographs of your librarians?" I ask Mr. Mutton Chops, and when he turns his gray eyes to me in surprise, I realize I have interrupted him rudely. I believe he was going on about the collection when my question flattened his diatribe. "Pardon me, sir. Do forgive me. I'm just terribly interested in the history of libraries, in the biographies of librarians, to be precise."

"A commendable pursuit in your education, Miss, but I am afraid I do not know of many photographs of the Bodleian's librarians. A few perhaps, scattered here and there. But you may ask away, young lady, and my substantial knowledge shall fill your hunger!" He beams at me proudly. Puffed like a peacock, he is, but I can't help but like the silly man.

"I heard tale of a ghost," I lower my voice conspiratorially. "A young child maybe? That haunts the books? This would have been, what?" I turn my gaze to Mr. Connelly for confirmation. "Recently? Within the last decade, certainly?"

Mr. Connelly ignores me; he seems distracted. He too, is running his hands along the spines of the old books. I feel like an interloper, a trespasser, and the touch of his hands is like a lover on skin. He does not seem to remember where we are, and I feel like I'm an intruder in his strange memories.

The mutton-chopped wonder does not seem to notice anything amiss, and he laughs when I mention the ghost.

"Ah! Yes! The ghost! How I've longed to see her myself, I have."

"Her?" I echo, curiously, as though I didn't know the sex.

"Yes, the murdered daughter of a French aristocrat. Or was it the murdered sister of a Belgian actress? The murdered mother of an English prostitute? Ah, well, the details don't matter, do they? The murdered someone of someone who roams our ancient aisles by night! Walking to and fro, she does, creaking the floor boards and shaking loose the dust. Softly murmuring your name, though she has no business knowing it, lifting the novels off your hands and dropping them upon the floor..."

He is making things up and yet the description is so fitting of what I experienced that night at Bedlam that I am uncomfortable and find myself rubbing my arms to get rid of the gooseflesh there.

"Just a legend then? Was there no child that lived here at the library, even for a short time? The daughter of a librarian, perhaps?"

"Aye, there was, but they were employed only a short while. Left quite suddenly, they did, and never came back."

"What happened to them? Did you know them?"

"No, not I. I'm not nearly old enough! This would have been... oh, dear me. The only librarian with a daughter was, if I'm not mistaken, was nearly a hundred years ago, to be sure. That's why she's just a ghost now, isn't it? Can't hardly be a ghost if you're alive, now can you?"

"Can you?" I wonder to myself. It seems she can. Because Rose haunts this library the same way she haunts Bedlam, and if Mr. Connelly isn't lying—which I don't believe him to be—Rose is very much alive.

But why the discrepancy in dates? There must be some sort of mistake somewhere. I look to Connelly again, but he acts as though he hasn't heard a word spoken, and he stares off into space. No help to me at all. It seems as though I must continue my investigation myself, so I plunge deeper.

"Will you be so kind as to point me towards Dante, sir? I'm afraid I am quite obsessed with him."

"But of course, child. Right this way."

We leave Connelly standing where he is, a sad expression on his face. Of course, I must be imagining things, but as I turn to leave him, he meets my eye, and the expression there is of such wistfulness and yearning that I am nearly undone. I feel as though I want to cry, and yet I do not know what I would be crying for.

*   *   *

I convince the librarian to leave me in the Dante area alone by telling him I hear the footsteps of other wandering patrons on the floor above us, and he bustles off to attend to them and their literary desires. I thumb through each volume patiently and slowly, partly so as not to miss anything, and partly to delay my search. I do not really expect to find anything of value to me, and when I do, my heart leaps into my throat. I shake so that I nearly drop the book when I see Rose's writing peering up at me from between the covers of Inferno. The original manuscript had been ripped out, and the edges of those old papers were jagged and torn and cradled a new sort of tale: that of Rose Gray. Trembling, I slip it under my coat as Connelly rounds the corner.

"Ah, there you are. Find anything useful?" His sorrowful demeanor is gone now, and I am left to wonder if I imagined it after all.

I hesitate, but only for the briefest of moments. Then I smile brightly.

"No, not really. It was a fool's errand, I suppose. Still, it was nice to get out of the hospital. I'm ready if you are."

"I thought we might stay a bit? I do find myself closer to Rose here than I thought. I would like to explore just a while? Would you mind very much?" His eyes, his nice eyes, peer into my heart it seems. He seems so...lost.

"That's fine. I'll stay here a spell, shall I? Never got to read much as a child, what with all the slave labor I was forced to perform at the orphanage. Ha ha, that was a joke. Don't mind catching up a little now." Again, my bright smile is back, and I wave him off.

"You won't come then? Take a tour with me?" He appears disappointed though I suppose it is only politeness that pricks his conscience enough to ask me.

"No, I'll stay right here where you can find me." I smile, brightly.

He leaves, though he glances backwards at me once, peculiarly. I busy myself with volumes I've no intention to read, though I do intend to look quite immersed in books should anyone happen upon me. I am only interested in one, and the heat from it feels as though it will burn a hole in my chest. I can nearly feel it beating like a heart beneath my coat and when I pull it out, nestled in Dante's arms, I breathe a sigh of relief.

Finally, I would know what happened after she left this place she loved to haunt.

I kept waiting, long after I knew he was never coming back, I kept waiting. Like a jilted lover, I kept waiting. I didn't eat, nor did I sleep, though that was usual for me. I couldn't believe Solomon would just discard me like a puppy or a bit of overcooked beef. I meant more to him than that, didn't I? His golden girl? His Goose?

Ah, but those missing drawings and designs of mine. Those damned him and his excuses. His disappearance I could fantasize explanations for, but my magic plans, my schemes and ideas? Why would he take those for a simple trip to the market? The swindler had swindled me, and I had been taken in.

I felt a white hot rage like none I had never felt before. The hatred I had felt for the girl who eventually felt my anger at the tip of a blade was nothing compared to what I felt for the emotions that consumed me now. Not hatred for Solomon exactly, but hatred at my stupidity. Him I still respected, still lauded, still loved. I could not merely stop; it would be like ceasing to breathe. He was all I ever had, and I could not despise him for what he was, when what he was was what made me love him so desperately.

No, what I felt was a rage so thick and smothering that everything else melted away in the heat. I was angry at losing him, not learning everything I could from him, being alone. It was the left behind feeling of my family, only worse. My family, such as they were, I barely remembered anyway. Memories of Solomon invaded every pore.

His fathering of me.

His instructions.

His nose when I threw the book at him.

The way he shielded me from the gypsies and their accusing looks.

The view I had of the top of his head from atop Vlad, that dark night we escaped.

Learning to read.

The books.

So I took my rage out on the books. I brought stacks, as heavy as I could carry and as high as I could heap them in my arms, and I dumped them in the street in front of the library. Of course, by my fourth trip, I had drawn a crowd. I lit a fire as quickly as I could, in our little kitchen hearth in our living quarters, and carried a burning twig.

I hadn't planned my little act of wrath out very well, and the twig was snatched before I could light the books. Someone yelled, and someone slapped me, and someone pulled the books to safety, out of the mud, and someone accused me of being the librarian's daughter, and someone took me to the police. I bit someone, and I scratched someone else, and then I cursed so passionately and in so many different languages that someone spoke in low tones of an exorcist. Someone asked where my shoes were, and someone tried to give me a blanket; I bit them too. Someone shouted for my father, and I shouted for him too, and eventually all the someones went away, and I was strapped to a bed in a place they called Bedlam.

And I grew up.

I feel tears on my cheeks, though I hadn't realized I was crying. I don't wipe them away, but allow them to drip silently down onto Rose's writing. A baptism of sorts. What a poor, wretched girl she was.

Chapter 10

At first I ignored everything and everyone around me, for weeks perhaps; I do not really know how much time went by. From the impression I got from the staff around me and the way they were wary of me and the way they spoke under their breath when they thought I was asleep, it seemed clear that I was in turn either extremely violent or extremely passive. It must have seemed like a strange pendulum in my moods to them, but I was simply too tired at times to be my normal, passionate self. I couldn't muster the energy to be wicked, so I sulked for a while, and then I struck out at them, only vocally of course, because I was nearly always strapped down to my bed or chair.

Escape was impossible. Besides the straps that bound my hands and arms, there were bars on my window and locks on my door. The lock I felt sure I could pick if I could only get to it—I used to skulk about Old Babba's door when she bolted me out, and made her nervous by finding ways back in—but the smallness of the room seemed immense to someone tied to the other end of it. The bars were too close together, even for my narrow frame. And the medicines they forced down my throat made me too tired to plot. They were full of poison in one form or another, I was sure of it.

So tired...

And then I realized that was the key. These past years I had been training myself to stay awake, so as not to leave Solomon. I had made sleep my enemy. Now it would be my ally and my way of escaping this place!

My little body revolted. My head ached. I was unaccustomed to long bouts of slumber; I had trained my body to revive itself every hour, at least. I could not seem to relax.

And there was a doctor. There was a doctor who fancied my brain.

"She's so very interesting, isn't she?" he mused one day to another doctor. They lurked over my bed like vultures. I feigned sleep.

"She has no one then? Alone completely? No one to miss her should something go wrong?"

"That's right. Her addition to science could be invaluable."

At first I thought they meant to slice me up and dissect me in order to learn more about me and why I did the things I did. I was not scared, only curious at how far they would go in their plan.

"Lobotomies are a risky business. What if it doesn't cure her but makes her worse?" the first doctor mused.

"Is that even possible?" the other joked and they both laughed.

Stupid men. "What a couple of asses," I thought.

"All joshing aside, my good man, she is an interesting case."

"Mmm," the other agreed, slowly. I could practically see him stroking his beard, though my eyes were still closed. I could smell his dreadful hair pomade. He probably combed it through his sparse whiskers. I coughed. Maybe even bathed in it. "Has the electroshock had no effect then?"

"Haven't tried it yet. Perhaps we combine the two? She is a difficult case, after all. Two birds with one stone, so to speak, eh? Or two stones with one bird, I suppose I should say."

Again, they chuckled. I didn't much care what they decided, so long as they went away.

It was impossible to fall asleep with those idiots near.

Do you know what they say about electroshock therapy, dear little reader of mine?

At this, I startle and nearly drop the journal. This is the first time she has ever addressed me, and I could not have been more surprised if she called me by name. I am disturbed and feel uneasy.

Sylvia Plath I think said it best. I read her later. Much later.

"By the roots of my hair some god got hold of me. I sizzled in his blue volts like a desert prophet. The nights snapped out of sight like a lizard's eyelid: A world of bald white days in a shadeless socket. A vulturous boredom pinned me in this tree. If he were I, he would do what I did."

Of course, you do not know Sylvia yet, but you will.

You do not know me either, do you?

You poor, pitiful thing.

I can't help but feel insulted, silly as it sounds. I snap shut the diary and untangle my legs from my perch. I should put away the books I pulled from their shelves willy-nilly, but I don't. I leave to find Mr. Connelly. I have questions I wonder if he might have the answers to.

He is speaking in whispers to the mutton-chopped man, and when they see me approaching, they stop.

"And did you find Dante entertaining enough?" the librarian asks me, brightly.

I am instantly suspicious of their little tete-a-tete. "What were you speaking of just now?" I keep my tone as bright as his on purpose, as I answer his question with a question.

"Ah, a sharp young thing," he nudges Mr. Connelly.

"Her?" Mr. Connelly pretends to eye me judgmentally and with an expression of feigned boredom. "She's quite obnoxious actually."

"Flattery will get you nowhere. Did you ask him about Rose?" I decide to jump right in and quit beating around the bush.

"I did." Connelly takes his cigarette from his breast pocket and lights it, calmly. "If she's been here, he didn't see her."

"Ah, well, she's a sneaky thing," I mutter. "Do you want to leave then?"

He puffs on his cigarette a moment and eyes me, thoughtfully. "I suppose I do. We should get you back to hospital. I don't want to be accused of kidnapping."

"I'm not a kid." I stand up straighter.

"Mmm." The corners of his mouth turn up again, in that maddening way I've come to learn is what he does when he's trying (not very hard) not to laugh at me. "Come along then, Grandmother."

We barely say a parting word to the librarian, who is urging us to return again someday.

"It's these braids," I protest, descending the stairs outside. "They make me look fourteen."

"I have the same problem when I do my hair that way," he teases. He opens the door to his magnificent chariot for me, and I climb in.

It has begun to rain lightly, a drizzle, and it splashes on the windshield in airy plops. Dancing splashes of water skitter and skate across the car like water skippers. I watch Connelly as he circles the Rolls-Royce: his hat askew, giving him a rakish appearance, his new cigarette in his mouth, those nice-looking lips hugging it.

Goodness, Lizzie! I give myself a mental shake. What schoolgirl, idiotic thoughts!

He is rather nice to look at though. Even my practical self has to admit it.

But he's entangled with a lunatic. Well, the best ones always are, I expect.

Being so young, they went slowly with me, and carefully. Oh yes, one must be careful if you are remove bits of bone and brain and matter. Of course, I don't recall it really; I'm only relaying what I was told after by the nurses. They read from my charts in dull, clipped voices. I didn't feel any different, and I wasn't sure how I felt about that. Did I want to be different? What was so wrong with me anyway?

I was just a little girl!

Recovering, I remember feeling very blurry. The world outside my little window was smudged. Everything in my room was smudged. I held my hand up to my face, and it was smudged. Blurred. Like it had rained upon my life and someone had smeared the colors: a bad watercolor painting. It got a little better later, but for the most part, life still looks like that to me, years later.

I sat there by my window, staring lethargically out, and the doctors came and went. I ignored them. They were pleased. I was not. I was becoming bored with them. Sleeping was coming easier, but I was not traveling. I was awaking in the same place in which I had fallen asleep, and it was maddening. I tried to sleep for longer and longer periods, and sometimes I would dream of being in some far off land, some distant or future time, and then I would wake. One morning a nurse shook me awake for my pills right in the middle of a lovely dream, when it had taken me so long to fall asleep. I was so angry; I slapped her hard and pulled out a chunk of her hair.

The doctors concluded my lobotomy was not a success. They became bored of me and left me tied for hours in bed.

One night I had an excruciating headache. I thought it was because of what they had done to me, and I pressed my fingers to my temple and rubbed the spot where they had taken out the bone fragments. It throbbed and ached and felt hot to the touch. I thought they had damaged me, but it turns out they must have heightened my abilities.

That night I finally traveled.

Old Babba had always known what my family was: Lost. She told me the barest bits of what I needed to know. She had "the sight," a vague term people coined back then to explain visions or over active imaginations. At first I thought she was batty, an old lunatic, but then I began to see that for the most part, her mutterings made sense, and her predictions always came true. Once, when she was in a talkative mood and both of us feeling passive, I asked her where my family was. She eyed me warily but obliged me by falling into one of her strange trances. It was as though she talked in her sleep when she did this. (I'd seen it before when villagers came to her to ask their futures. I would duplicate it later, faking of course, during the sideshow when it was my turn to tell fortunes). She murmured about a place called Italy, a villa near the sea, and a number: 1571. Why hadn't I gone with them when they left? I didn't know, but I certainly meant to find out. She had enough truth in her visions to know that my family was gone for good, and that hopefully she'd lose me in the same way someday. I never paid too much attention to her mutterings until I woke under that table in India; then I knew I really was something special.

Traveling again, leaving Bedlam, was bittersweet. I knew I had left Solomon behind for good, and there would be no reconciliation. I would never see him again. If I traveled to the future, he would be dead. If I traveled to the past, he would yet to be born.

I woke in a cornfield. A little boy, younger than I by a couple of years, was staring at me. He was sitting cross-legged and chewing on a piece of straw. He barely blinked when I opened my eyes. We stared at each other. Finally, he spoke first.

"My pa don't like no hobos, even if you is a girl."

"I'm not a hobo," I said. I didn't know what one was, but I was certain I wasn't. "Who are you?"

"None yer business. You better scat!"

"I don't have anywhere to go."

The boy sighed. He had an old man's sigh, deep and full of years. "Fine. Come home with me if you want, but you ain't gettin' any food."

I brushed off my dress which was really just the hospital's old dressing gown, my knobby knees sticking out, and followed him. I was barefoot, and I kept stepping on hard rocks and prickly weeds. We moved through the cornfield like it was a maze. I hoped he knew where he was going.

"Ma ain't gonna like you neither," he said.

"Why?"

"She just won't, that's all. Where's yer family?"

"I don't know. Dead, I guess."

He nodded and plucked a fresh weed out of the ground for chewing. "You sure? Cuz I don't want them showin' up, too. I'm gonna get in enough trouble just bringing you home with me. I don't need no scrawny brothers or sisters or nuttin', okay?"

I was silent.

He stopped and sighed again. "Okay?" he repeated, slowly, like I was a dumb animal.

"I don't know what that means," I mumbled. My English was good enough, but I didn't know this word. His accent was so strange.

"What? Okay? It means, you know," he paused. "Well, I don't know how to explain it! You not from around here? You talk funny."

"I do not. You do."

"Fine. Anyway, we're here."

I stopped short and stared. It was a small house, dingy white. There were three huge dogs chained up to a tree and a bony woman sitting on the porch, shelling peas. There was a rundown automobile nearby (though I didn't know what in the world it was at the time. I'd never seen a car). There was a naked baby playing in the dirt, and a girl about fifteen was swinging on the gate. She stared at me and quit swinging.

"Who's that, Daniel?" the woman asked, warily. "Who are you, girl?"

"Rose."

"What do you want? We ain't got nothin' to spare."

The boy, Daniel, looked at me triumphantly. "I told her so, Ma. She don't listen."

"Then she'll fit in real good 'round here," the girl on the gate said. "Nobody listens to nobody here."

The mother gave her a look that could have curdled cream. "Pipe down, Louise. Go get yer dad. It's time for supper. We ain't got nothin' to spare," she repeated, turning back to me.

"I'm eatin' at Bobby's, Ma. You can give Rose my share," Louise said over her shoulder as she left.

The mother sighed as she got up from the porch and picked up her bowl of peas. "Fine. Be gone by tomorrow. I'll give you a ride to town."

The thought of riding on that bony woman's back to town gave me the shivers. What a strange place I'd landed in. Still, it was better than the hospital, so I went in the house willingly enough.

It was dark, but that was nothing new to me. The place was dusty, but I was never one to care about that. There was a smell of something cooking, and I followed the mother into her kitchen.

"Wash up then," she ordered. I watched her throw the peas in some boiling water on top of a large oven. I stared at it curiously: the oven, I mean. I couldn't see the fire, and I was curious about the heat source. I wanted to reach out and touch it, but the mother looked like she wouldn't want me to.

"Is the river close?" I mumbled.

"Not particularly. You're a funny one. Use the sink," she gestured towards the place near the oven.

I waited until Daniel passed me by and used it first. The water came gushing out of a pipe right into his hands. I held my hands under it eagerly. It was cold, but it felt nice enough.

The father arrived, a big man, dirty from working in the fields all day and ill-tempered. Probably from being married to a shrew, I figured. He grunted when introduced to me. We sat down at the table and ate our supper. There was bread and meat and the peas and a jar of peaches. It wasn't the best food, but I was hungry enough to eat, especially the bread. I stuffed a whole piece in my mouth, and the mother moved the plate out of my reach with a glare. She didn't scare me, and I glared back.

That night I slept in a bed with Louise, who had come back from her beau, Bobby. She nearly talked me to death, like I was some sort of friend or sister or something, until I told her to shut up or I'd smother her with a pillow. I think she thought I was joking because she laughed, but I wasn't joking, and I didn't laugh with her, and she abruptly shut up.

The next morning the mother made us all line up for prayers, and when I wouldn't say them she tried to turn me over her knee for a swat. It was unsuccessful, and she ended up looking a fool, panting and angrier than a hornet. I laughed in her red face and went outside. Louise and Daniel looked after me with expressions that almost looked reverent.

I was sitting by the car (to me it was just an odd pile of metal) when it suddenly sprang to life. It roared and sputtered and moved, and I screamed. I wanted to run away but my legs wouldn't obey me, and so I just sat there, screaming until the father came out from the pile of metal and yelled at me to stop.

"Get her out of here!" the mother demanded, letting the screen slam shut behind her. The naked baby was on her hip.

The man opened a door in the metal thing and came toward me, and when I realized what he meant to do, I screamed louder and kicked him hard. He grabbed my wrists with one meaty hand and my kicking ankles with the other. I tried to bite, but he shook me like a dog. I felt my teeth knock together with such force I wondered if I broke any. He tossed me in the growling thing, and I hit my head. I thought he meant to cook me in there, like it was some sort of giant oven, and I was not going to die that way. Like the witch from the gingerbread cottage. Would he throw in wood and fire next? I pushed on the door, but it wouldn't open the way it had for him. Was there a magic word? Was there a key or a secret latch? I fumbled until I found it and pushed and pulled until it gave way and the door swung open. My body fell out. The father came around again, and the whole ordeal started over. This time the mother brought out a frying pan.

"You want me to knock her in the head, Bert?" She held it over her head with one hand, while she balanced the baby with the other.

"Naw, she'll behave," the father grunted. "If she don't, then we'll grind her up and feed her to the pigs. Ain't nobody to miss her, the goddamn little lunatic."

I figured he wouldn't really grind me up, but I stopped fighting. To my surprise, he followed me in the big steel container, and then it began to move. I put my hand on the window of the steel thing and stared at

Daniel as we moved away. He stared back, and he got smaller and smaller in the distance until he was gone forever.

Chapter 11

Such a strange little girl, I thought, as I put the diary down. Our own car, well, Mr. Connelly's car, was moving along too. Our hearts in synch, Rose and I were traveling down different paths in different times, she terrified and I not. I had asked Connelly if he minded me reading it in the car instead of conversing and he had chuckled.

"I'll try to get over your silence though it stings my heart a bit," he said.

"I could read aloud if you miss my voice so much," I offered, cheekily.

"All right then, little one. Enlighten me on Rose."

So I hear Rose's story in my own voice all the way back to Bedlam.

Being only eleven, I wasn't worried about every danger being in this predicament put me in. I wasn't scared at all of the father, though I should have been, but I was wholly unhinged over the contraption we were in. I saw the cornfield where I had met Daniel go whizzing by at a frightening speed. I felt every rock and gravel and pebble as they were trampled beneath our steel feet. I felt as though I was in Death's coach, the carriage to Hell with invisible horses that pulled us along at breakneck speed. I was certain of it.

"Where are you taking me?" I asked, hugging my knees to my chest. My hospital gown was becoming threadbare after its night in the cornfield and its subsequent wearing.

"Drop you off at the Wilkensen's, I 'spect," Bert grunted. "They shot my favorite dog last fall. Figure this'll make us even."

And drop me he did. The pile of metal screeched to a halt and the father leaned over my body to open the door. I slid out with relief, and my legs were so shaky, I nearly slid all the way to the ground.

"Keep walkin' down this road and you'll come to a house. Or don't. Just stay away from us, you hear?" He had to lean down to be seen by me.

"Yes, sir," I mumbled.

I had never spoken such polite words in my life, and I expect I never will again.

"We're here," Connelly interrupts. The hospital looms large out my window.

I sigh dramatically. All that work to be done now that I'd taken a day off… All I want to do is hide from Miss Helmes.

"I was hoping you could drop me at home instead?" I wheedle.

"I don't think that's a good idea. Better to let Miss Helmes see you safe and sound, and you can get back to scrubbing." He leans over me in the very same way I imagine the farmer had for Rose, and opens my door.

"A gentleman would get out and walk me to my door at least," I hint.

Connelly draws on his cigarette and regards me with amusement. "I never claimed to be a gentleman," he says, and the way he says it makes shivers go up and down my spine.

Mina meets me at the door. "Where have you been? I was so worried!" She hugs me quickly. "Were you off with him?" The way she says it, it sounds as though the H in him should be capitalized. "He seems… nice. And handsome."

"We were looking for his," I pause, and frown. "His… someone."

"Well, I'm glad you're back. I worry when I can't find you," Mina links arms with me and leads me inside.

"You're a ridiculous worry wart," I say, fondly. "Any riots or surgeries or gristly murders while I was away?"

"Nothing at all," she laughs. "Except Mr. Limpet has been asking for you."

"Oh, dear. I probably promised to dance with him again. Is it Monday already?"

"Speaking of dancing, Lizzie, dear, I'm having a party. You will come, won't you? It's to be the most lovely old-fashioned ball!" She claps her hands like a school girl and awaits my response with held breath.

"At your house?" I shrug out of my coat and hang it on the wall. "Oh, Mina, you know I don't fit in with your people." In so many, many ways...

"You'll be smashing, you'll see, and it will be good for you to get out of the hospital for a night. You're looking too pale."

"We're in England in April! Everyone is pale, you nitwit." I snort. "You look like a corpse yourself."

"Mother makes me wash my face with milk and lemons; it's not my fault. Say you'll come?"

"What will I wear?" I don my apron hurriedly and plop my nurse's hat over my braids. "I'm afraid my good apron is at the cleaners."

"Very funny," Mina wrinkles her nose the way she does when she's found something I've said to be distasteful. Her nose is going to stick that way someday, I swear. I'm constantly giving her reasons to wrinkle it. I imagine her mother will make me pay for the corrective surgery. "I'll loan you something pretty. Papa had several new dresses made for me, and I think one is more your color anyway; it's a beautiful periwinkle shade."

"Oh dear. Periwinkle, you say?" I feign distress. "Periwinkle washes me out. Do you have anything in ruby or emerald? Jewel tones make me feel rich." I wriggle my eyebrows. "By the way, I ate my lipstick."

"Oh, for goodness sake. Thursday evening. You won't forget now?"

"I will check my busy social calendar and get back to you, yes," I promise. "Now, scoot, before the old battleaxe finds us loitering."

"Oh, and Lizzie?" Mina calls before I round the corner. "Mack is coming along with me. You can bring someone if you like. A gentleman?"

I smile and laugh. "I'll try," I answer, knowing full well who she means. "But I'm afraid he's no gentleman. I have it on good authority."

Mr. Limpet finds me before Miss Helmes does. I am busily sweeping out the back hallway when he wheels his chair up to me. Most of the time, he's too frail to get around anywhere by himself, but occasionally he finds a spurt of energy and makes a round of the entire building, causing people to get their toes out of his way in a hurry. He squeals to a halt and regards me suspiciously.

"Do we need to oil that chair again, Mr. Limpet?" I ask, cheerfully. "Sounds like you're driving the Coach de Bauer."

His face relaxes into a wreath of wrinkles as he smiles. "Ah, Lizzie, it's only you," he says, fondly, reaching out for my hand. He pats it with clammy hands. "I'm so glad when it's only you."

"I'm glad to see you, too. Did you save me a dance later?"

His smile deepens. "I did! I did save one for you! The ragtime! Your favorite!"

"Is it?" I can't help laughing. "I don't recall, but if you say it is, then it must be." I smile down at the old man. Never mind that that dance went out of vogue before I was even born; I can't help but humor him with promises he'll never remember to cash in anyway. "Does it go like this?" I do a funny two step.

Mr. Limpet scowls at my dancing. "No, no, that's not right! Don't you remember? Why don't you ever remember?"

I sigh and bend down to kiss his bald head. "Never mind, Mr. Limpet. I'm just a forgetful girl. I'll brush up on my steps at home, okay?"

"That's good then. You're such a good girl, Lizzie." He wheels himself away.

"I must be," I mutter to myself. "Who else would do this wretched job?" I long, once again, for my assistance to be needed in a lovely surgery or the setting of a bone. Heck, even a nice batch of leaches to apply to someone who needed bloodletting would be welcome right about now. I have serious doubts about staying here at Bedlam if my medical expertise (well, all right, less medical expertise, more medical *passion* might be a better description) isn't wanted. I fluff some more pillows with more force than is strictly necessary and allow myself to wonder about Mina's ball and her periwinkle dress.

I've never had much cause for dressing up. It wasn't as though the orphanage threw a lot of parties, though we did wear our best when some parents-to-be came strolling through, usually hand in hand, cooing over the youngest ones, and ignoring the rest. Like puppies and kittens in a store we were: lined up, looking as adorable and well-behaved as possible, hoping against hope that this would be our chance for a real family. It never happened for me, like it never happened for so many there.

Ah, well. Such is life. No point in moping. Someday I'd have a brood of children, and I'd never leave them, not once. I'd give them crumpets and cocoa for breakfast each morning, and I'd braid each of my daughter's hair with brightly colored ribbons. We'd wear our best to church, and everyone would comment on our happiness and health. The girls would look like their mum, and the boys would have eyes that sparkled mischievously... a bit like Mr. Connelly's now that I peer a bit closer into my fantasy.

Perhaps I shouldn't be trying so hard to find Rose. After all, a girl has to look out for her own future.

I wonder what he would say should I ask him to accompany me to Mina's ball? He had said he was rather bored. A bored, rich young man. It was practically charitable of me to ask, really. I hated to think of him sitting in his big empty house, pining away for a mad girl, with nothing to do. He'd probably thank me for taking in an interest in him. After all, he did drive me in that lovely car to Bodleian, and he certainly didn't need to. He never thought Rose would be there anyway; that was all my idea. He really was quite agreeable. I stop fluffing pillows for a moment and think.

Why is he so agreeable?

Does he have a motive I'm not seeing?

Well, if he does, it can't be that bad. Sweet Fanny Adams, there's really no need for me to twist a handsome young man into Jack the Ripper. My imagination is always getting me into trouble. I resolve to ask him to Mina's ball the very next time I see him.

Chapter 12

Whoever the Wilkensen's were, I never found out. I sat in that damned cornfield, getting burned by the sun, for two days. I slept as much as possible, but my head hurt. I was thirsty, but didn't want to move. I was afraid of that steel contraption appearing out of nowhere and mowing me down in the prime of my short life. My lips were cracked and bloody, my hair stringy, my bare feet nearly black with dirt, and my skin bright pink. I just lay there and lay there; it felt like forever. I began to rub the spot on my forehead where the ache was, and it was both more painful and pleasant at once. I rubbed it with my thumb and thought of my time in the hospital. I rubbed and thought until I fell asleep, and that's how I woke back up in Bedlam.

The year was different. Same old Bedlam, same old walls, same old smell of decay and madness, but a different time. I can't say I was thrilled to be back, but I was certainly happy to be away from Bert and his evil machine, and the bony lady with the frying pan, and the dog-shooting Wilkensens.

I was in the main hallway, and there were too many people about. Some stared at me; some ignored me. They were all mad in their appearance, each and every one. If they hadn't been when they arrived, they certainly were teetering on the brink now. Their clothes were different than the gown I still wore, older styles, a little more like what I had seen in my early days with Old Babba, but maybe even earlier. The woman wore tight bodices with yards of skirts, and the men had ruffled shirts (or they had once been ruffled); now they just looked like wilted dead flowers hung around their necks. Why they were all packed in the hallway remained to be seen. Were there so many patients they had run out of room?

But no, that wasn't it. They had been herded here briefly so the employees could search for someone. A missing man, a patient, evidently. The staff wandered about, pushing their way through, opening and closing the doors of the rooms, shouting for MacAbee. They seemed quite annoyed at his lack of presence.

I hugged my scrawny knees to my chest on the floor and silently cheered on MacAbee. A man with a drooping mustache sat down by me and when I paid him no mind, he leaned over and whispered in my ear,

"They called me mad," he said, as if we were having a normal conversation. "And I called them mad, and damn them, they outvoted me."

By the time they located MacAbee (hiding in the potato bin) everyone was so mixed up and the workers so irritated that I was merely a distraction no one wanted to deal with. Tossed in with the patients, I suppose I could have found a way out, pretended to be someone else, maybe a tourist, but the thought was too exhausting, and the idea of food and water and a place to sleep too tempting. I allowed myself to be locked in a room with a woman named Ursula who had crossed eyes and wouldn't speak, and though all I had was a thin blanket and some thinner soup, it felt good to be home.

The feeling didn't last long. The next few years were spent crafting my abilities. I had come to learn that I could will myself to travel where I wanted, just by concentrating on the place and time and pressing on the spot on my head where they had played with my brain. I could go, but I could not stop myself from coming back. Oh, I could make myself return speedily enough (though why would I want to?), but I couldn't go anywhere else without Bedlam being my anchor eventually. Sometimes I could go to two or even three places without being pulled back to the hospital, but most often than not, I'd return in between each one. Off to Spain I would go, to enjoy the twelfth century, or some such thing, but no matter how I tried from there, I couldn't stay. I'd spend a summer in the New World in the year 1600, but I'd find myself back in my little prison soon enough. The years at Bedlam were always different though. Each time I'd reappear, no one would recognize me, because, in a mad, mad way, they were either dead or hadn't been born yet.

I wondered sometimes if they ever found my disappearances mysterious and if they ever looked for me in the potato bin.

But no, I don't think anyone ever looks for me at all.

Sometimes I picked places and eras from my favorite story books to travel to, but they always fell surprisingly short of my expectations. How could fiction be better than truth? But it was. There was no Scheherazade to greet me in Persia; there was only sand and hunger. The royals in France during the Revolution may have been interesting enough, but I could not get close enough to the palace to find out. Boston was the home of The Scarlet Letter, but Pearl and Hester were not real, and I found the city dull without them. All was not lost in Boston, as I visited the grave of Edgar Allan Poe: a macabre poet I was very fond of. By the time I was fifteen years of age, I had my traveling abilities nearly perfected. My stays, however, were becoming frustratingly short. It seemed I hardly had any time at all to enjoy my new surroundings, cherry-picked by me and my imagination, before I was yanked back to Bedlam. While I had spent a whole summer in Spain as a thirteen-year-old and had taken two months to cross the ocean on a boat of questionable moral integrity (piracy is not the romantic profession some make it out to be), the places I went afterwards were becoming shorter and shorter. Did each child of the Lost have a certain number of eras to visit and would then run out, I wondered? Was I using mine up too quickly? Would there come a day when I could no longer travel? I found the question both disturbing and comforting. It kept me up at night.

Eventually, my journeys became limited to usually only a few days and nights. Typically, once I fell asleep for more than a couple hours at a time, I would wake at Bedlam, year unknown. I could stay awake longer than most, but even so, my journeys were becoming frustratingly short. At best, I could stay anchored in one era, in one spot, for about three days.

When I was fifteen, I met Luke.

He was the most handsome boy I had ever seen. I had no time for boys, no interest, nothing but dislike and disdain for anyone. Somehow, he

I frown. Where is her young man now, I wonder? I thumb through the pages of the diary, curious if her writing would come to an abrupt halt and her story end. But no, there was plenty more to be read. Perhaps his absence would be explained, or—and this seemed more likely—perhaps he was with her still, wherever she was holing up.

The time traveling, this was strange stuff. Never had I seen in my time at Bedlam such fantastical story telling. She believed everything she wrote; that much was as plain as the nose on my face, and she never wavered in anything. Her delusions seemed to be her reality.

Though, it certainly would explain her disappearance... How silly. She was pulling me into her illusions now, and I wouldn't have that.

I set the diary aside and make myself a cheese sandwich and a hot cup of tea. I'd keep reading, but keep my wits about me and not let my imagination take over. Yes. Good plan. I like it.

I told him of my plan to find my family, my abandoners, my deserters. He frowned at me when I said I could control my traveling. He said I should prove it to him, so I asked him, where did he want to go? He thought for a moment, blowing on my cold fingers for it was December and my gloves had holes, and said perhaps someplace warm, with sunshine and the ocean. A place all to ourselves. An island, he said. What era, I asked. He said it hardly mattered; we'd be alone, wouldn't we? For a short time, I murmured, but he didn't seem to hear me.

That night he snuck into my room. Security was never much at Bedlam. You'd think it would be, reader, wouldn't you? But it isn't, not really. They let their patients fraternize, and oh yes, love affairs are frowned upon, but then again, it's entertaining for the staff.

Am I entertaining you?

I nearly choke on my cheese. I am beginning to dislike Rose more and more. While before I felt overwhelming sympathy for the wretched thing, now I am starting to see why she was friendless and hopeless.

It almost feels as though she watches me from the shadows, as though she's just out of my line of sight, her hand on my shoulder, her voice in my head, like she knows me. It's an unnerving, unsettling thought, and a shiver creeps up my back and settles in my neck.

I'd like to just forget her, forget she ever existed, but I cannot. It's too late.

For what exactly?

I don't know anymore.

Chapter 13

It was so late it was nearly morning before we fell asleep. Luke kept kissing me, and I kept telling him I had to concentrate. It was clear he didn't really believe we would wake in an island paradise.

"Though that would certainly confound the police and keep them from hanging me," was the last thing he said before sleeping.

I was so excited to show him my powers, my specialness, my abilities! I was almost too excited to sleep, but I finally did. I pressed on my forehead where there was always a dull ache, almost like a soft heartbeat in my head, and thought of blue waters and green trees and endless beaches.

The sound of waves crashing woke us up.

Luke was speechless. He was so handsome in the sunlight. He kept staring around us in amazement. I just lay on the beach and watched him take it all in, all this knowledge of what I could do. When he finally could speak, he whooped like a little boy and went running down the beach. He flung sand and splashed in the waves, making me laugh. I had never laughed from happiness before, so I did it again, and I wanted the moment to last forever.

Of course, we stayed awake as long as possible to make our paradise last as long as it could. As beautiful as our island was in the sun, it was even more beautiful in the moonlight. Two days later, though, Luke teased me that next time could I please order up a deserted island with a meal or two waiting on silver platters?

Boys eat too much. He's always hungry. We had to go home.

When we returned, it was a different century, as usual. The hospital was new, so this was as far back in time as I had ever traveled. Luke said he'd been further, said he'd been back to the very beginning, or very nearly so, but Luke lies. I don't mind. We all lie, don't you know?

For example, I told him I wanted to find my family to be reunited.

That was a lie.

I only wanted revenge.

Luke had blended into the crowd when we came back to Bedlam and was free to come and go as a visitor. I was never so lucky. I was always caught like a rabbit in a snare; the metal teeth of Bedlam always found my ankles and tripped me up. Oh, I could invent stories, and to myself I thought I was quite believable, but it never worked. They took one look at me and knew I belonged there.

I said I lied. I never said I was any good at it.

For a short time, while inwardly I formulated a plan for finding my family, outwardly we traveled. Luke's mind had always bent towards thievery and mayhem, and though I cared not a fig for money, I didn't mind a little adventure and it did my heart good to see him happy. I suppose it seems silly to some to steal and cause trouble and attempt to get rich when you can't keep much of any of your spoils, but for Luke, just knowing he could and that he was perfecting his skills was enough. He'd steal little things at first; picking pockets, seeing what he could get away with. Well, of course, that's typical and common behavior for the Lost: I too, have lifted my fair share of folding money. You have to survive. You don't have the luxury of working your way up in a proper and respectable position, do you? No, you have to eat and you have to find shelter. Of course, some Lost don't enjoy this part as much as we do.

Luke had been desperate to go someplace wealthy, someplace teeming with millionaires or ever billionaires, or pull off a scheme so large it could get us in the history books. He called us Bonnie and Clyde, though he had to explain to me who they were. A lovely enough young couple - I thought we would probably have been chums. Had I been the sort to have chums.

In New York City in an age where automobiles were all the rage and gangsters were in fashion, we nearly got ourselves killed by over-eager and underestimated police, when we held up a bank with stolen guns. I enjoyed the part I played in that particular heist: a pretty young thing, just opening her first bank account. I was coy and sweet and twirled my hair. I was never one for talking, not even when I was playacting, so I relied on hmming and hawing and in general, throwing myself on the wisdom of the young accountant. He was all too happy to sign me up for all sorts of things with his thinning hair and his proper suit coat, and I was demure and gentle and meek with his attentions. My red dress I almost always slept in to travel had not been fine enough for this robbery, and Luke had pinched me a smart dress with navy piping and shiny buttons. My hat was set at a saucy angle on my light hair, a feather tickling my left eye at times. I remember the smell of the bank and the back of the accountant's hands as he wrote and shuffled his papers, and the way he cleared his throat often, as though I made him particularly nervous.

When Luke leapt to the top of the counter, brandishing his weapon and gleefully shouting for order and respect and silence, I screamed like the lady I was pretending to be. I even huddled closer to the accountant, who had defied Luke by moving (around his desk, to me). What a gentleman, I suppose. I thought my scream sounded quite good – better than the woman across from me, who sounded like a wounded eagle. I wanted to shut her up permanently but we were here for other things. My brave and ever cheerful boy was nearly dancing along the counter tops. I think he fancied himself a sort of gangster and was enjoying the part immensely. Of course, we were only kids and we didn't think things through very completely, so things got out of hand rather quickly. Having landed in an age of notorious bank robbers, our intrepid bank employees were very well trained. Someone had tipped off the police and I knew who it was: a smug faced lady who had given me the once over when we arrived. Luke had spoken to her too, before he revealed his pistol, and who knows what he had said that wasn't to her satisfaction: I just know from my perspective, sitting demurely with the accountant's arm around my shoulders, she was up to something. She was far too calm and self-satisfied, and her eyes kept drifting to the back doorway, as if waiting for someone to appear. Perhaps she pressed a hidden button, perhaps she mouthed a code word to someone else who had slipped away, who knew. No matter. It hardly made a difference to Luke and me whether we slept in jail that night, or on the streets – though Luke, of course, would be disappointed in himself for getting caught. I sighed a bit at the turn of events, and then I turned on my accountant knight and pressed my pistol to his head. Luke laughed and leaned down from his counter top to plant a kiss on my hat.

"That's my girl," he said, fondly. "Now what do you say you bag up some money for us?"

We didn't get terribly far before the police stormed in, and I suppose it would have easier and less messy to just surrender, but you'd be surprised how much adrenaline kicks in when you're under duress like that. We nearly made it out the door before the shooting began. I was terribly irritated. I hadn't minded running the risk of prison (what is that compared to Bedlam?) or the hazard of having causalities in our adventure, but I was hardly prepared to lose my own life over it. The window beside the door, and right beside the hat on my head, shattered. It also gave a new escape route, and Luke shoved me through with all the grace of a hippopotamus mother, or maybe a terrified lover about to lose his girl. We tumbled like rubber balls onto the sidewalk, and got up running and laughing. They didn't catch us. Looking back, I wonder if they didn't try their best. After all, we were a couple of kids and we had dropped the money and they had other fish to fry.

Our Bonnie and Clyde escapades were all Luke's plans and desires, so he owed me one. I wanted to find my family now.

I thought about running the risk of leaving Luke behind. I wouldn't be gone long, but the fear of him not being where I left him won out. I remembered Old Babba's details: Italy, 1571, a villa by the sea. It was good information, and I knew I would be able to find my family eventually, even if I had to come back to the hospital and rest up between searches. It might take me a while, but I would find them, even if I had to go up and down every coastline, peek my head into every village window. And Luke would enjoy Italy, wouldn't he? Of course he would because I would be there. He only wanted to be with me.

It took me nearly a year to find them. I was getting discouraged. I wasn't eating much, and Luke would feed me Nightfall pills because he couldn't stay awake as long as I could.

Nightfall pills? What in the world? I wonder. Wonderful, now she's on drugs. Lovely. Really lovely. I'd like to throttle this Luke. Who did he think he was, dispensing medications like candy?

When I finally found her, my mother, I had been awake for three days. I was not at my best. Upon hindsight, I suppose I should have left, gone back to Bedlam for a few days of peace and quiet, gotten some rest, gone back later, but once I saw her, walking that cliff, I couldn't leave. I knew her at once.

Her dress, blue as cornflowers, was blowing in the wind. Her hair, half up, was blowing too. She looked like me. She should have known me instantly, but she didn't seem to. She seemed confused when I called her mother.

She said to get away from her. She said I was a cruel village girl, playing a mean trick on a grieving mother. She was angry.

I told her I was special, that she never should have left me, that I was better than my sister. She began to look less angry and more frightened. I think she started to believe me then, started to believe I really was Rose.

I held out my hand to her. Or was it she who held hers out to me? I don't remember now. How funny!

Someone held out their hand, and someone didn't...

Someone fell and someone didn't.

Wasn't me. I never fall.

Jack and Jill went up a hill...and Mother came tumbling after.

At this, I begin to long for my medical dictionary for my bedtime reading, but at least I have a reason now to keep searching for Rose. I need to find her before she harms anyone else, and I need to keep Mr. Connelly from getting too involved with her. It's clear he doesn't know what she is capable of.

If he is right, and if my strange night with the writing on the wall is to be believed, she hasn't gone far.

*   *   *

The next morning, instead of pestering a vague and cryptic Miss Helmes about Rose Gray again, I head straight for the doctor. I am annoyed to find the golden boy, Mack, already ahead of me in his office.

"Here to see Doc Ford?" Mack asks, cheerfully. He sets aside whatever book he had been reading when I walked in.

"Here to perform difficult surgeries?" I retort, sourly. I'm glad for my red lipstick today; I feel more grownup with it.

"Nah, just here to talk shop. You know, shoot the breeze?"

"Wonderful. Must be nice to be such chums."

"Shall I put in a good word for you? Tell him you've done your fair share of bed making and mopping?"

"No, thanks." I'll work my own way up, even if it kills me.

The door to the inner office opens, and Dr. Ford is suddenly filling the frame. He's a large man, a bit fat, and even his bones are big. His hands are large and red as they grip the door handle.

"Ah." A flicker of recognition passes over his face as he sees me. "Two visitors this morning? To what do I owe the honor of my sudden popularity?"

"Go ahead, doll," Mack nods to me generously.

I want to scowl, but instead I attempt a gracious smile. It probably looks like a grimace, but it's the best I can do. I stand and hold out my hand for the doctor to shake. He always looks a bit taken aback, like every man, when I greet him this masculine way, but the advance of women must start somewhere. I must take myself seriously, even if he doesn't. Yet.

"What can I do for you?" Dr. Ford pauses a minute as we take a seat in his office. I can tell he is struggling to find my name in his memory. "Lizzie, is it?"

"Yes, sir. I'm looking for a former patient, sir, a young woman named Rose Gray. She's stayed at the hospital off and on since she was about eleven, I believe. Are you familiar with her? It's imperative I locate her whereabouts now."

"Is it?" The good doctor looks intrigued. He sets aside the papers he'd been shuffling, and gives me his attention. "And why is that?"

"I believe she's quite dangerous, sir, and I don't think she should be wandering around London. She may harm someone, or even herself."

"Ah. A diagnosis." Dr. Ford smiles, and even though I don't know that he means it to be, it feels very patronizing. "Remember, I am quite new here. Haven't been here long enough to know everyone, and I must say, I am unused to nurses making diagnoses." His words are a warning. He has moved from kind to cautionary in one fell swoop.

"So, you have never met Rose Gray?" I persist, ignoring his barb. I'll probably pay for it later with a decrease in pay, more bedpan duty, or getting canned. Bloody hell, I hope my impertinence doesn't get me canned.

"I didn't say that. I met her once. Just once. I peeked my head in her room when I was touring the place before I settled on my position here.

She was asleep though so I'm afraid I didn't get a very good look, and I wasn't able to interview her. Very interesting case, very interesting indeed. I hoped she would stay longer, but," he snapped his large fingers. "She was gone, just like that. As if she'd never been here at all."

"She couldn't have just disappeared!" I frowned. I was not prepared to accept Rose's peculiar notions of nighttime time traveling as a means for an explanation.

"Oh, she didn't disappear, my dear. A young man signed her out."

"Who? Was his name Luke, by any chance?"

"I don't think it was chance; I don't believe in chance; I'm a science man. But yes, it was a Luke. Luke Dawes. Do you know him then?" Dr. Ford leans closer to me. He looks intrigued.

"Only by reputation," I sigh. "Why ever did you agree to let her go, sir? You surely couldn't have thought she was cured?"

"Dr. Dawes seemed to think immersion therapy was the answer. That perhaps she needed a dose of reality. He seemed quite knowledgeable. A doctor himself, you know."

I snort. "Naturally, he would be. Probably a lawyer and the King of Transylvania, as well."

Dr. Ford begins to rustle the papers around on his desk again. I can tell he is becoming bored with me, and I have been summarily dismissed from his attentions. I'd best leave before he assigns me to kitchen duty. I can just see myself peeling potatoes for all of eternity, and not only do I not care for spuds, I am also afraid I'll never get the image of escaped patients jumping out at me from inside the bins out of my head. Sweet Fanny Adams, I may never eat another potato as long as I live.

Chapter 14

After the sudden death of my mother, I was extremely agitated. I remember being shaken, not with sadness or regret, but with sudden bursts and lapses of memory. For a while, I wandered the cliffs, hearing the waves crash below, my cloak billowing out from me like the heroine in one of Solomon's novels. I felt like Cathy searching for Heathcliff, Jane searching for Mr. Rochester.

For a moment, I couldn't remember my love's name. I felt so very unanchored. Lost. I couldn't recall who else I had been looking for. Then, in a spasm of understanding, I remembered: my father and sister. Of course! Such a ninny, Rose. Don't be silly now; it's time to focus.

But, no, on reflection, I simply had no energy left over for them. Revenge on my mother had left me tired and weak. I only wanted to go back to Luke, and oddly enough, to Bedlam. At least I could get some sleep and eat something.

"Perhaps one day I'd come back for the rest of my family," I thought. I stored that thought away for later in the shrinking area of my head where I kept my memories and plans.

I told Luke what had happened on the cliffs, but he was only concerned that I looked pale. I could no longer piece together exactly what had transpired. I told him Mr. Rochester was nearby, and then Luke firmly told me we had to go home, that I'd had enough excitement for one day. I yawned and agreed. He always looks out for me that way. Most times I like it; sometimes, though, I don't like being told what to do. He should tread carefully, my Luke.

When I awoke the next morning at Bedlam, he was already gone. I had a momentary twinge of jealousy at Luke's ability to blend into his surroundings, while I was once again snared in a hospital bed, trapped like a rabbit, but the bed felt warm and comfortable, and I knew someone would bring me tea and something to eat soon enough. As if beckoned by my thirsty thoughts, a stiff young woman, thin as a rail except for a heaving bosom, entered my cell. She pulled my blanket back without so much as a by-your-leave, and set a bowl of broth down on the only other piece of furniture in the room: a very small chair.

"I don't like mysterious men checking in young ladies without all the necessary paperwork being finished, but I suppose you're here, and there's nothing I can do about it. Don't dawdle over your breakfast. The doctor wants to see you straight away." She didn't wait for me to answer, but slammed shut the door behind her as she stomped away.

A perfect description of Miss Helmes if ever I saw one, though I'd hardly call her young myself. I suppose young is a relative term, a matter of opinion?

Excitedly, I realize Rose's account could not have been made that long ago now. We were nearly up to the present time; I was almost sure of it. Mr. Connelly had said once that Rose is about my age, and she must be so—or almost so—at this point in her diary. If I've made sense of her ramblings, she'd be about sixteen now. That didn't explain Miss Helmes being so young, but perhaps it isn't Miss Helmes; perhaps the hospital only hires this type of skinny, antisocial employees? The thought makes me smile.

I was irritated by the woman nurse, but still tired, so I contented myself by plotting her death as I sipped on my broth. Really, all I wanted to do was sleep some more, but I was worried about Luke and where he had gone off to. Sometimes I wanted to ask him more about his life, but I always thought about it when he wasn't there, and then when he was, I forgot. I was forgetting more and more. As if particles of my brain were disappearing. My whole life seemed like a dream sometimes: blurred around the edges usually or sometimes crystal clear but without any sound. You won't understand this, but it's like a television with the sound turned off, or a radio tuned in to static

Maddening.

*Exhausting, too. Which was a nice feeling actually, because I was getting better at sleeping. I could now lie down, and it wouldn't take me hours and hours to fall asleep. Especially if I knew I'd be traveling, I could practically will myself to lose consciousness. I stayed for about a month that time, resting up. Luke came by every day and I knew he wasn't far away at night. I hadn't been pulled into one of **his** travelings yet, which I found curious. I think I was using up our lifetime supply.*

When I felt well enough, we traveled far and wide. We went as far into the future as Luke had ever been: twenty-first century America. He said the technology at the time was advanced enough to locate the whereabouts of my family.

It was an odd place, this futuristic America. We went to New York City.

People looked the same, and yet, very different. It was a strange mixture of fashions and noises and smells. No one person dressed the same as the next, which was unexpected, but made me fit in nicely. I wore my favorite red calico dress that Luke bought me, and I didn't even feel out of place. Everyone was strange and different and odd and bizarre, and I kind of loved it actually.

I couldn't learn the difficulties of the technologies that Luke said would do our research for us. They confused me and irritated me so that he told me to find something else to amuse myself and he would work alone. So, while he spent hours holed up in the libraries, I would wander the city.

Once I followed a group of girls my age into their school.

What a funny place! I had never been in one before, not ever. Of course, I had read plenty about schools, and most of my favorite novels had made mention of them. I had not read a whole novel since Solomon.

No one paid any attention to me, even when I sat down in a classroom. The teacher, an ugly woman, asked my name and sighed and said, why didn't anyone ever tell her anything about new students? and then she told me to sit down and everyone else to be quiet. The girl closest to me kept chewing something loudly, and I wondered why she didn't just swallow whatever it was and get it over with. I wanted to smack it out of her mouth, but I also wanted to stay longer, so I behaved myself.

I soon found out this was a history class, and they were studying the Civil War in the Americas. None of the students looked interested, and most of them were doing things with small boxes that lit up, and some were talking. The teacher droned on about slavery and Abraham Lincoln.

Eventually, I couldn't stand it anymore, and I told her she was not only wrong concerning everything she just said, but also that she was a donkey's ass. The students howled with laughter. To my surprise, she didn't seem offended or shocked by what I said, but she did tell me my smart mouth would cost me my grade. I shrugged and left, amidst laughter. One boy lifted his hand up to me as I passed him. I didn't know what he wanted (me to hand him something? I didn't have anything), so I walked on by.

"Hold up!" he said, following me into the hallway. "Nice work in there, baby."

"I'm not a baby," I spoke slowly, as he seemed like an idiot. Handsome, but an idiot.

"What's your name then, sweet thing?" Yes, his face was handsome enough, but he must have been a simpleton because his trousers were nearly on the ground like some sort of village idiot.

"You don't want to know."

"I don't? Ah. I get you. Mysterious and beautiful. You're like a vintage puzzle, sweet thing. Walk with me?"

I shrugged. I didn't have anything else to do. If I got bored, I'd find new amusements.

"You know, this place has a million rules no one ever follows, but you should probably put on shoes, just because I wouldn't want to see those pretty feet step in something nasty."

I looked down at my bare feet. I didn't like shoes.

"I'll be fine," I muttered. "What do you do around here?"

"You mean for fun? Ah, baby, I got you covered there. Why don't you hang with me?"

"Hang?"

"Today and forevermore, sweet thing."

Lord, what an idiot. I sighed.

"Come on, baby, let me show you what you'd be getting." He reached out, fast as a snake, and pushed me up against the wall, one hand on my waist, the other reaching under my skirt. Calmly, I looked into his handsome eyes and entwined my fingers through his. I yanked back on his wrists, and he crumpled like a paper doll.

I don't condone violence usually, but I couldn't help a silent cheer in my gut for Rose.

Bored with the school and everyone in it, I wandered off, and I stayed close to Luke for the rest of the night. He was tired—staring at what he patiently explained for the fifth time was a computer—but he was determined to find enough of a trace of my father or sister before we slept and found ourselves back at the hospital. I sat on the table next to him, twirling my hair and yawning.

"Here's something!" he finally exclaimed. "Look!"

I peered at the brightly lit screen. There it was indeed. My father's name, Noah Alexander Gray. Thank you, Old Babba, for muttering under your breath how much you hated my parents and for burning their full names into my head. It was an arrest notice for public drunkenness, along with a very helpful address and year.

I slept happy. It wouldn't be long now before our reunion.

They were going to be so surprised when I showed up!

We went back to Bedlam for a time. I had to think. Had to arrange my priorities, you see. Couldn't just show up without a plan, could I?

Of course not, I think. That'd be crazy. I shake my head silently, and check the clock. Do I have time for a few more pages?

Luke didn't seem overly interested in my plans for my family. I think he was in a hurry to get it over with; he had a yearning to visit our island again. The stays in the hospital were more bearable when we had a little vacation to look forward to. But I was getting more and more concerned about using up all my traveling abilities and getting stuck somewhere, without having done what I wanted with my father and sister. So, I rested up for a just a bit and told him we'd spend some lovely time together, just us, soon enough.

"I just have to do this, darling," I said, one day when he visited me. He looked so handsome. I loved him so.

"All right, love," he agreed. "I'll be here tonight if you're ready."

"I'm ready."

"You're sure? What if they don't want you?" he looked worried. "Do you plan on keeping them?"

"What, like a batch of puppies?" I laughed. I liked laughing with Luke, even though I did it so infrequently it sounded rusty, like nails on a chalkboard.

"Yes," he grinned. "Like puppies. I don't want puppies. I hate puppies. I just want you."

"I won't keep them," I promised. "It will always just be us. But I have a role for you to play."

I shared my plan with him. He agreed to everything.

Of course he did.

I couldn't get a handle on this Luke Dawes. What a shyster. That much was true. But he was an interesting mix of villain and meek accomplice. Who was the real Luke? I wonder. And did Rose really know herself?

The gods seemed to be kind to me this trip. I think they must have approved of my plans because I managed to stay in one place and time for a longer period than normal. We found my father and sister, Sonnet, right where we knew they would be. I sent Luke to them first.

He did such a good job.

He posed as a photographer. We even found an empty, tiny room for him. I went in through a busted window in the back and we set up shop, with old cameras from a pawn shop that we bought with stolen money. We made it look lived in, hung a sign and everything. Sonnet was stupid to believe us, but believe us she did. Or Luke rather. I hadn't made an appearance quite yet.

We stayed in an abandoned house, outside of town, which was perfect in so many ways. It was falling apart, on the outside and the inside, and there was a notice on the door that I didn't read. There was canned food in the kitchen that we took a pickax to in order to open, and once I even started to read a book I found. It was dull and badly written, and I left it open after a few pages. I hadn't read since Solomon, and I was relived I still knew how, though the desire for books was gone. I explored all the nooks and crannies, like a little child, when Luke was gone. I pretended to be a little girl, and sometimes I let my big sister come along. I'd talk to her in a child's voice, and we'd play hide and seek like sisters do. I'd always win. She wasn't as smart as me. And she always played by the rules, my imaginary Sonnet. Silly girl. If you want to win, you have to break the rules.

I decided to concentrate my energies on the real Sonnet.

She was a strange girl: taller than I, and darker, too, but with the same ice blue eyes. A kind of clumsy beauty, a careless sort of pretty, with a throaty voice and legs that tripped over one another. Somehow I think I would have known her anywhere, though we were so young when we were separated. I felt no affection for the creature; after all, she stole away my half of our parent's love and attention. She had them all to herself, and I had no one. Who were my mother and father figures? A crazy old bat with The Sight and a man who deceived me.

It's amazing I grew up sane.

Sonnet deserved everything bad I could throw her way. So, being a generous soul, I threw her a lot.

I confused her, which I found fitting. Hadn't I spent most my life confused? Seemed fair. I walked by when she could barely glimpse me. I was good at that, being the library ghost. Once, I sat in the back of a crowded shop when she played her guitar. Like a fool, she tripped when she saw me. I couldn't have planned it better. I left before she could stand again. Like the mist, I was gone. I was surprised she couldn't hear me laugh! For days after, I couldn't stop my bubbling laughter every time I thought of her startled, hopeful face. I laughed all the way down the alleyway, my hand over my mouth. I stifled my laughter when I doubled back and saw Luke comfort her, take her tissues to wipe her tears. He was so very good at the part he played. If I had been the jealous type, I would have been fretful at the attentions he paid her. No matter. I didn't believe his flirting, but she certainly did, and that was what mattered. Once I did become a trifle concerned, asked him if he was falling for her—Sonnet, I mean. He smoothed my hair back and kissed my mouth and didn't even have to speak. I was winning again, you see.

The next time I saw Sonnet, I couldn't really see her. It was dark. Dark in her room, where I hid. I watched her from her closet as she readied for bed. I had known for a few days where she lived, even had studied the people who lived with her. They were a strange bunch, and I wasn't too much interested in them. There were a couple of old men who didn't leave the house much, a fat old lady who smelled like gravy, a completely dull married couple, and a tall, black man I found a bit frightening. Well, frightening isn't the word exactly... I just wanted to avoid him, and he was tricky to avoid because he came and went entirely too much and at odd times. He drove a huge blue car, and once I saw Sonnet take it and drive away at a snail's pace. She could have walked backwards faster than she drove that car. Anyway, I wasn't interested in any of these. Only Sonnet and our father mattered, and it was becoming less about our father somehow, and all about Sonnet.

She was distracted in her thoughts that night in her room; that much was certain. It took her a bit to fall asleep. I hummed a while out of boredom, in the closet, but she didn't stir. I crept out and sat on her bed next to her. The last time we would have done this, we would have been small children, with different colored hair and the same eyes. Now look at us, I thought. Nearly grown. I reached for her hand and with the other, I stroked her cheek, gently. My gentleness was partly ruse, partly curiosity. I felt for no love for this girl. I simply wanted her to sleep deeply and, maybe in her sleep, remember. I remembered, so why shouldn't she?

She murmured something in her sleep. I knew she was dreaming. What did she dream of? Loving parents? Friends? Talents? Never being alone? Handsome photographers? Didn't she think of me at all?

Angry, I pulled my hand from hers, and as I did so, I scratched her wrist rather brutally. I hadn't planned that, but my emotions had gotten the best of me. Sometimes that happens with me. I took advantage of her shock and frightened reaction and also the dark, and left like a ghost.

Indeed, I was a ghost. I slipped through their horrid little house without anyone seeing me.

No one ever sees me if I don't want them to.

Chapter 15

The next time I wanted her to, I was standing beneath her window. The rain came down that night in sheets, but I was patient. I knew she was restless, knew she'd be having a hard time sleeping, knew she'd look out her window that night, knew, because I would have done the same thing, and were not we sisters? The same blood coursed through our veins. I could predict her every move.

She was so very easy to predict and play. Like the old deck of cards I used to practice my tricks, she fell so neatly into my hands just the way I knew she would.

I stood there, ever so patiently, while my yellow hair hung down in a solid mass around my face. My red dress was plastered to me, and my feet were cold. Still I waited, and when she pulled aside her curtain, I was there.

Like a painting, she stayed motionless for a time. But eventually, she whirled away from the window, and I knew I had to be quick. I ducked inside the truck Luke stole (my fear of automobiles had been lifted once I knew what they were). We waited in the dark while she drove off in her friend's car. She was going right where I knew she would. Hadn't I planned this, too? Had already subtly put the idea in her head when I told Luke to take her to our temporary home? She had felt me there and couldn't shake me. I knew she'd go back, and go she did. I told Luke to take me there, but quietly, with no lights glaring on the front of the truck. He dropped me off in the darkness, and I told him to leave us. He didn't want to, but of course, he indulged me. He always spoils me like that. Such a good boy. He probably spent the next little while playing with his new cameras. He did have a knack for them.

I waited until she went upstairs and then snuck in the house quietly. For a moment, I flirted with the idea of pushing her down the stairs. Hadn't I done that once? Pushed someone? Our mother, wasn't it? But it wasn't stairs, I don't think. Sometimes I forget.

But I didn't push Sonnet. I whispered her name, and that seemed to frighten her sufficiently. I was so very close to her, and the fool couldn't see me. I swung the door shut, with her trapped inside the little room. She was playing into my hands perfectly! I had already nailed the window shut, and there was no way out.

I turned the key in the lock and locked her inside. She was silent for a moment as she realized what had happened, silent for a moment before she tried the knob. Then came the banging, the kicking, the crying out.

I couldn't help myself; I laughed a bit as I left and wondered if Luke had found any cake for me.

Poor big sister, I think. What a mess she found herself in, if this crazy retelling was to be believed. Or perhaps none of this ever happened? Was it all in Rose's head? Who could even know?

I think Mr. Connelly might. I think it's time he came clean about some things. Rose hasn't mentioned him once, *not even once,* in her diary. If he's known her like he's claimed, shouldn't she speak of him once or twice or a hundred times?

I resolve to confront him as soon as possible. Either he doesn't know the depth of Rose's illness, or he knows but doesn't care.

I'm not sure which is worse.

The only row Luke and I ever had was after that night. He was irritated with me for locking Sonnet in. I got angry. He got angry. He wanted to go home, he said.

"Home? Home, where? Where is home?" I shouted at him. Normally, I don't shout, not now that I'm older and grown up. Shouting isn't ladylike. But sometimes, I forget myself, like I forget everything else.

He was done playing this silly game, he said. I was acting like a child, he said. I couldn't believe he could be so harsh with me. Weren't we having fun?

He left.

I felt cold and sick inside.

I think I have always been cold and sick inside, but that was the first and only time I knew it.

Oh pet, we all knew it all along, I think. I want to read further, but I pace myself. There are questions that need to be answered by a certain cigarette-smoking individual.

*   *   *

"What business do you want with him?" Mack had asked earlier, impertinently, I think. Or concerned? I couldn't tell which.

"None of your beeswax, doctor," I drawled out the last word, even though I knew it was immature of me. He didn't even have the decency to look affronted. The nonplussed nonchalance of youth strikes again. Anyway, I got nowhere in my queries of Mr. Connelly last night.

It dawns on me this morning, as I braid my hair, that I don't even know Mr. Connelly's place of residence. He never spoke of himself. What had he told me? That he was rich and bored. I muse on that a bit while I unbraid my hair, in an attempt to look older. I study myself in my cracked mirror, as I sweep it up and pin it. I look like a little girl playing dress up. More red lipstick helps, but still. Will I always be so small and insignificant looking? I indulge myself and allow a few moments to picture myself sweeping down a staircase at Mina's house in one of her dresses, my hair piled high and glittering with diamonds. All right, the diamonds are a bit much. No diamonds then. My hair would sparkle all on its own.

Naturally, there would be a handsome prince waiting at the bottom, his heart beating only for me. I'd lose my shoe at midnight and...

All right, silly girl, enough fantasies. The hair becomes braided again in order to ground me and my imagination, and at the last minute, I wind the plaits around my head and pin them. There. A sort of compromise.

I look like a Swiss maid.

Heavy sigh, and my mind drifts on to a different sort of fantasy: one where I am dressed in a smart uniform, capable of leading teams of nurses, skilled in the surgery, saving lives. I'd write a book perhaps, and smoke a pipe while writing it, in my own amazing library, one that went up to the ceilings, and had ladders! Yes, this was more my style. Perhaps my handsome prince would be in possession of a heart defect or something delicious like that. I could save him by inventing a cure. Why, I'd practically have to marry him after that kind of bonding. It'd be cruel not to.

A glance at my clock told me my dreams have cost me my punctuality, and I race to the hospital, the laces in my boots undone and flying in the breeze that my feet make as I run. By the time I arrive, my lovely hairdo is a wreck; I don't have to look in a mirror to know it's frizzy and fuzzy, and one of the ends of the braids is sticking up. I lick my hand hurriedly and smooth it down as best I can and stoop to lace my dirty, black boots. The hospital is eerily quiet, and I see no one at first. I hang my cloak and finish smoothing my hair.

"Good morning," says a sharp voice.

My eyes adjust to the gloom of the room, and I am startled to find Mina's mother there. I met her once, briefly, and it's safe to say we didn't exactly fall in love with one another. She's a tall woman, imposing, and nothing like her daughter. She's a bit rude, a bit insensitive, and altogether very rich. Add to that, she doesn't approve of the time Mina spends here, and yours truly will never measure up.

"Mrs. Dobson," I greet her as warmly as possible and extend my hand in my usual fashion. Not surprisingly, she doesn't even glance at it (I would have fainted), but she does do me the courtesy of cracking a thin smile.

"Lizzie, is it?" My name feels brittle and distasteful rolling off her sharp tongue.

"Yes, ma'am," I feel obligated to drop a curtsy and do so. The woman feels like royalty, I a peasant, or an orphan, a peasant orphan. Why can't I be a rich orphan? Or a peasant with family? Talk about drawing the short straw in life. Really, I have nothing good going for me at all. It's depressing.

"I'm told Mina has invited you into our home." Mrs. Dobson seems to be choosing her words very carefully; either that, or she is speaking slowly because she feels I am dimwitted. "I do not approve." She lets those words sink in. "You are not—not someone I feel comfortable with, my dear. No fault of your own, of course. Just as you probably wouldn't feel comfortable there, yourself, would you?" She leaves no time for reply, and her words sail on, oblivious to me. "I think it is best that you rethink what you are doing and where you would like to be in the future. Everything we do now is a road to our future, isn't it, Lizzie? A block, a beam, a brick in the road. We must be careful to build the right road, mustn't we? There are very specific destinations in providence for you, my dear. Very specific, and they lead to specific places. We mustn't play around with roads that lead to nowhere. Such a waste of time, and time wasting is a sin."

I am unclear what my response should be, or indeed if my very presence is even required in this one-sided conversation, so I merely stand still, an orphan with her arms behind her back, hands clasped, seen and not heard, just like I was taught all those years ago. I feel eight years old again. I wouldn't be surprised if she boxed my ears next, or took away supper.

"Of course, I'll speak with the doctors, as well. Perhaps I'm mistaken, but I'm sure I'm not. I doubt they'll want to let you out of their sight anyway, will they, dear? Such a busy time at the hospital, and so much to do, so many treatments to administer, I suppose." She exaggerates every syllable as though it will lend sincerity to her words.

A busy time? I let my eyes wander around to the stillness. If I concentrate, I suppose I can hear Mr. Limpet's wheelchair creak. Yes, we're certainly bustling. I don't know how the doctor could spare me; why, the whole place might fall apart without me here to change linens. Someone's corners could come untucked, and then where would we all be? Up a creek without a blanket, that's where.

"I agree, Mrs. Dobson," I say, cheerily. "Balls aren't really my cup of tea, as you well know. I'm much better suited to cleaning out the fireplace, and besides, the mice here are dreadfully difficult to catch. For the coachmen, I mean."

She blinks.

"Anyway, ma'am, I tried telling Mina the same sort of thing, but you know how she gets. She has it in her head that having an orphan around will be good for, I think she said, your social reputation? Some such thing. Evidently, Jane Wilcox took a servant girl under her wing recently and everyone is all agog at such charity. I heard her social status went through the roof. Such silliness! But I quite agree, ma'am, it is entirely unnecessary and inappropriate for me attend your function."

Mrs. Dobson looks taken aback for a moment. "Well, I, that is, I didn't mean to make your decision for you, and naturally if Mina wants you there, I suppose..." She trails off, but her eyes narrow at me as if not sure what to make of me.

"I assure you, ma'am," I respond, lightly. "I wasn't being cheeky. I merely spoke the truth, and if Jane has had three marriage proposals this year, I'm sure it's a coincidence, not a nod to her benevolent activities. Although, with the size of her, I was surprised it was three... but again, I'm sure it's a coincidence. Some gentlemen do like quantity over quality, don't they? But Mina doesn't need any help in that department, does she?

The marriage department, I mean."

"Of course not! And I'm not attempting to marry her off."

"Of course not!" I echo. I give an exaggerated sigh as if my heavy burdens have lifted. "Well, Mrs. Dobson, I'm certainly glad we had this little talk."

"Yes." She frowns at me. "You have a nice day, Lizzie. And if," she pauses, and once again her eyes narrow as she peers at me. "If Mina wants you there and if you can find something suitable to wear and promise to be on your best behavior, well, then I will be happy to see you."

"Yes, ma'am. Thank you, ma'am. If I finish picking the peas out of the hearth, then I'll do my best to attend."

"You're a peculiar thing," Mrs. Dobson sniffs. "I must confess, I don't know what my daughter sees in you, but she's always been of a softer character than I. She gets it from her father." She doesn't seem too pleased with this revelation. I'm not sure who she is insulting now: Mina, Mina's father, or still me.

"I'm sure he's a lovely man. I like him already. Well, I'd best be off to work. It certainly was wonderful seeing you, Mrs. Dobson."

She doesn't grace me with a reply, but sweeps out of the room like a grand duchess.

I can't decide now if I want more than ever to go to her blasted ball or if I wouldn't be caught dead there. In my endeavor to confuse the barmy woman, I've confused myself.

* * *

The day drags like the proverbial molasses in January. I'm bored out of my mind with nearly nothing to do, and Mr. Connelly is a no-show, blast him. He always seems to pop up when I am thinking of him, but not today, it seems. Miss Helmes has me reading aloud to one of the patients, an elderly woman named Nora. Just Nora apparently; she is a bit of a mystery, and if she knows her own surname, she isn't telling it. Probably a street woman, I suppose, with a colorful past that has left her a shell of her former glory. Her mind is nearly gone, poor thing.

I read from Ethan Frome (which is a bit dull and was never my favorite), and she has no reaction to my words.

"I don't see there's much difference between the Fromes up at the farm and the Fromes down at the graveyard; 'cept that down there they're all quiet, and the women have got to hold their tongues," I drone on. I peek at Nora. Still no reaction. I snap shut the book. "So, the Fromes up at the farm met up with the Fromes down at the graveyard and they all had strawberry cordials and went to the ball. There was scandalous dancing and heavy petting in the corners and no one minded in the least."

Nora continues to stare past my shoulder, not meeting my eyes, not really looking at me at all. What has made her this way? Was she like this from the start? No one has ever come to claim her. She was dropped off by someone, a family member, but they never came back. Typical, sadly. Did she have no one who loved her, I wondered? If someone dropped me off, would anyone come looking? I pat her hand then. It's soft, like crepe paper, and dry. She snatches it from me, but still doesn't meet my gaze.

"All right, Nora. I won't touch you. Do you want more of the story?" I sigh, dreading her answer though she probably won't give one. "Book?" I hold it up in front of her face. "More?" I feel silly, like I'm talking to a baby, but in a way, she is one. Most of the patients have to be handled like this, at least the ones that aren't dangerous.

"Okay."

I'm staggered she has finally spoken to me, and also a little taken aback by the word choice. I remember Rose when the farmer's son said that to her, and she didn't know the meaning.

"Okay," I repeat, and smile. "But we could switch books if you like. Little Women is much better, I'm just letting you know."

"This one is fine." Now that she strings more words together, I detect an indeterminate accent.

I sigh again and open Ethan Frome. As I open my mouth to pick up where
we left off, Nora speaks again.

"I don't care so much about the ending of this one, so it's best." French? I
think she's French.

"Um, all right. I don't care much either, but why is that best?" I keep my
voice soothing, like I've been trained to do with our patients.

"In case I don't get to hear the ending."

"But why wouldn't you hear the ending, Nora? Are you firing me so
soon?" I smile.

"No, but I won't be here long." She looks down at her crepe paper hands
and wrings them like a dish towel.

"Oh, that's right." All the patients say this. "Well, in case you stay longer
than expected, we'll just get into the story, all right?"

"It's not all right!" She bursts out. She is still wringing her hands,
practically wringing the skin right off. No wonder they look like they are
made of the frailest tissue. "No one understands! I won't be here forever,
and I don't know where I'll go! I don't know where I'll go. I don't know
where I'll go." Her voice fades away, softly, trailing.

"You don't have to go anywhere, Nora," I say, gently. "You can stay here
as long as you like."

"I don't know where I'll go."

"Then stay here."

"I don't know where I'll go. I don't know where I'll go. I don't know where
I'll go."

Her chanting is becoming eerie now. She finally turns her head to look at me, carefully, as if it costs her a great deal to do so.

"Don't you find it fearsome?" she says. "To be someplace different? To be so lost?"

Perhaps it's the abundance of late night diary readings, but I swear the inflection in her voice sounds as though she had said *"to be so Lost."*

Chapter 16

I struggle through more of Ethan Frome, but my mind isn't in it. I keep eyeing Nora uneasily, but she doesn't interrupt me, and her chanting has stopped. I'm being perfectly ridiculous even entertaining the thought of the Lost, but now it's in my head, and I can't force it out.

"What did you mean, Nora?" I finally blurt out, right in the middle of a sentence. She reacts to her own name, I can tell. "Why do you think you don't know where you're going? Are you afraid to be someplace new? When?"

"Anytime. Soon. Not soon. You don't understand." No, not French… Spanish?

"I'd like to understand. Will you tell me? I promise…" I falter, just a bit, and even look over my shoulder at the door I've left ajar. "I won't tell anyone if you like. Just between us."

She leans forward, like a little girl with a secret, and smiles. "I can't tell you, silly," she whispers in my ear. "You'll think I'm crazy."

This is a common enough fear at Bedlam, ironically enough. Inwardly I sigh, but outwardly, I just give Nora an encouraging smile. "No, I won't! You can say anything you like to me."

"Can I?" Nora leans back in her chair, fretfully, and tugs her afghan over her knobby knees. "I don't think so."

Rather than beg (which I feel like doing), I pat her knee under the afghan. "Some other time then," I murmur. "Never mind. Why don't you take your nap, now? I'll be back to check on you later." And if you aren't here, I'll know I'm the one who should be committed to this place, I think.

Nora doesn't acknowledge me when I leave. She's switched her emotions off, as effectively as turning a knob or pushing a button. Some people have that ability, and she's one of them. I, on the other hand, tend to wear my emotions on my sleeve, as they say, and for the rest of the afternoon, I grumble through work. I'm irritated by the lack of Connelly, irritated by myself and my thoughts, irritated with Mack and Mrs. Dobson and Nora. I feel as though I'd like to jump out of my skin. The thought of changing one more bedpan or unpacking one more box nearly has me flying into hysterics.

I'm saved from embarrassing myself by Mr. Connelly strolling through the doors. Finally! And it's nearly time for me to be off work altogether. My stomach is growling for its supper, but I wouldn't miss this time with him for any amount of food. I make short work of polite pleasantries and get straight to the point.

"Walk with me outside a moment, sir?" I gesture towards the doors he just strolled through.

Mr. Connelly pauses in his task of removing his coat. He hangs in time for a moment, still, and then makes a great show of putting it back on. He even sighs, which I find a bit overdone and insulting. I snag my shawl and lead the way outside. It's a rare English evening, still warm, no breeze. I spot his wonderful car parked haphazardly nearby. You can be sure, if ever I were to own such a beautiful thing, I'd learn to park it perfectly. I suppose it's yet another example of the wealthy taking for granted their riches.

"Mr. Connelly," I begin, in what I hope is my most mature and no-nonsense voice. "This business with Rose has me quite consumed, I'm afraid."

"So I've noticed," he seems to be smiling, though his cigarette and what would have been a five o'clock shadow a week ago hide it well enough. So does the fact that he is so very tall. Has he always been this tall? "I'm sure she'd be delighted to learn someone has taken such an interest in her. Your hair is very unusual today, by the way, little one."

I shove a pin back in and glare at him. I'd forgotten my Swiss maid look.

"It was windy this morning, and I was late. Also, a patient hit me with a pillow. As I was saying— Are you laughing at me?"

"No, no. Not at all. I was thinking of something else. Go on." He **is** laughing, sod it!

I switch tactics and attempt to take him off guard. "What is your name, Mr. Connelly? Your first name, I mean."

"Sam. Why? Are we so intimate then?" He helps me with another pin.

"Don't tease. Ow! It goes in the hair, not in the scalp. It just struck me this morning that I don't know very much about you."

"True. And you probably shouldn't be running off in cars with me or taking lonely strolls through the woods with me, either." He makes a show of looking dangerous and ferocious, but he mostly looks like a diseased bear.

"Don't be silly. This isn't a wood, and I can take care of myself, should you decide to—" I trail off. Decide to, what? Get frisky? Kidnap me? Rearrange my hairdo?

"Ravish you? Ruin you?" Now there's no mistaking; he is definitely laughing. "Well, the thought had crossed my mind once or twice, but I promise to behave. Now what else do you want to know in this sudden burst in inquisitiveness?"

"Stop teasing! And stop doing that thing with your eyes." I say, crossly.

"What thing?"

"That twinkling, sparkling thing. It's distracting."

The diseased bear with impossibly sparkling eyes, snorts. "I apologize for the state of my eyeballs. I'll try to contain their – um, twinkling."

"Thank you."

"Maybe I could douse them with ashes or something if they get out of hand. Or throw dust in them. Rub some mud in them."

"I'm considering all those at the moment." I pull my shawl tighter around my shoulders. I think of Nora's bony knees as I feel my own shoulders through the thin fabric. Had he really been thinking of ravishing me? "You don't look like a Sam."

"Don't I? Well, you can call me Samson if you like."

"Really? That is unusual."

"It's also not my name, but you can call me it if you like," he continues, cheerfully.

"Look, *Samuel,*" I glare up at him. "You are being awfully immature and full of codswallop. I'm trying to have a grown up conversation and get to the bottom of things and you keep..." I almost say "flirting" but stop myself. That couldn't be what he is doing, is it? I am unaccustomed to flirting, unless it's with rowdy teenage boys, whom I mostly ignore. Had he really thought of ruining me? "... keep annoying me and getting me off track. Besides, I don't have a lot of time to talk; I'm positively starving, and I want to go home and eat."

"I have a better idea," Mr. Connelly—Sam—tosses his cigarette down and grinds it out with the toe of his lovely shoes. "I'll buy you a nice supper, as an apology for being a rake and for very nearly, almost, practically, considering the mere possibility of ravishing you. You can talk all you like over a nice steak and butter beans."

I'd like to feign indifference to the invitation, but my mouth is already watering. I'm afraid to open my lips to speak, for fear of salivating all over those lovely shoes. I manage not to clap my hands in glee like a little girl, but I do smile in what is probably an idiotic manner.

"That sounds nice enough. Thank you, Sam."

"You're very welcome. Do we need to check with Miss Helmes?"

"Of course not. I'm off work now. She is only my warden between the hours of eight and six, you know."

"Ah." We are at the Rolls Royce Phantom now, and she is just as sleek as I remember. "Hop in."

Hopping in is just what I do, a little hop of excitement that I can't contain. After a rotten day, things are looking up for me. I have to cross my legs at the ankles just to keep them from happily bouncing in the car and to keep my toes from tapping. I debate asking to drive again, but squelch the desire, since I already know the answer.

"Where to?" I ask, breezily as we pull away from the hospital. I ask out of curiosity and something to fill the silence with, not because I am well versed in restaurants. Odds are, I won't have heard of his answer anyway.

"There's a nice place I know of. You'll like it."

"Thanks," I pause for a moment, "Sam. So, one of the things I wanted to talk to you about—"

Sam shakes his head, firmly. "No inquisitions until I have a steak sitting in front of me. Be quiet, and enjoy the scenery."

"It's London. I've seen it," I wrinkle my nose, "especially this part. I liked Oxford better. I liked the library."

"We're not going to Oxford; now hush. Good Lord, it's like having a toddler in the car."

I swat at him playfully, but when he nearly runs down a dog, I leave him be. Eventually, we pull up at a wonderful looking club, and Sam gives the keys to the Rolls to a young man for parking. I eye him carefully.

"How do you know he won't just steal it?" I wonder aloud.

"Turn about is fair play," Sam replies, mildly.

Whatever does that mean? But there is no time to ask, and the desire is gone anyway, as we have entered the restaurant. Low lighting, rich looking patrons (oh, why didn't I ask him to let me change first? I smooth down my wretched skirt), the smell of delicious food wafting by my nostrils. The women wear jewelry that sparkles; even in the dim lighting their bracelets and necklaces catch the reflection of candles and bulbs and twinkle merrily. The men are smartly dressed and handsome. The smoke is thick, and I can't help but cough. It seems a crude and childlike thing to do, so I try covering it up with a fake sneeze. Sam looks down at me, amused.

"You shouldn't have brought me here," I hiss. "Not that I'm not grateful—and hungry—but I look so out of place! I look like the maid."

"You're fine."

"People are going to give me their coats. Just watch."

"Then we'll go through the pockets for change. Come along," Sam nods to someone I don't see, and he presses his hand in the small of my back, urging me to walk. We pass a sign that advertises Live Lobsters as a delicacy. Right beneath it is another that boasts, Dancing Nightly. I stifle an urge to giggle.

When my eyes adjust to the lack of lighting and the smoke, I see who we're following: a waiter who is impeccably dressed (I'm not even dressed well enough to be the Coat Girl on reflection). He leads us all the way to the back, and I feel like a sideshow freak on display. Gertie and Lulu would have nothing on me, I find myself thinking. In my head, I can see the sign now: *Come see the Urchin Girl! Two bits!*

I pull at my braids, which had come down from their pins finally, and wish, desperately, for my red lipstick. I might as well be a dancing lobster;

I am so out of place. Thankfully, beyond a few curious glances from the men and dismissive looks from the women, I am mostly ignored. The waiter pulls my chair out for me and even bows. I sit down stiffly and sip from the icy goblet of water near my plate. Suddenly, I choke on it and narrowly stop myself from spitting all over Sam.

I gesture towards something, covering my mouth with my large cloth napkin. I sputter my frantic words into it.

"What?" Sam puts down his own water and looks at me in confusion. "Are you having a fit?"

I gesture again, frenetically, towards two women not far from us. They sip drinks, and one of them, the blonde one, catches my eye and smiles politely. I want to die.

"It's Lillian Gish and Mary Pickford!" I attempt to talk coherently through my huge smile. I have finished coughing and sputtering, but now I am having a difficult time speaking English. Mary Pickford just smiled at me!

"Who?" Sam squints across the room.

"Stop it!" I hiss, yanking his arm and nearly spilling our water. "Stop looking conspicuous! Don't stare! Oh blimey, I can't believe it's them. Stop looking!"

"You told me to look!" Sam laughs. "Quit having a coronary. Are these chums of yours?"

"Chums?" I stare at him, incredulous. "Chums? Me? Chums with Mary Pickford and Lillian Gish? Are you knackered?"

"You're squeaking."

"That's because I cannot believe you just asked me that. Of course we are not chums! What a ridiculous notion. Are you truly telling me you don't know who they are?"

"Sorry, little one. Not chums. Enemies then?"

"Oh, for Pete's sake. They're movie stars! Huge movie stars! Haven't you ever seen a picture?"

"Ah. Yes, of course, a good many of them. Can I have my arm back now?" He disentangles himself from my clutches, but I barely notice. I am staring dreamily at the women, out of the corner of my eye.

"You look like you're having an epileptic fit," Sam continues, mildly.

"I'm trying not to stare. Just keep talking to me, and I'll keep my head pointed your direction. I'll smile and nod a lot. Go ahead!"

"You're going to give yourself a headache. Leave the poor things alone, and let them eat their supper. What do you want to eat?"

"Whatever." I dismiss my options with a wave of my hand. He's right though; I can feel my head begin to ache a bit from my awkward position. I am about to give it up and finally concentrate on Sam and food when they both stand and push their chairs into the table. "They're leaving. Oh my, they're so beautiful. They're coming over here!" I begin to squeak again, frantically this time. "They're coming over here! Sam! What do I do?" I want to slide under the table and disappear.

"Don't ask me," Sam has lit another cigarette and looks at me, amused. "Hello, ladies."

It takes all my will power to keep my knees from turning to jelly and sliding down my chair, into a puddle on the floor. I smile, weakly.

"Hello, yourself, handsome," Miss Pickford says, in a voice smooth as honey. Her bias cut gown shimmers like a mermaid's tale. It is cream colored and has nary a crease as it hugs her small hips and clings to every curve. Long strands of pearls dangle over her breasts, and when she turns a little to wave farewell someone across the room, I get a peek at the back of the gown: a deep V that ends at the small of her back, with a cheekily placed bow. She isn't as tall as I would have thought, given her larger than life impression in the pictures, even in her high heels. I can't help noticing her glamorous cosmetics: liner that wings up at the edge, and lashes that can't possibly be God's gift. Her shade of lipstick looks like mine, which gives me some small comfort. It'd be a larger comfort had I been wearing any tonight.

"And hello to your little dame." Miss Pickford winks at me. "I thought you might like an autographed photograph? I saw you recognize us."

I swallow very loudly. "Thank you, Miss Pickford!" I manage not to squeal this time. Instead, I sound like a bleating goat. Too loud, stammering, and full of longing. "Thank you so much. I, I just loved you in Coquette. It's my favorite picture! Well, after La Boheme!" I hastily turn to Lillian Gish to shower my awkward praises on her next. She smokes a cigarette from a long-handled, decorated holder as I bleat on. "The whole orphanage got to watch that one! We had a benefactor who paid for us all to go. It was lovely."

Lillian is dressed in the same type of gown as her friend, only in a deep jewel-tone blue color. She shimmers like peacock feathers, and her heels are silver, and her necklaces are diamonds instead of pearls. Her hair is dark and exquisite, curled just so.

"That is sweet. Who shall I write it to then? Hold this, handsome?" Miss Gish hands her cigarette holder to Sam, with a smile. Was she flirting?

"Umm." why do I feel as though I've lost my own name? "Lizzie, Miss. Thank you, Miss. So much, Miss!"

"Perhaps the orphanage would like a stack of these. Do you think, Mary?"

"We could arrange that," Miss Pickford muses, as she signs her photograph with a flourish and hands it to me. "And you're very beautiful, Lizzie. Have you thought of going into the movies?"

I gape. Like a flounder, my jaw hangs slack. Am I drooling? I snap out of it. Was there room in pictures for a drooling lobster?

"No, Miss. I'm a nurse."

"Well, keep it in mind. You have a very unforgettable look about you. Come along, Lil. We don't want to keep the boys waiting. Goodnight, handsome. Goodnight, Lizzie."

They are gone, in a cloud of perfume and glamour, before I have enough wits about me to respond. I stare after them in shock, my photos clutched to my chest.

"Hallelujah, they left. Now we can order! I kept looking at all that beauty, and all I could think of was steak, steak, steak." Sam beckons for the waiter, who had been hanging back patiently.

"You're cracked. How can you even think to eat at a time like this?" I feel dreamy.

"You're cracked. When would be a better time? I'm ordering for you since you look like you've severed all ties with reality. Two steaks, medium rare—"

"Well-done," I interrupt, still in my dreamy, sing song voice.

"Don't listen to her; she doesn't know what she wants. Butter beans, a whole mess of 'em. A couple of potatoes, drowned in cheddar and onions. Do you have some of that brown bread? A big plate of that, please. Coffee. Apple pie. Off with you, young man, and step lively! I don't want to faint from hunger in your fine establishment, but I may, so for the love of God, be nimble!"

The waiter scampers off. Literally, he scampers. I marvel at his sprightliness before finally shaking myself out of my icon induced stupor.

"That was wonderful! Really. The best night of my life."

"We must get you out more," Sam teases. "You haven't even tried the steak yet. It will erase all memories of movie stars right out of your head."

"I doubt it. I won't even taste it. I'm just... shell shocked. They were just lovely, weren't they?"

"I suppose so. If you go in for glamour and jewels and minks and all that jazz."

"Oh, you don't?" I laugh. "What do you go in for?"

"Braids and lipstick." He winks. "Every time."

Chapter 17

The meal is nearly wonderful enough to erase my memory of my star sightings, but not quite. I imagine every line of Lillian's gorgeous gown as I tear into my steak with reckless abandon. The entire potato in, my stomach finally stops growling, and I can come up for air. I savor my beans, one by one, and resolve to find the answers to my questions. That is, after all, the whole point of tonight; movie stars and brown bread aside.

"Why doesn't she speak of you? Rose, I mean. You said you know her well?" I am very interested in my question, but I pretend nonchalance as I experiment with how many beans can be stabbed on one fork.

"Quite. And I haven't read the diary, so I don't know."

"A long time you've known her? Her whole life?" Nine beans, but they're terribly squished. I feel bad for ruining their perfect, buttery roundness.

"No, not that long. It only feels like it. Are you going to finish your pie?"

"Yes. What do you make of what she thinks she did to her family? Is she telling the truth, do you think?"

"Which part?" Sam inquires, dryly. "The part with Mommy Dearest, or Father Goose, or Big Sister?"

"Any and all of it. Well, let's start with the mother." I drum my fingertips on my lips as I rest my chin on my hand. Elbows on the table would never have happened at the orphanage, I remember out of nowhere. "Do you really think she killed her? Her own mother? She said herself she was very confused that day. She thought she saw Mr. Rochester or some such literary character. Maybe the whole thing was in her head?"

Sam pushes his plate away and leans back in the chair, regarding me. "What do you think?" He turns the table on my inquisition smoothly.

"Oh, no, I asked you first."

"I asked you second."

I scowl. "Someone has to be mature here."

"Not it."

"Fine. I'll go first. I think she invents wild things in her head and imagination to keep herself occupied in the hospital. We already know she comes up with some pretty crazy scenarios, so we can judge from that; we can't believe everything she says."

"So, you'll just disbelieve all the frightening things? Is that it? Not face them. I see." He looks—disappointed in me.

"Don't be condescending. I'm simply giving you my version of things. But fine, all right, let's say she really did kill her mother that night. How'd she get there? How'd she get out of Bedlam?"

"How'd she get out this last time? Doesn't seem to be a problem, does it?"

"Why do you keep answering questions with questions? It's terribly annoying."

"Is it?"

I throw a piece of bread at him. "You're impossible."

Sam smiles and raises his eyebrows. "Not impossible. Quite possible and highly likely."

I roll my eyes and dig into my pie. It's melt in your mouth good, with cinnamon and brown sugar. We don't get food like this at Bedlam. I'm so full; I feel I could burst.

"You're really no help to me at all." I grumble. "Lord, this pie is heavenly."

"I'm sure He had a hand in it, at least with the crust. How does the diary say she keeps getting out of the hospital?"

I swallow, and wonder how he'll react to the response I'm about to give him. "Well, she *says* she—" I don't know whether to lower my voice, laugh a little, sound skeptical, or simply come out with it. I choose the latter. "She says she can time travel." There I said it. I had been worried it would sound silly, and now I know it does.

"Well, that would explain it."

"You're not surprised?" I certainly am.

"I told you. I've known Rose for a long time." Calmly, Sam butters the bread I had tossed at him.

"Actually, you said it hadn't been a long time," I argue, crossly. I'm too full, and I push my last few bites of pie away. "Make up your mind."

"That's just it. A 'long time' is rather relative, don't you think?"

"No. No, I don't. I may be willing to believe she murdered her mother and terrorized her sister, but I'm certainly not going to entertain any thoughts of time traveling. I'm sorry. I'm just too practical for that kind of nonsense." And I'm disappointed in him if he isn't.

"You think it's merely a symptomatic side effect of—" Sam looks uncomfortable, and I realize he is not meeting my eyes; rather, he is staring at my shoulder somewhere, or maybe my forehead, but not my eyes. "Of her condition?"

"Her condition? All right, we'll call it that if you like." I can think of other names: madness being at the forefront. "Her *condition* is not unlike most others at the hospital really."

"They all think they can time travel?" This is said wryly. "I had no idea it was such a common *condition*. Can I finish your pie?"

"No, and all right, already! Here. Naturally, they don't all think they can time travel, but we once had an old woman who thought she was the Queen of Persia, and we all had to bow to her whenever she came in a room. And then there was the man who thought rats were living in his clothes. That was an interesting case. Constantly undressing himself. Not good!"

Sam chuckles around his mouthful of apples. "I can imagine."

"Yes, well, no you can't. Did I mention he was nearly four hundred pounds? Yes, imagine that."

"I'd rather not! Your point being what?"

"My point being this: everyone in Bedlam has delusions; otherwise they'd be nice, quiet members of society and not locked up, right?"

"You could use better locks. What?" He feigns innocence. "That should be your next point, is all I'm saying."

I glare at him. "Look. If it's our fault Rose is missing, then I'm sorry. But I'm hardly the security team, am I? I'm the one helping you, so don't continually get your jabs in with me. Take it up with Miss Helmes."

"Hell, no! That woman scares me. And like I said, Rose will turn up. I'm only teasing you about the locks." Sam reaches over and squeezes my hand, reassuredly. I pretend his touch doesn't make me glow inside.

"Well, it isn't funny! I'm worried about her. I feel like I know her somehow, because of the diary. She's in my head." I run my fingers through my hair until they snarl on what's left of my braids. I pull out the bands and a stray pin, and comb through the mess with my fingers. "And I have to say, it's not always the nicest feeling to have her there."

"I know." Sam lights up yet another cigarette, and leans back in his chair. He's watching me comb through my tangles, and it feels an intimate sort of inappropriate thing to be doing at dinner. I put my hands down.

"Believe me, I know the feeling. Look!"

I turn, and watch a striking woman in a deep, red gown, positively dripping with accessories, take the nearby stage. As she steps up to the large, silver microphone, several men whistle. Other than those whistles, a hush falls over the crowded restaurant. A five-piece band is near her, all the men dressed in perfectly pressed, white suits and black ties. The tips of their shoes even put Sam's to shame, they shine so well. The band leader waves his arm, and they start to play a lively tune. I watch the beautiful lady sway and wait for her cue. Her hand cups the microphone like she would cup a lover's face, and she looks completely at home on the stage. Once she begins to sing, she sounds like an angel.

"She reminds me of Sonnet." I smile.

"What? Damn!" Sam jumps up and wipes at his trousers, where he evidently has just deposited his coffee.

"Are you burnt?" I should pay more attention to his dilemma, but I don't want to take my eyes off the performer. Besides, I'm not going to lend a hand to his lap anyway.

"No, I'm fine." Sam sits back down, gingerly. "I didn't want children anyway. What did you say earlier?"

"She reminds me of Sonnet. Rose's sister? Singing up on stage, that's all. I mean, I don't know what Sonnet looks like, but I picture her like this."

"I know who Sonnet is, thank you, and she's chubby and hairy. Doesn't look anything like this woman."

"Oh, you know her? Of course, you do." I finally rip my eyes off the Not-Sonnet look-alike. "Do you know how to get in touch with her? Is she in England?"

"I don't think that'd be a good idea. Sonnet and Rose are rather estranged, I believe. I highly doubt she's harboring her sister somewhere."

"Well, I haven't gotten very deeply into their story yet. Maybe tonight, if I don't slip into a food induced coma first, I can read some more. Is she really hairy and chubby?"

Sam has a smile playing at the corner of his mouth. "Not really, no. I think you'll be getting into an interesting part of the story soon. Maybe she'll finally mention me, eh?"

"I'm beginning to think you don't exist," I respond, pointedly. "Either that, or she's mad at you and has literally written you out of her life."

"Don't say that," he looks wounded. "I'm sure I'll be in there somewhere. When she speaks of a darkly handsome devil, that's me. She'll probably use the words rugged… dangerous… desirable…" Words like that. They'll mostly likely be a lot of swooning and bosom heaving in my general direction."

I roll my eyes, but can't help laughing. He's so easy to talk to. Just when things get too serious and mysterious, he does me in and makes me laugh. I've never been a silly girl, never been one of those ninnies who goes weak in the knees over the opposite gender, but oh, how this particular man/boy threatens to unravel the threads of my carefully knit together life. Falling for him would be beyond silly.

And, yet…

I've always loved the frightening, thrilling, beautiful feeling of falling.

*   *   *

We argued some more, and frankly, I got bored with him. He was being slow witted, and I didn't have time to baby him. I knew he'd let my sister out of that house, so I decided to simply let him. Normally, I stay awake during the day: I don't like traveling without Luke unless it's necessary. I'm always concerned I'll forget where I left him, and then it'd be difficult to get back, wouldn't it? But I was feeling petulant and even took a nap once, alone. Luke was upset when he found out, and after shouting at me a bit, we forgave one another. I couldn't help but be pleased that maybe he had learned his lesson. He should never have stood up to me, but then again, would I love him so if he ever stopped? We're either the perfect pair, or doomed for all eternity.

And when you're Lost, eternity seems even longer than most.

Now that he wasn't angry, he was my willing partner again. The next time we left, that very night, I was yanked back to Bedlam, per usual. The only thing was, I inadvertently took everyone with me. I hadn't really counted on that, hadn't even considered moving everyone, but it was perfect. Simply being so near was enough to pull anyone of the Lost along with me in my traveling. It had never happened before, not with anyone but Luke, who slept next to me, but perhaps my powers were growing? I was delighted. Of course, not at first; first I woke up in the hospital, with only Luke and I didn't realize how many people I had pulled along with us.

Things were dismal in dear old London. I was upset at being there, and extremely bewildered, too. My confusion after traveling was getting worse, and it was taking me longer to come back to myself and right my head. I was in quite a mood in Bedlam that day, throwing fits and yelling. They strapped me down to a bed and refused even water after I spit at a doctor. Luke was there, but he knows me better than anyone and he knew not to try to calm me down just yet. I will not be willed to calm down. At least one day passed – or perhaps it was even more – and Luke came and went. When he told me that the others were out there, in London, I could hardly believe my luck. My head was still fuzzy but I remembered enough of them to know I hated them.

Now what? What to do with them, here? I needed a plan. But as it turned out, necessity is the mother of invention and a brilliant opportunity presented itself. I became sweet as pie long enough for the staff to unstrap me, and in my wandering through the old familiar hallways, I met someone. Though I had not had much in the way of schooling, I knew enough of the Ripper to know him when I saw him. No one else knew who he was or who he was destined to be, naturally, but I think people of a kind come together like magnets, don't you? The legend was well known – I'd spent just enough time in the nineteenth century to have heard of the fellow. Bedlam is full of strange and wonderful people. They're all a bit crazy, don't you know?

Jack was incarcerated for murder. Luke was brought there for murder. I was brought there for being me, which I found patently unfair, but that's beside the point.

The friendship between my sister and the prostitute, Emme, was simply too good to pass up. I had never really planned to murder Sonnet, and I hadn't yet decided what to do with my dear old father, but doing in Emme was just lovely. A kind of revenge that would shock them back to their senses. What did they think they were doing anyway? Replacing me? Me: her sister, his daughter? They shouldn't have been so callous as to do that.

I hadn't gone and replaced them, had I?

It was a good plan. I liked it very much. I didn't even have to get my own hands dirty, thanks to Jack. Not that I minded doing the deed myself, but, well, it was just cleaner this way. All Jack needed was someone to listen to him; someone to understand his hatred and his desires. I only had to soothe his tortured soul and whisper in his ear. I am a very good listener. It's one of my finest qualities. By the time Luke got us out of the hospital, Jack was in a black mood.

Power like that can make one a bit giddy. Who else can do what I can do? I can redirect the Lost's path like a dam redirects water. Their future lays helpless in my hands. The things I can do...wonderful!

Luke was happy to help; our quarrel from before had made him contrite. "Just don't hurt Prue," he had warned. "She's off limits." I had nodded, but I hadn't really been listening. I don't like ultimatums or anyone telling me what to do. Don't hurt Prue? Watch me.)

We scampered off from Bedlam like children. Luke stole me a piece of cake, and we kept our distance for a bit longer as the others acclimated to where I had deposited them.

When next I saw Sonnet, or I should say, when next she saw me—as the two things are not always one and the same—Luke had already made his appearance. I had watched, from a distance, as he did exactly what we had rehearsed. Yes, I made him rehearse with me; of course, I did. I had spent those precious years of my youth with Solomon, hadn't I? The master actor, the magician. Rehearsal is very important, crucial to a good performance. "If you want the audience to believe you," Solomon would say, "you have to perfect every move, every cadence, every lilt to your voice, every tilt of your head."

"Golden Goose," he would say. "Practice, practice, practice. Practice makes perfect."

Chapter 18

Luke was a good actor. Naturally, Sonnet was thrilled to see him; like a ninny, she suspected nothing. Really, the girl had no survivor's edge to her, no trace of suspicion, no cynical view of the world. You could tell she had lived too soft of a life. No one had taught her to expect the worst from people. Fooling her was almost too easy.

The manifestation of Emme earlier had been another reunion I had watched, and that one had nearly boiled my blood. Embracing as though they had been lost without one another. Disgusting. They weren't sisters. It was time they remembered that, and remembered me.

I let some more time go by, but when I saw Sonnet out walking one day, in a yellow dress laced so tight she walked strangely, I didn't let the moment pass by unmarked. We were near where we had all woken up together, and she was staring out at the water. I wondered what she thought about: probably about having a love affair with my Luke or spending time with that hateful Emme.

I walked right up to her, right by her, and stared with her. We stared, the two of us, me barely controlling a smile and her, entwined in her own imagination. We were so close I could smell her: a kind of nutmeg scent that probably came from her hair. And a mothball scent that came from her dress. I wrinkled my nose over the nutmeg. She didn't even turn to glance at me until I spoke.

"Hello, sister," I said. "I knew you'd find me."

She turned then to look at me, and her light blue eyes were wide. I thought I looked very fetching, with my gray cape and the way the wet wind from the Thames had put waves in my hair. I stared back at her, solemnly, although really I wanted to laugh a little. I had wondered if I would feel the urge to hug her the way Emme had, but I didn't feel it. Evidently, she didn't either, for she didn't move at all, except to speak.

"I've been looking for you. I thought I'd never see you again." Sonnet has a deep voice for a girl, throaty and husky. It's not at all like my voice, yet another example of how different we are. I'm beginning to suspect different fathers. Perhaps Mother had been busy. Too bad I forgot to ask her before she fell. Or was she pushed?

"Why would you think that?" I asked. I really didn't understand the question. "I'm your sister, aren't I? Don't we belong together, you and I?"

It was a simple enough query; I still don't know why she gaped at me, wide eyed and slack jawed, like a fish.

"Yes," she finally agreed. "We do. But we've been apart so long. Are you...?"

I wanted to roll my eyes. Really, she was messing up our reunion. Starting with pleasantries? As if I had time for such nonsense.

"Oh, I'm fine, Sister. You?" I played her game and tried to be polite. "You've been well all these years? Living with our father?" I made sure to say, **our** *father. I hoped she recognized that she had hoarded him to herself all these years, like the spoiled brat she was.*

"Yes. He'll be so anxious to see you and so happy, too."

"Oh, will he?" I thought. Doubtful.

"Will you come and see him?" Sonnet asked.

I declined, said I was very busy. Another time, perhaps? Weren't we striving for politeness, after all? Always be hospitable, even if you don't feel like it. That's what Solomon said.

"Rose, please come with me." Sonnet sounded very confused, and she reached out to me.

I didn't want her mussing up my lovely cape, and I don't like people touching me without permission, so I pulled away. I wanted to frown at her, but instead I smiled a little. I don't remember what I said, but she reached out for me again! Doesn't she ever listen?

"No, no, don't pull on me. I don't like it." Fine, if she's going to be impolite, then I've tried my best, Solomon. She started it.

For some reason, Sonnet started asking about doctors. I patiently tried to stay with the conversation, but she seemed very dim. Not very bright, my sister, I'm afraid. She asked me where I was staying.

I don't remember much past that. We spoke some more, but I felt puzzled and no longer sure of why I was there. I had a headache, and I had forgotten the next part of my plan. I think I ended up inviting her for tea, a silly thing to do, but it turned out it couldn't have been better if I tried.

It was Boxing Day when Sonnet came to visit me. She showed up at my door, looking uncomfortable and unsure of herself. I'm always sure of myself; I think I've always been that way. I just know who I am, and what I want, and I don't see any need to apologize or shirk away from that. Sonnet, on the other hand, can't seem to figure out who she is or what she wants. It's not an attractive trait, really, and makes her seem very flighty.

I made her tea, which I thought was very nice of me, but I noticed she wasn't really drinking it. She seemed rather nervous, which was to be expected, I suppose, seeing as how we didn't know one another very well. Family get togethers can be so awkward. I read that once in a magazine when I was visiting another era, and it is true. Awkward, awkward, awkward.

I tried to put her at ease by my conversation; really, I did, but evidently I made her mad when I started mentioning Mother. I even told her my secret, that I could control my traveling. I thought she'd be proud of me, but nothing could have been farther from the truth. She was upset.

She went on and on about Mother. She was completely missing the point. I hate people who can't see the big picture! Caught up on the details, she was. Details don't matter, it's the end result. Mother died; so what? Everyone dies. The big picture is how special my abilities are, and she didn't seem to care about that at all. I was taken aback; how could she not see how splendid my powers were?

I've heard about the competition between siblings and how they always must outdo one another, but really, I expected better of my elder sister. I suppose I must have thrown her out, though I don't remember now. I think I chucked a teacup at her head—that seems familiar—but I'm fairly certain she ducked.

Luke came home and brought me cake.

Such a dear boy.

The next part of my plan had already been set in motion. Emme was as good as dead, and my hands were clean. Well, very nearly so.

The only thing I hadn't predicted was Luke blowing his cover, but really, it hardly mattered at that point, anyway. I came home one night to find him barricaded in a closet, of all places. It took me what felt like forever to move the heavy furniture my sister and her lover had pushed in front of the door. I am very small, and sometimes I forget to eat, so I can be a bit frail when it comes to physical strength. Luke was having a fit in there. When he stumbled out, all righteously angry and upset, I had to kiss him back down to a rational place. He can get so angry sometimes. Really, it can't be good for him to lose his temper the way he does. It's like he doesn't even know himself or what he's capable of when he's like that. It took all my womanly charms to calm him down.

The next time—the last time—I saw Sonnet and our father, was at the girl's funeral, Emme's funeral. Everything had gone according to my plans, the way I knew they would. Jack took care of her for me. He's a dear. Very misunderstood on the whole.

I wondered what he could do in other centuries? Why, he'd never be caught if he traveled with me. Interesting thought. I need to think more on that.

At the church yard, we kept our distance, Luke and I; of course we did. We aren't stupid. But I was curious. The last funeral I had been to had been Old Babba's, and that was a festive affair with only me. This one (from what I could tell from such a remote location under several trees and near a crumbling crypt) was a sober event, at least at first. I had forgotten the prostitute had a mother and a brother. That was very nearly sad, but I shook off any sympathy. The big picture, remember? The big picture was I had gotten a revenge of sorts, by taking away someone my family loved - loved instead of me. That was the big picture, indeed. If I had unintentionally made a small child sad; well, it was simply a casualty.

Someone made me sad once.

I survived.

The little boy would survive, too. Perhaps he'd grow up strong and influential, like me. Perhaps I had done him a favor. I can be kind, you know.

They were a sorrowful, pitiful bunch, I'll say. Things had worked out for the best. I wasn't sure I wanted them anyway; my drunk father, my odd sister, her strange and frightening Israel. Maybe I had been meant to be alone, after all. I hadn't done so badly, had I? A feel of exclusion still lingered though. I couldn't help wondering if we all could have been happy together, if circumstances had been different. Would I bring Luke home for Christmas? Would Father someday give me away, walk me down the aisle? Would I be Auntie to Sonnet's children? In my fairy tale land, would we all live happily ever after?

I laughed at the thought. Silly me, getting romantic notions. And here I thought Austen had been wasted on me, all those years ago at the library! Obviously, some fluffy ideals had seeped through and taken root. Solomon would have tousled my hair and teased me.

If they had bothered to look over, they would have noticed us, Luke and me. They were absorbed in their grief, their shared sorrow, and didn't glance our way. I watched as Sonnet's ebony veil blew across her face, and the folds of her black skirt whipped in the wind. It began to snow, and I saw her lift her head up to face it head on. The gesture made me wonder if maybe she wasn't braver than I had given her credit for. After all, she had sought me out, and most people don't do that.

Most people leave me alone. Forever, they leave me alone.

Why won't you?

I really hate when she does that, addresses me as if she knows me. It gives me the chills and makes me feel as though she watches me, curled up on my window seat, drying my freshly washed hair. I sip my tea and pull my shawl closer over my nightgown. My hair smells of apples and leaves and—though it needs a good scrubbing, and I'll be glad I did it tomorrow—right now it is frigid in my little flat, and my sopping wet mane is not helping. I pull my winter cap out from its place in my bureau and slap it on my head. My hair will not dry well, but I am freezing suddenly. Whether that's due to temperature or Rose's cryptic comments and murderous confessions, I do not know.

I only have a few pages left of the little diary. Rose's handwriting is difficult again, small and cramped. It strains my eyes; I feel like they've been rubbed with sandpaper. I debate whether to finish it all tonight or save some for later. Why am I so reluctant to give her up? I should be happy at the thought, but I have found no clues in recent readings as to where she could have gone and still no mention of Sam either. Would this diary end the abrupt way the first had? Did I need to skim the pages, playing detective, looking for locations she could have stashed the next installment? Or was she writing the next installment now, as I read her words, several weeks or months behind her? Was she curled up somewhere in a flat of her own, penning words for me to find?

How ridiculous. She doesn't even know of my existence.

"Thank God," I mutter aloud. The thought of actually meeting Rose Gray gives me the willies. Insanity I am used to, but she's a special case, and now that I have been privy to her private thoughts, it's somehow worse to think of her face to face with me. And yet, hasn't that been my goal these past few weeks? To find her?

I groan. What do I want? Maybe I only want to find her to discover her exact connection to Sam. And why would I want that? I pester myself. Blimey, this interrogation in my head is ludicrous!

I decide to force myself to submit to questioning anyway.

Why do I want to know her exact connection to Sam?

"Because you are falling in love with him, you dolt," I mutter.

I was unsure of my next step. It was as if my life's work was closing in on me. I had accomplished so much, but was it enough for me? Should I leave them alone, what was left of my family, or continue to destroy them, one at a time, until they were gone?

Luke wanted to be finished with them, although there was enough pent up rage in him over being shoved in a wardrobe that talking him into another confrontation with at least Israel wouldn't have proved impossible. But he was tired, too, and worried about me. He missed our island, he said. We deserved a holiday.

I was sorely tempted, but I wasn't sure I should leave them. It would be odd for them to travel so soon after arriving in London, but I didn't know if their inner clocks would be ticking at a faster pace due to my interference. Would they still be here when we returned? "Just a week," Luke pestered. "We can come back and find them again; they won't have gone far." We didn't argue about it—our last row had left us careful of each other and wary of tempers—but we could not seem to agree on what was the best course of action. I wanted to stay, follow them a bit, lest they get away forever. Luke, I was beginning to think, wanted them to get away forever, not because he had any love for them, but because he wanted to move onto other things.

"What would you have us do?" he asked, the night after Emme's funeral. "There will be no reconciliation now. Will you send your father to meet your mother?"

I wave away the notion. "I'm not convinced my father is my father. He doesn't interest me much. And neither does Prue, so don't get up in arms! Just Sonnet. I don't even know why anymore. Do you think I'm obsessed, darling?"

Luke smiled at me, ruefully, and then laughed. "Only a bit. But I like it. I like you."

"I know," I frowned. "Stop being silly, this is serious. Wouldn't you like a chance at retribution with the Rhode fellow?"

"I do owe Israel a little something. I never liked him, right from the start." Luke glowered, and took out his knife to clean under his nails, something he's always done when he's concentrating and thinking of things. When that doesn't relax him, he usually rubs my shoulders, but he could tell that I was in no mood to sit still. I was fidgety and anxious. Besides, rubbing my shoulders was distracting, and I needed to focus.

"See? I told you. We can't just let them go."

"All right. We'll stay near them, if you like and if it means so much to you. On one condition?" He looks up from his knife and points it at me playfully.

"What?" I frown harder. Luke's never given me conditions before. He knows I won't tolerate them.

"I'll let you plan whatever you like with your dreadful family; I'll even help you accomplish whatever you decide needs to be done, but first—"

"What?"

"Marry me," he said.

Chapter 19

I can't help but feel a twinge of happiness for Rose, though I quickly squelch it with rationality and a strong sip of very hot tea. She didn't particularly deserve romance and happiness, not after what she had done, and yet—.

I'm incurably romantic, I suppose. I've read my Austen, too.

Perhaps love will turn her brain to all things pure? Sunshine, charity, hope, and puppies? Maybe a husband will calm her down. She can learn to knit, bake, shop...put down her deadly scissors and pick up some mending? Rock babies instead of pushing people off cliffs? Burn dinner instead of throwing teacups at heads?

I snort into my tea. I feel I know Rose well enough now to predict that marriage will not change her.

Luke knew her well enough, too. It sits uneasily with me her association with Jack the Ripper. Could Luke—? But no, that was taking things too far. But she spoke of moving Jack...as if he were Lost, too. And she's forever moving Luke. Well, not in reality; only in her head, I guess.

No. I'm beginning to be fond of the fellow, even if he harbored a passionate love for a mad woman and seemed a bit dangerous himself. More than a bit, actually. But perhaps I was reading Rose's view of him; who knew who he really was? Was he with her now? Helping her hide away? Did they marry?

I want to read on, but my inner clock is telling me to sleep. I don't need to report to Bedlam tomorrow; it's my day off, so I could sleep late. I yawn, and even the tea isn't helping to keep me awake. Curiosity, as usual, kills the cat, and I turn another page.

Our wedding was a low key affair. I would have gone down to the rectory, in my homespun, red calico, and taken my vows there, but Luke wanted a wedding. Being underage and having no parents to recommend me, we did what we could do: we eloped to Gretna Green.

Luke said I deserved a dress, a real gown, with a veil and gloves and everything. He stole me flowers, too, and a ring, a beautiful ring that sparkled when I turned it to the sun, with a tiny pearl nestled in the band. I felt like a real lady, a respectable lady. I wasn't the ragtag orphan that Old Babba grudgingly took in. I wasn't the performing girl, embarrassed by her peers at the sideshow. I wasn't even Golden Goose, loved and then abandoned by Solomon. I was a real, gentle lady, one worthy of respect and admiration. I dreamt of entertaining callers and pouring them tea. Better yet, having my maid pour our tea. I'd wear the finest hats and be highly regarded in the city.

At least until I ended up back at Bedlam. But I tried not to think of that on my wedding day.

The only piece of finery I balked at was the shoes: dainty, pointy, lace up boots with pearls. White, like my fine gown, and beautiful, too, but I hate shoes. Oh, I wear them when I have to, but I didn't have to in the church that day. I married Luke barefoot, same as the day we met. He carried me in his arms when we stepped outside, just like a proper bridegroom.

I knew I looked stunning; he told me so, but I would have known even if he hadn't. I felt stunning. My gown was so lovely, and I had washed my hair and everything. It fell nearly to my waist in shiny, yellow waves. I have never had the patience to plait it or pin it or do any of the other tens of dozens of styles other girls perfect. Of course, I never had a mother to teach me, nor an elder sister to practice on.

No matter. I have gotten along fine without them. Here I was, marrying the most handsome and intelligent man in the world. If they had been half the family they should have been, they would have been so proud. They would have been there to see my husband lift my veil and kiss me. They would have seen the priests bless us, even though I don't think they were real priests, just witnesses who worked at the blacksmith shop. But they had eyes, they could see we were respectable folk.

I'm shocked when I find the tiny snapshot photos. I simply stare for several seconds, my mind not processing what I'm seeing.

I've kept some of these sewn into the hem of my red dress, but I took them out. I'll keep them here for a bit, since I know how to get back to you if I need to. And here is the one from our wedding.

I pull them out gently. There are only three, all printed on old fashioned card portraits. They are sepia in tone, and I know it's from their age and the ink turning. I stare at the wedding portrait first. Rose is beautiful, stunning really. Her dress is Victorian in style, and so is the veil. It looks as though all the yards of fabric could consume her if she let it, but her bearing and her confidence won't allow it. She is standing sideways, nearly turned away from the camera, and she looks over her shoulder. Flowers trail, almost drip, from her fingertips.

I kept a flower from our wedding. Isn't it beautiful?

There is a pressed flower, or what's left of it, glued to the next page. It looks as though a small child has been practicing her pasting skills. It has been painstakingly done, but that has not saved it: it is really only the spiny remains of the stalk. It, too, will be gone soon, especially if I keep carrying the diary around and opening and shutting it. I feel guilty for the destruction of the flower; I can't even tell what species it once was. Hastily, I try to put the disintegrating pieces that had crumbled into the deep recesses of the diary's fold back together. It's hopeless. They are one touch away from dust. I feel a chill, and can nearly sense Rose's disapproval. A palpable thing, it looms and chastises me, and never before have I felt so sad and miserable, not so suddenly and immediately anyway. It's as though she leans over me, upset and frustrated that I have ruined her pretty flower.

The other photos are taken from her days at the sideshow, days I had hoped she had only imagined. She is a tiny thing in a tutu, her hair curled and wild about her head. Her ribbons on her ballet slippers lace up to her knees. In the first picture, she is merely posing. In the second, she holds a knife. It's a chilling photo, at least to me, not the least reason that it is at least 40 years older than the wedding portrait, and yet it's unmistakably the same girl, only less than ten years apart. On the back of the one with the knife, someone has penned 1846. They could be mistaken, of course. That's nearly one hundred years ago.

I don't want to read anymore, and I set aside the diary and crawl into bed, heavy as a body made of lead.

I don't want to think about the fact that earlier I had come to the conclusion that this entry was made recently. If that were so, a pressed flower would hardly have turned to dust, not if the diary had been sitting in with Dante this whole time.

It's almost as though the flower really is half a century old. What is going on?

*　*　*

The next morning, I could kick myself for having spent an entire evening with Sam and still not finding out his residence. Not that I could march right up to his step necessarily; I may not be wonderful at being a lady, but I do have some standards. But really, I still have more questions: mainly, what the heck happened to Luke, Rose's husband? I am beginning to worry about the bloke. Had a lover's quarrel changed things? She wasn't above murder, and I am beginning to be concerned for Luke's safety, or had she "traveled" without him, this time losing him entirely?

I'm not prepared to entertain that last notion, not really. I'll dwell on murder before I dwell on fantasies.

I debate going to the hospital even though it's my day off. I wouldn't mind talking to Nora again, but the threat of Miss Helmes with never ending spoons to polish, or Mack, rubbing in his surgeon tasks, wins out. I would just end up being sucked into the hospital, as usual, and there would go my only day off in weeks. I shouldn't waste it. I'd visit Mina for a bit, and if I wanted to, I'm sure she would know how to find Sam.

My mind made up, I walk briskly. It's a very long walk to Mina's, and if I were smart, I would have called her and asked her to send round the car, but it's a lovely enough morning, and I can use the exercise and the fresh air. Sometimes I spend so much time confined to Bedlam's walls, I worry my pasty skin will make me look like a cadaver when I finally emerge in public. My hair, freshly washed, is doing its freshly washed thing: being wild and out of control and blowing about my head. I hadn't braided it this morning. After the loveliness of Mary Pickford and Lillian Gish had shown me the error of my ways, how could I? I'll let Mina fix it for me; she'll know all the latest styles. And we'll see then if Sam would tease me about being a child! He'd be swooning and heaving his own bosom at me for a change.

I set my pace to something brisker and pull my shawl tighter as I walk. It's a windy morning, and suddenly a fat drop of rain hits me square on the nose. I scowl. Before I am halfway to the Dobson's estate, I am completely drenched. And after all that work, drying my hair in the freezing cold last night. Wretched weather! What I wouldn't give to be on Rose and Luke's island!

The imaginary one? I chide myself. Yes, that one. I'd imagine up enough sunshine to turn my skin nut brown.

I knock forcefully, and when it takes a minute for anyone to answer, I find myself wishing Mina lived in a flat like mine, where I could barge in at any time. I'm tempted to anyway, sopping wet and shivering, but when I push on the door it is already being opened by the butler. I don't wait for an invitation, but step in quickly.

"Hello, Danvers. I'm going to show myself to the parlor, if you don't mind. Is there a fire in there?" I'm already nearly there, and I have to turn my head to speak to him behind me.

Of course, Danvers, being the perfect butler, impeccably trained, and ever so proper, doesn't show emotion, though he's probably appalled at my behavior. He merely nods his stiff head and doesn't blink. Blinking is beneath him.

"Very good, miss. I will alert Miss Dobson, Miss."

"Thank you, Danvers," I call, cheerfully, from inside the parlor.

I've only been in here one other time, and it was during a sewing circle Mina made me come to. I had to sit for hours, plucking at thread and trying to make sense of all of her friend's petty conversations. Well-raised, bored rich girls don't really talk about the same things poor, bored orphan girls talk about. By the time the afternoon was up, we had two quilt tops for charity, and I wanted to kill myself. I had decided I didn't enjoy charity in any form: receiving it or bestowing it. It probably reserves me a special place in Purgatory, but alas, it's how I feel.

Now there is no one here, and a lovely fire is burning merrily. I plop down, grateful, and toss my drenched shawl aside on the floor. It smells like a wet dog, or perhaps that's me. I pull off my shoes and get my frigid toes as close to the flames as I dare. I love a good fire.

"Lizzie? Is that you?" Mina's voice is surprised. "What are you doing here? Gracious, girl, did you walk?"

"Sorry, can't speak. Defrosting. Needs all my focus."

"You silly thing," she says, fondly, and bends down to rub my arms briskly. "I would have sent the car; you know that."

"Well, it didn't start out raining. It seemed like a sensible thing to do at the time. Isn't your sewing circle always harping about young ladies getting exercise?" My teeth chatter.

"Yes, wealthy, complacent young ladies. The kind who sit around their mansions all day, eating. Like me! Not like you."

"You don't sit around all day," I yawn. "You work harder than most of us who are actually employed for a living."

She looks uncomfortable, like I knew she would. "Well, I like to be busy, that's all. Does Miss Helmes know you're here?" Now she's moved on from uncomfortable, to concerned.

"No, why? It's my day off. I'm free!" I throw my arms out in an exaggerated fashion. I'm sure Miss Helmes is doing the same, somewhere. There isn't too much love lost between the two of us, or perhaps all the love between us is lost? I've never quite understood the expression.

"Then we'll make a whole day of it," Mina answers, kindly. Sometimes I do feel like her personal charity, just a little bit, but somehow I don't mind too much. I should; it really should bother me, yet somehow it is worth the price to have her friendship. She doesn't mean to make me feel like a charity case, and besides, I'm quite certain she likes me and treasures my friendship as well. It's simply awkward for the rest of the world when the two of us are pals. Plus, she has to put up with nasty looks from her mother, and those cannot be underestimated. "First, let's get you something to eat. I know you; you've probably had nothing but your tea this morning?"

"Ha! That's where you're wrong! I found a jar of marmalade in the back of my cupboard when I was toasting bread."

"Did you eat some?" Mina puts her hands on her hips, and eyes me sternly.

"Um, I think I forgot, no. I was distracted by my thoughts, I'm afraid. So, yes, please, food would be lovely." My mind wanders back to last night's meal, when I was so stuffed with steak and butter beans, that I thought I'd never be hungry again. Although, Sam did finish my plate.

"Let me ring for some refreshments." She crosses the room, but tosses her next words over her shoulder at me. "What were you distracted by?"

"Hmm? Oh. Nothing much, really, just a little thing. I'm sure you wouldn't be interested at all... Forget I said anything." I drift off, knowing she'd take the bait.

"What? What happened last night? Yes, will you bring a tray of refreshments, please? Thank you." Danvers nods and is gone again before I've even finished laying out my socks in front of the fire. My, but he is efficient. "Well? What was your big distraction?"

I debate keeping her tenterhooks a tad longer, but her fresh faced, eager expression makes me laugh. I give in promptly. "Mr. Connelly took me to dinner, and you'll never believe who we saw! Mary Pickford and Lillian Gish. They even talked to us, Mina! It was wonderful. Oh, they signed photographs for me. Blast! I should have brought them to show you."

"You'd only have drowned them. Here, give me those socks. You're going to burn my house down."

"They were even prettier in person, honestly. Though Sam was not impressed."

"Sam, is it? Hmm." Mina raises her eyebrows, suggestively. "How far we've come."

"Not that far," I reply, tartly. "You people in the higher classes just hold onto those rules longer, that's all. I don't go around calling my own siblings and nearest and dearest Mister and Miss and Sir That and Lady This, the way you do."

"All right," she laughs. "That's probably true enough. But how was it? Did you—" She leans in. "Feel anything for him?"

"What are you talking about?"

"You know…romantically speaking?"

"Oh my heavens, Mina, you're the silliest thing when it comes to boys." I make a show of turning my socks over.

"Oh, darling, he's not a boy," she chides, and her eyebrows wiggle up into her curly hair. "Here, let me do that. Seriously, I like this house and would prefer not to watch it go up in flames. Scoot back; I think your knees are smoldering."

"He's far too rich and exciting for me. Besides, we're just helping one another, that's all." Isn't it?

"Helping one another? With what? Oh, thank you, this looks delicious!" Mina takes a tray, laden with food, from the butler and nods him out the door. "Here, have a pastry, but talk around it; I want to hear more. More about Sammmmmmm." She drawls out his name in a teasing way, and once again, her eyebrows wiggle up and take residence in her hair.

"I didn't say it like that! Mmm, this is really good. What is this? Liver? I've never had liver like this before. Anyway, we have a patient in common. That's really why we have been spending time together." I debate telling her about the diary and about Rose Gray. Somehow I still don't want to; I want to keep Rose to myself, though she frightens me. "Really? It's liver, really and truly? Blimey. The orphanage used to do dreadful things to liver. I'd tell you but you'd be frightened. It involved sweated onions and broken teeth."

"A patient? Really?"

And then I want to smack myself upside my dull head. Mina has volunteered at Bedlam much longer than I have been there. She probably knows Rose.

"Her name is Rose Gray. She's a young woman, very violent. Evidently, her own husband signed her out not too long ago, pretending to be a doctor." I look for signs of recognition in Mina's face.

Mina looks appalled and puts aside her sandwich. "He isn't a real doctor?"

"Well, I don't believe so," I proceed, cautiously. "But then again, I'm only going off what she says and believes, and she's as loony as they come— really, truly, beyond doubt, a crazy."

"She's talked to you?" Mina looks confused and worried. She bites down on her sandwich delicately. "You've seen her? Heard her?"

I sigh. I'll have to start at the beginning.

Chapter 20

"No, she's not spoken to me, not exactly." (We'll just leave out the part where I thought she whispered at me that night I found her name written on the wall. That odd night is going with me to the grave.) "I found her diary, and I've been reading it. I know, I know, I should have turned it over to Miss Helmes, but it's been a nice distraction from all those boring, tedious chores she gives me. Anyway, I've been a bit obsessed with it." I probably look sheepish. I feel sheepish. Also, hungry, so I finish off another pastry.

"Obsessed?" Now she really looks concerned. "Are you sure this is good for you?" Mina looks positively ashen. "I don't like it."

I laugh. "It's harmless, just something for me to do. You saw how dreadfully I sew; what else am I going to do with my free time? Anyway, Sam knows her. He says she'll be back in Bedlam because she always comes back. I suppose Luke will readmit her when he realizes he can't control her."

"Luke?"

"Yes, her husband. The one who took her out? The not-doctor?"

"Oh, yes. A fantastic story. I don't blame you for getting caught up in it, I guess. It does sound a little more thrilling than quilt tops. I think I'm rather jealous."

"Do you know her then? Miss Helmes seems to remember her, though she's a bit like conversing with a clam, so I can't get anything out of her."

"Who, Rose?" Mina hands me back my socks. "Here, they're dry enough. Yes, I remember her, I think. I think Miss Helmes took care of her single-handedly. She was, as you say, rather violent. You know they don't let the volunteers near the aggressive ones."

"Oh." My face falls. I hadn't thought of that. "I was hoping you'd know her and could corroborate some of her stories. So far, all I have to go on is her diary, and it's a bit like reading The Jabberwocky poem. You know, 'Twas brillig and the slivy toves,' and all that bit."

"Mother made me memorize more substantial poetry. Like, 'ask ye why these sad tears stream,' and all that bit. Are you sure you want to find her?" Mina sounds doubtful. "Maybe it's better she stays lost."

Lost. An interesting choice of words. Of course, I'm letting my imagination get the best of me. Still, the word takes me aback, and I choose my next phrasing carefully.

"I'm a bit worried that she's out in society somewhere," I point out. I take a bite of something square shaped that is evidently filled with molten lava. "Oh my word, these are hotter than a June bride in a featherbed!" I curl my toes with a yelp.

"Lizzie!" Mina smacks me on the shoulder. "You can't talk like that!" But she's stifling a giggle behind her hand. "What if Mother hears?"

"Sorry, sorry. These are hotter than…a petit-four right out of the oven?"

"That's better. Now come on, silly girl. Have you had enough to eat? I want you to come and try on some dresses for the ball. Did I tell you it's going to be a masquerade?"

"No, you didn't mention it. Can you do something with my hair? I need a new…something." I let her pull me up to standing. "I'm too old for braids."

"Mmm. Did Sammmmm tell you that?"

"Oh, stop! Fine, I'll just braid it then," I grouse. I think I may be blushing, and knowledge of the fact only makes me blush brighter. Then the annoyance that I'm blushing harder makes me blush even more. I may burst into flames at any second. I hide my embarrassment by beating

Mina to the hallway and running like a hellcat up the stairs. I can blame
my pink cheeks on the exertion.

"Wait up!" Mina laughs, but of course, she doesn't run; she takes the steps
like a lady, skirt in her hand. "I'll do your hair, promise, but first you have
to see what you think of my gown, and pick one out for yourself. I can
alter it tonight. And we must decide on a mask for you!"

I'm already sprawled on her bed by now and can only hear every third
word or so. Mina's room is luscious; everything is plump and sumptuous.
I curl up on a dreamy pillow, but keep my hot feet atop the blankets.

"Oh no, you don't! No napping! Up!" Mina pokes me. "We have to focus."

"It takes focus to pick out clothes?" I'm skeptical. I haven't had much
experience—all right, no experience—when it comes to picking out ball
gowns, but I would have assumed it came down to color and...well,
mainly color.

"Of course, it does. Here, I'm going to toss you a few, and you hold them
up to your face."

"Whatever for? I won't be wearing them on my face." But I oblige by
draping a green silk over my face as I sprawl.

"You're so childish," Mina sighs, and yanks it down. "I was right, too
washed out. Doesn't bring out your eyes at all."

"That's because they're closed."

"You need to take this seriously! Don't you want Sammmm to see you as a
beautiful woman? He is coming with you, isn't he?"

"I have no idea. That's my answer to both questions, by the way." I hold
up a peach colored gown, under my chin, and wait for approval.

"Hmm. Better. Definitely better. A little dull for a party though. Why don't you have any idea? What'd he say when you asked him? Oh, Lizzie, you did ask him, didn't you?" Mina looks dismayed.

"Don't be disappointed in me, Mina. I just forgot. I'll ask him when I see him next. When is the party again?"

"Tomorrow night. Let's hope his social calendar isn't full. Waiting until the last minute indeed. Well, at least he knows you aren't desperate for him, I suppose." From the depths of her wardrobe, she tosses a mountain of gold silk at me. "This one?"

"For goodness sake, how many gowns do you have back there? Is there a false bottom?" I drape the gold one over the peach one. I'm starting to look like a giant, silken pillow, with a tiny head peeking out.

"I love dresses. I've kept all mine and all of Mother's. Some are dreadfully outdated, but that's what makes a costume ball so fun. You can be anyone, dress in anything! Besides, I'm a wizard with a needle, so we can make alterations. We can even do them tomorrow, during the sewing circle, instead of quilting! You are coming, aren't you?"

I suppress a shudder. "I have to empty bedpans, thank you. I'll be very busy. I like the gold one, I think. It's...sparkly. Sparkly is good, isn't it?"

"I like this one." Mina holds up shimmering umber colored gown, the shade of orange fire. "Your hair will look nice against it. It's a bit Elizabethan court, but that gives it a lovely waist, don't you think?"

"I'm a little behind on my Elizabethan court fashion history, but it's very nice. Are you sure your mother won't mind me borrowing something?" I finger the pretty fabric.

"Of course not." Her words don't match her tone though. "Besides, it's my dress, and I'm letting a couple of the girls borrow things, so you aren't the only one. Not that it matters. Want to see mine?" Her tone changes immediately.

"Of course! I'm ready to be dazzled. Did I mention Mary Pickford's dress?"

"Name dropper. What do you think?" Mina shows off her midnight blue gown. It's much more straight and simply cut than mine, with much less fabric. There is beading up and down the bodice, and the back is daringly low cut. "With gloves, of course, and plenty of jewelry? And here's my mask." She holds out a bird inspired mask in shades of blue, with peacock inspired feathers. Or maybe they are actually peacock feathers. The rich! They never cease to amaze me. Here some bird is walking around, plucked and embarrassed, so grown adults can dress like children...

"Lovely. You'll be beautiful, as always. But you'll have to move the beak if you want to kiss Mack, or you'll put his eye out." I tease.

Mina laughs. "I'll try to remember that. Now, a mask for you! Oh, I know." She nearly disappears into the wardrobe again. "Hang on. I know I have it somewhere. Ugh, smells like mothballs in here. Here we are!" She emerges, beaming, and holding a gem encrusted, cat shaped mask. The ends curl up, with white feathers. It's rather enchanting, even though it brings to mind the cat that ate the canary.

"Goodness, Mina! I'm not sure I want to be responsible for all those jewels," I reply, doubtfully. "The dress is expensive enough."

Mina laughs again. "They aren't real, honey. I'm a wealthy socialite, not the Queen of Sheba! Mother hasn't trusted me with a single real piece of jewelry yet. She says I'll take it off to push wheelchairs around and forget where I put it. She's right, of course. All of mine are paste, but they still twinkle. Here, try it all on so I know what to take in. You're so tiny."

I crawl in the gown. There's no other word for it. I simply step in and the whole thing eats me alive. Mina looks distressed. The gown hangs around me like a little child playing dress up. I giggle.

"Oh, dear. Why do you have to be so impossibly small? I'd need a month of Sundays to fix this. Well, this will never do.”

“Do you have anything smaller? From when you were say, eleven?” I quip.

“Very funny. We’re just going to have to think of something else, that’s all. You’re sure you don’t have anything at all? Anything we could gussy up?”

I make a great show of pondering. “Well, let’s see, there’s what I wore to the queen’s coronation, and the gown I inherited from my wealthy aunt, and the lovely one from my fairy godmother, though I think I left it in the pumpkin after the prince and I got carried away that night...my shoe wasn’t the only thing that was tossed to the wind that evening...”

“Funny. Focus. Nothing?” She looks fretful. She wants me to have a good time, the sweet thing.

“I’m sure. I’m sorry to put you out, Mina.”

“Hmm. Not your fault you were born an orphan,” she says, kindly.

“I think it was a bit after the birth, actually. The orphan part, I mean.” I’m met by a blank look. “Never mind.”

“Well, let’s see. Alice is nearly as small as you; she has dreadful taste, though. She always strays into the brown territory of frocks, and then she looks like, well...”

“A turd?” I suggest.

“Lizzie!”

“Sorry, I mean to say, a pile of sh—.”

“Shh!” But she’s laughing behind her hand again. “Yes, you’re right, but I didn’t say it! Well, there’s nothing to be done but what needs to be done, that’s all.”

"I don't even know what that means."

"Neither do I, actually. It's something Mother says all the time. I'll figure it out. You just make sure you remember to arrive on time. And bring Sammmm. You won't forget that important detail, will you?"

I eye her, warily. "Why do you keep bringing that up? I told you, I'll try."

"I know, but..." Mina picks at a thread on her sleeve.

"But, what?" I'm feeling impatient now. Whatever is she beating around the bush for? Polite society is so polite that it annoys me greatly. "Come out and say it, for goodness sake!"

"It's just—" Now she's abandoned her sleeve picking and moved on to gnawing on her lower lip. "Most of the young men who will probably come don't know you, and I don't want you to feel slighted if no one asks you to dance, that's all. They can be a snobby bunch, I know. And they will mostly be here to flirt or to look for prospective wives, and I just don't want you to feel left out. You won't, will you, Lizzie, dear?"

"Mina, I have not been entertaining fantasies of one of your rich boys sweeping me off my feet!" I laugh. "The thought hadn't crossed my mind. You're the one who keeps telling me I have to be there, remember?"

She looks guilty. "Yes, I suppose it's me, having romantic fantasies for you. But I do want you to have a good time, and really, some of my mother's friends are dreadful snobs. If they're rude to you, you just send them to me! I'll dispatch them home immediately."

"I'm fairly adept at dispatching my own enemies, but thank you for looking out for me. Now, can we talk about something else? Like, why you're bringing along Mack, the wonder kid, when you have millions of rich boys to toy with? You don't really like him, do you?"

"Don't you?"

"No, he's insufferable!"

"Oh, Mack is fine." Mina waves my notion aside. "He's a dear. And he'll look out for us, you know, in case things get out of hand. The other young men there wouldn't know how to handle anything in an emergency."

"You're expecting emergencies? At a ball? Gracious, what kind of den of iniquity are you bringing me to?" I widen my eyes, in mock horror.

Mina laughs. "The very worst kind. Cook might serve the wrong liver mousse and chaos will erupt. You have no idea how dreadful these affairs can be when things go wrong. Once, Mother accidentally shuffled the seating arrangement around the wrong way, and I can't even tell you the awkwardness that permeated that evening. You could have cut the tension with a sword."

"Sounds terrifying," I deadpan. I'm starting to regret my promise to come. Liver mousse and small talk, in a dress that's so large, it could fall off me at any time, all while no one asks me to dance. What a way to spend the night. I'm wishing suddenly I could cry off and spend my time finishing Rose's diary.

Just as suddenly as the thought comes, I'm desperate for closure over Rose Gray once again. Just when I had thought my life was my own (such as it is), and was beginning to enjoy myself and forget her, she manages to yank me back into her head and soul. How must the people in her life— Sonnet, their father, and Luke—have felt? They actually knew her and loved her, or tried to. I'm simply an observer, and I feel completely engulfed in Rose. She swallows me whole like the gown did, and I eye the pile of suffocating satin with distrust.

Chapter 21

The feeling of being somewhat possessed by Rose hasn't left by the time I take my leave of Mina. I've pocketed a few sandwiches, or really, Mina has pocketed them for me, and I feel like Little Red Riding Hood with her basketful of goodies and sweets for Grandmother. Instead of skipping merrily through the forest, I trudge around the puddles dotting the streets of London. Not for the first time, I wonder what life would be like elsewhere. Would I still be me? Could I be anyone else? The Lost, imaginary though they are, had some things going for them, I reckon: to start off new in exciting places, to never be tied down, to wander like gypsies, and see the world, in so many different centuries? I suppose it would have its drawbacks, but to me, it sounds rather heavenly.

I wonder what it would have been like for Rose to travel to so many different eras, yet always be yanked back to Bedlam. Of course, it hadn't happened that way, but she believed it did, and so the result is the same really. She believes it to be true, so it affects her as if it's true. At least I think that's what the doctors would say about it. No matter that it can't possibly happen, this time traveling she speaks of, she still is who she is because of what she feels in her bones is fact. Poor Rose. Not for the first time, I feel sorry for her. I wouldn't want to meet her in a dark alley, but I do feel sorry for her.

I pass by the shops and see an advertisement for a Jack the Ripper tour through White Chapel. I remember Rose's supposed connection to him with a chill. Naturally, she's too young to have ever met him in any place other than her imagination. I finger the advertisement and eye the crude pen drawing of the infamous killer. "Would Rose draw his likeness like that?" I wonder. "Only fifty years ago," I muse. Theoretically the man could still be alive. After all, they never caught him. If it even was a him. For a moment, the idea of my very own murderous Rose Gray being Jack the Ripper fills my head. I pull my shawl around me. That's taking things too far. Suppose Rose did meet him, only not back then of course, but more recently? He could have killed the girl named Emme for her after his reign of terror in the 1880s. He could have killed her just last month, or last year. Supposing Emme ever even existed in the first place.

But picking apart sense in her ramblings is pointless. There may be some truth, no truth, or a bit of truth, in all her memoirs, but who is to say which parts? I can't say. Trying to find out is useless, yet I still want to try.

I let my fingers linger over the drawing of Jack and stare at the date and times of the tours. The orphan director would never have let us go to such sensationalistic fodder, I'm sure. And Mrs. Dobson would never allow Mina to go: too unseemly. I don't even really want to go, but suddenly I wonder if *she* would. Rose.

After all, killers usually return to the scene of their crimes; do they not?

Being Mrs. Dawes was harder than I expected, but so worthwhile! Marriage agreed with Luke. He was happier than I had ever seen him. He introduced me to everyone we met, as his lovely wife. Why, he would even invent reasons to meet people just so he could introduce me. I think in a way, he was trying to distract me, and it certainly worked. I forgot for a spell why we had come to London in 1888 in the first place. I spent some time keeping house until we were kicked out for squatting. I learned to bake cake, though I had no gift for it. Luke would make me feel better by eating it, but I usually stole the better stuff from the bakery around the corner.

I had very nearly forgotten all about Sonnet. By the time I remembered and could hold the thought in my head long enough and found the energy to do something about her, she was gone again. Traveled? I doubted it. She hadn't been here long, though as I had said before, perhaps my interference in her inner clock messed things up. But I leaned towards a different theory: that she had simply run away.

Silly coward.

It wouldn't be that difficult to track her, but did I even have the desire anymore? I liked being Mrs. Luke Dawes. Couldn't we just stay here and be normal? He wanted it. Part of me wanted it.

And then I dreamed, a horrid dream, and I knew my past wasn't over. I saw Mother in her blue dress, floating in slow motion over that cliff. Her skirts billowed out around her like a parachute, but not one that could save her from the dreadful crash at the bottom. She stared at me, reproach in her dead eyes. She wasn't proud of me. She didn't love me any longer. I had messed everything up. She was upset at me, even in death.

She wanted me with her, I thought. Death came to me in a cornflower blue dress.

I was sure of it, and I was paralyzed with fear. I hadn't been afraid of anything in who knows how long! What a peculiar feeling it was. Was this clammy feeling, this shaky emotion, this pit in my stomach how I made others feel? The last time I was scared was when I realized Solomon had left me at the Bodley. And that wasn't necessarily fear… more sorrow and anger than anything.

I awoke, and I knew I had to find Sonnet and finish what I had started.

Luke was disappointed, of course, but you make sacrifices in a marriage. Of course you do. All the research and the experts say so. You give up things for those you love, and he loved me, so he didn't fight me too hard. Besides, he didn't like London any more than I did, and he wasn't really serious about settling down. Luke with a gentleman's career? A job? A respectable life? Don't make me laugh.

We started with the doctor they left behind and his annoying Chinese wife. Sonnet and Israel had been playing house with them. Why, I'm sure I don't know. Some sort of friendship, I suppose. I can't imagine such a thing, but then again, I'm not very like my sister. Luke was spitting nails over how the wife had interfered anyway (if it hadn't been for her, it's very likely Israel would have died that night, and possibly even Sonnet), so neither of us would have felt any remorse doing her in. It turned out though that they had left as suddenly as my family. I toyed with the idea of them being Lost as well, but their neighbors claimed they went to Africa to start a hospital, and I believed them. Sounded like the type of idiotic thing philanthropists and do-gooders like to do.

Sonnet and Father had no one. But Israel... I wondered if Israel had anyone. And who had been those old men in America? The brothers? Would they know where my family could have slunk off to?

Then there was Prue, the old cooking woman. She was still here, still in 1888 with us, too old to want to travel, whether through time or across town. They had apparently left her behind. Maybe they wanted to keep her away from them, and thus, from me, but they hadn't followed that thought through very well, had they? Instead, they left her behind with me. Not smart.

We started with Prue.

Naturally, Luke was dragging his feet a bit, but I promised him we weren't going to hurt her, not as long as she cooperated anyway. "That's the problem," he growled. "Prue won't cooperate with anyone."

She'll know where they went, I promised. They wouldn't have left her forever without letting her know their plans. She was like their adopted grandmother. She should have been like my grandmother, but no. They'd all seen to that.

So into Sir Halloway's home we went, where Prue was employed as a cook. Truth be told, I was getting a bit tired of slinking around like a criminal, even if I was one. I remembered my days being on stage with Solomon, and missed them sorely. I missed the audience and the way they respected me and what I could do with the knives. Now here I was, a married and respectable gentlewoman, and I was still breaking into homes and trying to put my past to rest. I just needed to finish all this business so I could start the life I was meant to live.

I just had to win, that was all.

Prue snored like an inebriated old man, but she slept light enough and jerked awake when I reached out to touch her. I didn't want to—I don't like touching strangers—but Luke was still being difficult over being in the house to begin with, and he was sitting in the arm chair by her bed, glowering. At me, or at Prue; I wasn't sure. He can be a pain sometimes.

Anyway, she jerked awake like I had shot her, though I hadn't even made contact with her blanket yet, and she stared at me with recognition in her black eyes. It was a full moon outside her window. Plus, she slept with a candle burning, whether by accident or design, I don't know, but we could see one another well enough. She knew me. I felt pleased.

"Rose Elanora Gray," she said, flatly.

I startled. I had never known my own middle name until then.

"Didn't think I'd ever see you face to face. Not too happy to have been proven wrong. You," she sniffed towards Luke, as if she wanted to acknowledge him but not let his name pass her lips. "Another one I ain't happy to see."

"Don't be difficult, Prue," Luke said. "Just talk to Rose, give her what she wants."

"And what is that? Your sister's head on a silver platter? Is that it? Your sister, who ain't never done nothing to you?"

"What do you know about it?" I answered, coldly. "You're just an old, feeble woman, and your mind is most likely full of mold. Tell me where they went."

"Not in a month of Sundays," Prue answered cheerfully. "Mold, indeed. Now go away before I start screaming bloody murder, and you know I will. I might have just enough love for the Gray family to let you go in peace, since you're one of them, but I certainly won't lie here quietly while you murder me in my bed. Now, scat, if you have a brain cell left in that wicked head!"

"Knock her out," I instructed Luke. "We'll take her with us."

"I told you. I'm not hurting Prue. You want her out cold; you'll have to do it." He was cleaning his nails with his knife again.

"Thank you so much for the chivalry, and here I thought it was dead," Prue snapped. "I don't need any hitting over the head, thank you. I probably wouldn't wake up from that, and I don't plan on dying tonight. You want to talk to me, talk. But hand a poor old woman her slippers. It's powerful cold tonight."

"Tell me a story then," I said, and unbelievably, I handed her the slippers. How did she do that? "I want to hear about Sonnet's life."

I think she knew why I wanted to know, to give me clues to where they might have run to, but she started to oblige. Luke was right; Prue wasn't stupid.

Only she didn't start out with "Once Upon a Time" like a proper story should. That bothered me, but I kept my mouth shut for once. I know how to listen when the need serves me. She blathered something completely unhelpful about how devastated they all were when they had left me behind.

"Tell me about America," I said. "Where she was living and working. Tell me where her favorite places where before that. Where she wanted to go. And Israel Rhode. Where is his family? Where would he go?"

She looked at me like I'd gone round the bend. "If I knew, I wouldn't tell, not when you have revenge on your mind. Noah is a good man, and I'm sorry you don't feel no love for him inside, but you can't go around killing off your family members."

"I can do whatever I like. I'm special. Aren't I, Luke?"

He nodded. "She can control it."

"I know," Prue sniffed. "So could your grandmother, and it didn't turn out too well for her."

"What are you talking about?" My blood ran cold. What grandmother? Who?

"Carolina's mother. You don't know about her? No, I guess you wouldn't. She died in a mental institution, or at least that's what we all assume. After a while, she got so bad she couldn't even travel anymore, on purpose or by accident, like the rest of us. She was just completely lost. Didn't know who she was. Was never homicidal like her granddaughter though." Here she glared at me like I was a naughty child.

Could I believe her? Was she really telling the truth about my grandmother? Was I not so very special then? Was there just something different about the Grays? Then why couldn't Sonnet control her traveling? Unless she simply hadn't figured it out yet. She was a bit dull.

"Did the traveling make her worse?" Luke asked, softly. Concerned. Concerned for me and my mind, I suppose. He put down his knife.

Prue didn't answer; she just looked at him. Then she nodded, slightly. Did they think I didn't see? Did they think I was so stupid? Something inside me snapped.

"I'm not getting worse! I'm not! I'm not! I'm not!" I yelled. I picked up Prue's water glass that was near the arm chair and threw it with all my might at the wall. It shattered and the water dripped down the wall, like blood.

Luke sprang up from the arm chair in alarm. Not alarm that I had gone off on one of my fits of temper, but alarm that I had been so loud in a house we were not supposed to be in. Prue looked triumphant, damn her.

We heard a shout from another part of the house, and then footsteps. I had gone and awoken half the household. No matter. I had gotten some kind of information, though not the kind I had come for.

"In here! Help! Burglars!" Prue shouted, as the footsteps came closer.

"What happened to her grandmother?" Luke asked Prue, as we climbed out the window like thieves. "Please tell me!"

"She died alone, I suppose," I heard Prue answer, as I dropped to the ground. "She never got her mind back, poor thing. Didn't know any of her loved ones, not even her own daughter. It wasn't her fault, poor thing. Poor Nora."

Chapter 22

The coincidence about Nora is almost more than I can bear. I want to shake it off, this dreadful feeling there may be more truth to Rose's tale than I originally thought, but I'm not ready to make that leap. So, there are suddenly two women in my life with the name of Nora. So what? It's not as though it's an uncommon name. Two women named Hildegard in my life suddenly; now that would warrant some alarm.

Even if my Nora **is** Rose's Nora, there is still no reason for anxiety. After all, she's the appropriate age to be Rose's grandmother, and besides, if they met at the hospital, then it's no small wonder Rose includes her into her delusions.

Right?

Even so, I want to talk to Nora again. First thing in the morning, as soon as I check in with Miss Helmes, I'm going to speak to her and find out what she may know about Rose. My mind made up, I settle back down into bed and check on my candle. My torch had died recently, and my lantern is out of oil, so I've resorted to old fashioned lighting. It should feel romantic and warm and cozy; instead it feels as though it doesn't light up a single corner and my flat is dark and cold and a bit fearsome. I have forced Hamlet to abandon his midnight wanderings and confine himself to my bed. He lies obediently at my feet, washing himself. He makes me sneeze, but I love his company. It gets so lonely here at night. Sometimes I even miss the orphanage. I am unused to silence; it unnerves me, even after a year of living alone. I miss the noisiness of the other orphans, the routine, the structure, the predictability, the chaos. Even the quiet days had their noises: the clink of dishes, the humming of the girls, the doors opening and closing. Here, in my flat, it's silence all the time. Some people would love that, but not me. I think that's why I don't mind Bedlam so much. The noise agrees with me.

I wonder if Mina would live with me. Not here, of course, but someplace nicer. We could study medicine together and walk to work together. Her mother would hate it, of course, but Mina would be game; I'm sure of it. I'll have to ask her what she thinks. Most girls lived with their parents until they married, but Mina is a modern woman, and she's in no hurry to marry, as far as I can see. It's not a bad idea, not bad at all. A lot of modern girls are getting their own places these days. It's very chic. Mina loves chic.

My thoughts turn back to Rose. I wonder if she's hiding out in the old hospital. In order to say why I think it's a possibility, I'd have to tell someone about my night there, and I'm not about to do that. For one thing, it's completely against the law for me to have been there in the first place, and I wouldn't put it past Miss Helmes to can me over it; for another, I can't be sure about anything that happened. I can't chalk it up to imagination—it was far too real—but there was something supernatural about it. Mostly I just want to forget about it, I certainly am not going to go back.

I could drop some kind of a hint to Sam though. Maybe he could check. If they are as close as he claims, she might not attempt to scare the living daylights out of him. I could admit to him that I went back there that night, for the diary, and I could simply say I felt like someone was watching me. I could mention her name on the wall. He'd believe me. The more I learn about Rose and her violent ways, the more I don't really want her wandering around society. I don't exactly want to lock her back up where I'd ironically have to take care of her, empty her bedpan, tuck her in at night, read her Ethan Frome, but I don't want her in the outside world either. As a nurse, I have a duty to my patients.

My candle is burnt nearly all the way. I watch it flicker, waver, lose its luster. I feel the heat leave even before I see the flame go out. The cold envelopes me faster than the dark.

* * *

Nora is in a mood this morning. She hasn't spoken a word to me; in fact, she acts like I'm not even in the room. It's highly irritating. I usually have patience with my patients, but she's wearing me out. Plus, I didn't sleep very well—I dreamt of Rose chasing me through White Chapel, and I couldn't run fast enough because of my cursed ball gown. I woke up when I ran into Jack the Ripper, literally ran into him. I think I looked straight into his eyes, but then I woke, and the whole dream was fuzzy and blurry around the edges. I couldn't remember what he looked like in my dream, but I had a funny feeling I knew him at the time. Try as I might, I couldn't manifest his looks after I woke. I only remember he smelled like blood, the way my hands smelled when I scrubbed the not-stew off the wall that day. I blow my hair out of my eyes with an impatient puff of breath. I haven't braided it since yesterday afternoon with Mina; she taught me how to set it at night so that it falls in waves, and I've pinned one side back with my one and only sparkly clip. The side that isn't pinned tickles my face. It's irksome.

"Nora? Come on, dear. Won't you talk to me? I have to go check on the other patients now. I wish you'd talk to me. Tell me about your friends here." Nothing. A different tactic then. "Tell me about the Grays."

She startles. Just a bit, but I saw it: the tremor in her hands, the blink of her eyes.

"Do you remember them? Was your daughter Carolina Gray?" I come closer, and sit down. I had found her all alone at the big dining table. "Do you remember your daughter?"

"No," Nora finally speaks, and her voice is shaky, like she hasn't used it in too long. "I don't remember anyone."

"Do you remember Rose? From not so long ago, not like Carolina. From the hospital?"

"I don't remember anyone," she repeats, hollowly. "Not anyone. I don't remember me."

How unbearably sad. I blink back a tear and swallow the lump in my throat. I hate crying; it gives me a headache and once I start, I can't stop for ages.

"Well, I remember you," I say, brightly. "I remember how much you don't like Ethan Frome and would like to switch to Pride and Prejudice. Now, tuck your feet in, and I'll read to you a bit."

"Don't you have chores?" She sounds a bit more cheerful now. I'm still trying to place her accent.

"Nothing that can't wait. Here we go. '*It is a truth universally acknowledged that a single man in possession of a good fortune must be in want of a wife...*' "

* * *

I don't like thinking about what Prue told me about my grandmother. It gives me the creeps that she was like me and that it didn't go so well for her, not in the long run. Perhaps she abused her powers? Perhaps she wasn't quite as adept as I at turning the tide? Who knew? I wouldn't waste time wondering about it. I needed another plan to track Sonnet and my father. Luke and I wasted time, wandering through London, in case they were hiding in plain sight, laughing at us. It seemed as though wretched Emme's family had disappeared with my own, too.

I was beginning to regret our wedding and the delay it had caused everything. I was short tempered and given to long periods of silence, when I fumed. I bit my nails so far down that my fingertips bled almost constantly. Luke was at his wits' end with me. Nothing he could say or do or suggest made anything any better, but I couldn't bring myself to tell him one thing: that I was seeing my mother all over the place. Was she watching me, or haunting me, or was my mind playing tricks on me? I didn't know. I only knew she unnerved me. I felt as though she had come for me, to drag me down with her into death. I tried to ignore her. She never came too close, the vision of my mother, and she never touched me.

Yet.

But she did stop me from things. Once, we decided to take a train out of

London, and when I stepped up on the platform, I saw my mother inside. She was watching me. I faltered, and I couldn't go in.

Another time, I saw her across a busy street, right before Luke and I were about to cross. I had to stay on the opposite side until she faded away. Luke couldn't cajole me away, or convince me to move. He was patient with me, but he didn't understand.

I had even lost my appetite for cake, which meant I was eating almost nothing. This made it difficult for Luke to hide my medication. He thought I never knew when he was slipping me something, but I always do. The cake tastes grainier, and chalky, when there's a foreign substance tucked inside. After eating it, I would feel drowsy and my senses would be dulled. But I wouldn't see my mother for a while, and that was... nice. For the first time, I would take the medicine with a glass of water, and Luke wouldn't have to hide it. He was pleased with my progress in that regard.

I hadn't been back to Bedlam in a while. It had been curious that my last travel, the one that brought my whole family plus their miserable guests, had deposited me on the streets of London and not inside the hospital, like usual. I suppose London itself was close enough? Knowing me and my sad luck though, I'd end up back there soon enough. If not after my next travel or two, then because I'd be bound to do something stupid and someone would take me in forcibly. It had happened before; I remembered after the Bodley, kicking and biting as the people drug me to my new home. I think it had even crossed Luke's mind recently to take me in. Oh, he wouldn't say it, but I think he thought it, once or twice, during one of my silent spells or my violent fits. The last place he likes to see me is there, but I know he always hopes eventually a doctor will be able to help me find normalcy. They didn't help my grandmother though, did they? Or did they? Perhaps she's found rest and happiness, after all. But to never travel again? What sadness. Poor grandmother! I resolve not to end up like her. I wish I had her recipe though, so I could write my own ending.

Finally, Luke ran out of patience. He realized I had to do something to put my past to bed, and staying in London was making me worse. I couldn't seem to make myself board a train, and obviously Sonnet and everyone were long gone. For all I knew, they had all gone to Africa with that doctor and his griddle-wielding wife. I had been to Africa before; it's ridiculously large. The thought of searching it—with my luck, in the dead of summer with its humid heat—made me tired. We needed something more substantial to go on.

"Harry and Matthias," Luke convinced me. They were the old brothers from America, from when I first met my sister. "It's easy enough to go back and find them. They'll be right where we left them. They don't know you. They know me, but they won't know I'm Lost, and they won't know of my connection to you, or anything that happened in London. I can simply reconnect with them. They might have an educated guess at least where they would go if the year were 1888. Hell, we can go back to the very next day, after your family disappeared. We can live in Sonnet's house if you want. Maybe we'll find something there even. All right, love?"

It was a good enough plan, better than anything else I could come up with. I couldn't explain why I was nervous about traveling again. Probably all that talk about my grandmother. Did she really get worse with every travel?

We went to sleep that night, me in my red calico dress, Luke in his white collared shirt and brown pants. I set my inner clock, as it were, and remembered the old lady's house across the street from Sonnet's home. I remembered the old abandoned house outside of town, where I had locked my sister inside and wondered if she'd die there. I remembered the smells of the coffee shop, and the soup kitchen where I had eaten a couple times when I got bored waiting for Luke. I fell asleep thinking of Sonnet's bed, where I had curled up once before, over a hundred years from now, and when we woke, I was in that same bed.

I have a headache from deciphering Rose's handwriting. I wish she'd pop over to a more modern century and steal a typewriter, for goodness sake. At times, her writing is studious and painstaking, like a grammar schoolgirl learning her letters, but most of the time, it's a loopy, scrawling mess of spider leg marks, rubbed out words, and downward spirals. I'm sure a handwriting expert could tell me all sorts of interesting things about my Rose Gray.

"See how the 'I's loop up at the corners? Yes, that's a sign of a murderous mind. And how the 'O's are more oval shaped than circular? Yes, she has mother issues. And the tightly wound 'S's? Yes, she has a way of invading one's personal space and taking up residence there." And how!

I rub my temples and set the diary aside. I'm nearly finished with it. I thought I would want to savor the last few entries, but instead, I am dreading them. I'm not certain why, but I worry about what I will find at the end, or perhaps what I won't find. Will there be another journal for me to locate somewhere? It doesn't seem as though there will, but I don't know how I know that. My inclination is that this one was not penned so long ago. I am nearly up to present time with Rose, though present time, and time in general, is a funny thing with her.

Where is she hiding? Is she holing up in the old hospital? I feel a stab of guilt in the pit of my stomach, wondering if I've left her there and been too cowardly to ferret her out. What is to become of that place? My thoughts turn to the old building. Will it stand forever, abandoned and teeming with ghosts of the past? But back to Rose and the situation at hand: did she lose Luke in their travels to confront the men she called Harry and Matthias? Obviously, she came back, from wherever it is they go, or the diary wouldn't be here...unless of course, she planted it at the Bodley and then traveled. By traveled, of course I don't mean jumps through time; I don't think I do anyway. I hardly know what I mean anymore.

Groaning, I rub my temples again. I hardly feel like a party, yet here it is: the day of Mina's masquerade ball. I should be giddy as a schoolgirl, but I'm not looking forward to it at all. Sam hasn't been around since our dinner together, so I wasn't able to ask him to accompany me (though I most likely would have choked anyway, so no harm done, I suppose), I still don't have anything to wear unless Mina has conjured up something like my fairy godmother would have, and my head hurts. Plus, Nora has been ignoring me again, as though we never bonded over Pride and Prejudice at all, and Mr. Limpet has really gone off the deep end somehow. He's gotten positively bizarre in his behavior, trying to escape the hospital in his creaky chair, and acting frightened of everything. I overheard him whispering frantically to Mack, "She's here. She's here. Didn't you see her?" and it was just the saddest thing. No one knows what he's talking about, though we do have some new patients. He just blathers on. He finally had to be sedated, and now he drools more than ever and doesn't seem to know anyone. I even long for him to ask me to dance, though the idea used to fill me with shivers, and I typically found an excuse to decline. Now I'd happily waltz around the hospital with his creaky old wheelchair if he'd just be himself again.

Miss Helmes had sent me home early today, probably because it was one of those days where nothing seems to go right. When those days come, she gets extremely independent and wants to do everything by herself. We all just get in her way. Mack walked wide circles around her, and I avoided her as much as possible. The new crew (who isn't very new anymore and is considerably less shiny and polished and much more haggard looking) learned their lessons, one at a time, mostly for trying to be helpful and anticipating what she might want from them, and she sent a few of them home early as well.

Still groaning dramatically about my poor head, I trudge down the stairs of my flat. There's a telephone on the wall downstairs, and I may as well call Mina and tell her I won't be coming. Well, call Danvers, actually. Mrs. Dobson finds the phone vulgar and only the servants are allowed to use it.

Just my luck, a girl from my building is on it already, and as she has entangled herself in the cord, twirling a section, and giggling, it looks as though it may be a while. My groaning intensifies, which will probably only make the throbbing in my cranium intensify, too. This girl, Marianne, can really talk; I know from experience. Once, she nearly chattered me into an early grave, going on and on about gossip at her employment, a department store. I do envy a little bit her job; she spritzes perfume on patrons as they walk by. I suppose it'd only be fun the first few dozen times though. After that, I'd be longing for wall scrubbing. She constantly smells like a bottle of perfume, which is probably lovely in smaller quantities, and I try to breathe through my mouth. Her twin brother, Arthur, lives with her, and the poor man smells like a woman drowning in gardenias.

"Marianne." I tap her shoulder. She turns and mouths a cheerful hello at me. "Are you going to be a while?" I inquire politely.

Marianne taps the phone, ever jolly, as if I couldn't see she is on the phone. Groan.

"Are you near the end of your conversation?" I persist, a bit louder this time.

She giggled again into the mouthpiece. "Hold on, sugar," she says, and then tells me. "It's my soldier boy. You know, the American."

"Mmm hmm. Should I come back later then?"

"No, no, honey. I'll only be a minute! Soldier Boy is going to get me an audition with the Roxyettes!" Marianne trades the phone cord for a lock of her gorgeous hair and twirls that instead for a bit. She begins telling Soldier Boy about several things that happened at work today, including what she bought with her paycheck, which seems to be an overabundance of lacey underpants.

Giving up, I walk the short distance to the front doors and go outside. Maybe the air will clear my head. I smell something delicious waft by my nose, probably from the diner across the street, and my stomach rumbles. What I wouldn't give for a steak dinner right about now! Suddenly, the scrambled eggs I had planned for dinner sound about as appetizing as boiled eels. Maybe I should go to Mina's party... There's bound to be some enticing fare there to sample. Would it be rude to only go for the refreshments and then scamper home to an early bed?

Deep in thought, it takes me a moment to recognize the Rolls Royce

Phantom. Stupefied, I simply stand and stare for a moment. Whatever is he doing here? I'd recognize that lovely car anywhere as well as the silhouette of the man inside. I march over and rap on the window. After a moment's hesitation, it is lowered, and I see Sam's sheepish expression.

"Whatever is going on?" I demand. "What are you doing here?"

"Nothing. That is, I happened to be nearby."

"You did not. Whatever do you think you're doing? How did you know where I live?" My inner suspicions were dead on. Sam isn't as trustworthy as my heart had insisted. I could be flattered at his attention (Marianne probably would be), but instead I'm put off. The only way he could know my residence is if he had been cavorting with Miss Helmes or if he'd been following me. Either scenario is sinister, if you ask me. Plus, I can't imagine Miss Helmes giving out my address; she's very close mouthed, and she certainly wouldn't find it proper. Though, now that I think on it, the two of them had seemed as though they knew one another. I remember back to the first day I met Sam. What had Miss Helmes said?

Mr. Connelly says a lot of things. I hadn't noticed then, but it seems a tad cryptic now. Still. I don't think she'd give him my address, which only leaves the other answer: he's followed me home. I swallow my fear. I read the newspapers. I see bad things at the hospital. I know what happens when poor, young women get in over their head with dangerous men.

"You have two minutes to explain yourself, Mr. Connelly," I say, coldly, going back to the use of his surname. Why had I ever treated him so intimately? I could kick myself. "And then I'm going back in and dialing Scotland Yard."

"Hold on. Hold on, Lizzie." Sam holds up his hands, as though surrendering. "Get in. We can talk. I'll explain myself. I promise."

I stand firm.

"Get in, please," he pleads, gently.

"No."

"Then can I come up?"

"No."

"It's cold out, and you're without a coat."

"I'm fine. And your two minutes are seriously ticking by."

"You're just going to stand there, half in the street and talk to me through the car window. Is that it?"

"That's it." I cross my arms over my chest, partly to look intimidating, partly to keep from freezing.

"I brought you something. For the ball?" He motions to the seat beside him. It's a very large box. I scowl.

"What ball? I don't recall inviting you."

"Yes, well, I'm sure you meant to." Now his voice is teasing. "Mina spoke to me about it earlier. She practically insisted I accompany you."

"Lovely," I snap. "I'm so glad you could be persuaded. That doesn't explain why you know where I live."
"Yes, it does. Mina has a big mouth. Did I mention I brought you something?"

My resolve is melting a bit, only a bit though. Now I'm just beginning to be embarrassed, which is almost worse than angry. Embarrassed at my mistake of Sam being a deranged killer stalking his prey or embarrassed that Mina had to beg him to take me to the ball? I'm not sure yet.

"Yes, you mentioned it. I'm afraid I still don't understand."

"That's probably because your brain is frozen solid. Please get in?"

I tap my toes and debate. Plus, the motion keeps my extremities from snapping off.

"Please?"

It's the please that does me in and the gentle way in which he says it. I've never really been treated with much respect in my short life, especially by a handsome man. Lord, am I really dumb enough to fall in love with him? I want to kick myself, but I also want to enjoy the fall.

"All right," I grouse, going around to the other side of the Rolls, "but if you kidnap me, I swear I'll beat you to a bloody pulp. I have had self defense training because of the patients, you know."

I didn't actually think he could hear me, being inside the car and all, but I clearly see the corners of his mouth turn up. I get in grudgingly and slam the door a bit. Immediately, I feel sorry for abusing the car.

Chapter 23

"I still think you're being," I pause, "forward."

He looks shocked. "Forward? God, no. I've been called a lot of things, but you wound me, madam. I would never be forward. A sexy brute, a wayward man, a rake who has sold his soul to the devil for a meal, but never forward. Good Lord."

I don't do him the favor of laughing, though I'm sure Marianne would have giggled her head off. I'm still wondering what I've gotten myself into with this man/boy, and just how far over my head I am. The knowledge that he was lurking outside my flat doesn't sit well with me. Perhaps it's the over cautious orphan in me, or perhaps I've just never walked out with a boy before.

"Truce?" Sam offers me his hand. After a slight hesitation, I take it. It's calloused but warm. It feels familiar even. Like we fit together. The thought, or his touch—I'm not sure which—sends chills up my arm.

"I promise not to hurt you, Lizzie. You can trust me." His voice is low and disconcerting in its frankness, especially after his joking just seconds before. It seems important that I believe him, like he will be disappointed and grieved if I don't.

"Truce. Now what did you bring me?" Nothing like gifts to melt my stubborn resolve, evidently.

"Open it." Sam had moved the package over off the passenger seat when I had slid in, and now he hands it to me. He waits with all the patience of a small child. "Go on! Open it! Here, there's a seal here. No, like this. Turn it over. Here, let me."

"Oh, for goodness sake. Would you like to do this for me?"

"You're one of those girls who open their birthday presents at a snail's pace, aren't you? Just rip into it!"

"I've never gotten a birthday present actually."

"Oh. I'm sorry. I should have remembered that. That was terribly stupid of me."

"Don't be sorry; why would you have remembered something you didn't know? It's not a big deal." The box is finally pried open of its tape and glue and whatever else had held it together. I move a layer of fine paper. I know what it is, even before I've finished pulling it out. A ball gown. A beautiful ball gown of black gossamer and tulle with gold trim. There's also a mask, gold and black filigree. I've never seen anything so gorgeous, not even in Mina's closet. I'm speechless. I simply sit and stare at my lap, the black and gold layers spreading over me and spilling over and in and through my fingers.

"Do you like it?" Sam sounds anxious. "We can get you something else if it's not your style. I'm a man, after all, I don't know dresses very well."

"You do," I cleared my throat. "You do know dresses very well, actually. It's wonderful. I just don't know what to say."

"Say you like it. And say you'll wear it tonight. With me."

"Are you being forward again, young man?" I say, lightly. "What have I told you about that?"

"Something about a bloody pulp, I believe. I'll take the risk just to see you in that gown."

"Sam."

"Yes?"

"What do you want with me? I'm just a nurse. Not even that hardly. You could ask anyone to Mina's ball."

"I don't want anyone. I want to go with you."

"Did Mina put you up to this?" I'm still confused as to why he'd want to be with me.

"I don't let myself be bossed around by rich little girls, so no. She didn't." He sighed. "Now are you going to quit being so difficult?"

"Thank you for the dress."

"You're very welcome. Happy birthday."

"It's not my birthday."

"Isn't it?" The playful smile is back. Lord, my heart.

I can't take it. I have to change the subject. "Have you had any luck locating Rose? I haven't seen you at the hospital lately."

His smile disappears. "Not really, no. Sometimes I think I catch a glimpse of her, but no."

A glimpse of her? It sounds like she could be playing with him the same way she played with Sonnet, allowing herself to be seen once in a while, on her turf so to speak. The thought gives me chills.

"Sam, I don't think you understand how dangerous she may be. Her diary is so disturbing. She's in a lot of trouble. I don't know what's true and what's in her head."

"The stuff that's true doesn't bother me." Sam sighed again. "It's what is in her head that has me worried. She became quite delusional in the last year or so." He looks at me with an apologetic, hangdog kind of look. "I've been at a loss as to how to handle her. I know the doctors felt the same way. No one knew how to help her anymore."

"What of her husband?" I broach the subject of Luke finally.

"What of him?"

"Where is he?" I gesture with my hands impatiently. "Why isn't he searching for her? What's happened to him? Why isn't he helping?"

"Ah, well. It's a delicate subject, little one. And he's hardly a gentleman. I wouldn't be surprised if he has taken off for good. She was far too young to get married anyway, barely more than a child. He's probably running from the law somewhere, to be truthful. I never liked him."

"You knew him then?" This surprises me, though I can't say why.

"Of course. Not well; no one did. He showed a different face to whomever he chose."

"So she's really alone then? With no one? Wandering around London?" I feel sad for her. Scared of her, but sad for her.

"Essentially. She has me, a few others perhaps, but no one she will confide in or come to of her own free will." Sam looks at me apprehensively, as if he's concerned about what I will think or say. "I've tried everything I can think of. I'm starting to get worried. She's never stayed away so long."

"You still think she'll just pop back up at Bedlam?" I can't help the skepticism that creeps into my voice. "That's your plan?"

"I do best without plans."

I hold up the dress. "This took substantial planning, liar. Oodles and oodles of planning. Positively Machiavellian planning, I'd say."

"Are you kidding? That old thing? Was sitting on a curb I happened to drive by. No one else wanted such an ugly waste of fabric, so I took it home out of pity."

"Liar," I say again, but this time with fondness. I finger the gossamer lovingly. Sam watches my fingertips and suddenly I feel flushed. "I should go."

"You should indeed. Get those wretched rags out of my fine car."

I laugh as I leave, lugging my precious gift in my arms. I'm careful not to drag it on the ground.

"Be ready at eight," Sam pulls his hat lower over his eyes, but not before I see him wink.

Her sheets smelled of her, of Sonnet, and the whole house gave me the shivers. I didn't like the homey touches, the things here and there that reminded me my family had called this home. I had never had things like they did; I found it unnatural. A monogrammed towel in the bathroom, a mug half empty in the kitchen, the pillows on the couch where I knew my father had slept, odd containers of odd food in the refrigerator (probably Prue's), her food cart parked in the covered porch, the giant blue car that I had seen Israel drive, and once, Sonnet, park at the curb, the same curb I had stood at, in the pouring rain, that night long ago. Not so long ago now. Probably only, what? Two days ago? How funny. Time is funny stuff. But dwelling on it makes my head hurt worse.

I went back to bed on Sonnet's bed. I covered my head in the blankets, like a child, and wouldn't get up when Luke prodded me. I was in a mood. One of my black moods. I couldn't quite remember why we had come, but I didn't want to admit it to Luke. Hadn't we already taken care of Sonnet? She wasn't here any longer, was she? Or was she? Why had we come back? Or had we never left at all?

I laid there and tried to regain my scattered thoughts. They were bouncing around like sunbeams through glass; I couldn't catch them and line them up properly. Everything was out of order. Once again, the television in my mind had no sound. Luke bent over me, and I could see his lips moving, talking to me, but it was useless; I couldn't hear. I scowled at him, and when he got tired of being ignored, he left for a bit.

Was the traveling making me worse? What if I finally caught up with my family, but couldn't recall them any longer or why I was searching for them to begin with? My life's work was in danger of slipping away, due to my blasted, flawed, wounded brain. The gift the doctors had given me might be the death of me yet. How ironic.

Eventually, I got tired of feeling sorry for myself and got up to make tea. I used a mug with a ridiculous looking fat cat on the front. The tail curled into the handle. It was ugly, but it held a massive amount of bad tea. I picked through the food containers and ate something that tasted of squirrel. Soon enough, I began to notice sounds again: the whistling of the wind through a crack in the window, the hum of the refrigerator, traffic going by. Mentally, I put myself back together, even took a bath which I don't do often, and was more cheerful when Luke returned. There were all sorts of bath oils and lotions and soaps lined up by the bathtub, and I used every one. I smelled nice.

"Harry and Matthias were happy to see me," he announced, settling into the couch. He had kissed me like we hadn't just quarreled, which is one of my favorite things about him. He never holds a grudge with me. He is happy to start over, each and every day if necessary. He teases me sometimes that I am a high maintenance wife. I tell him beggars can't be choosers, and who else but me would want a thieving murderer for a husband? That always make him laugh, and I love to hear him laugh.

I had located the missing part of my memory concerning our visit here, so I knew of whom he was speaking. "Were they not suspicious at all?"

"Of course not. We were chums well enough, remember? They have no idea what happened after the Grays left here. For all they know, they are living in a castle in medieval Scotland right about now. Of course, they don't know I know anything about the Lost, so they made up a story about how they moved away suddenly and didn't leave a forwarding address. I went along with it, though I played the jilted lover quite well, I think. Tried for a hangdog look, and ran my hands through my hair as much possible. Felt like I was in a damn soap opera. Anyway, they had nothing to lose by telling me a bunch of back story on

your dad, since they know he's long gone. They don't realize we mean to find them, no matter the century. I'm going to heat up some of Prue's cooking. She's a darn fine cook."

"Stupid old men," I rolled my eyes, and combed through my wet hair with my fingers. "Why are people so gullible?"

"Because they aren't as smart as us, love. That's why. Oh well, they're good enough chaps, but I may need another day with them to get more leads. Mmm, you smell good."

"What did they tell you so far?" I'm done with my hair and leave it to drip down my back onto Sonnet's blouse. I had tried on all her clothes in her closet. There weren't many, and most were strange, but I felt like being her for a bit. Also, I knew it would annoy her to know I was dressing in her things, sleeping in her bed, eating her food, like Goldilocks. The blouse was far too large, but it was a comfortable T-shirt material and was a pretty blue color. It brought out my eyes. It probably brought out her eyes too, but I didn't care. I was the beautiful one, after all.

"Let's see," Luke propped up his feet on my lap. "There was some substantial time in Portugal we could look at. That's where they picked up Israel, I believe. I also think we need to focus on that buggar a bit more; if he and Sonnet are going to make a love match of it like I suspect they will, they might do a little tour of his homeland, look up relatives—I don't know, stuff you do when you're honeymooning."

"We didn't," I pointed out.

"Sure we did. We're doing it now, aren't we? Looking up your relatives."

"To kill them, not drop by for the holidays," I responded.

"Tomato, tomahto. Besides, you don't want to kill them. Come on, love, you saw how much they want you in their life. It's not too late for that."

I'm skeptical and let it show on my face. Besides, I don't care if he's right about them letting me in; I'm not interested. "What else?"

"Well, to focus on Israel again: I was thinking about where he'd go to be the most helpful in 1888. He'd probably stay in a city, partly to find work, and partly to stay hidden from us."

"If they haven't traveled centuries yet." I frown. I hoped we had enough time to locate them before they really made it difficult.

"We found them once; we can do it again, but yes, it'd be easier if they'd stay put in 1888 for a time. Another interesting tidbit: they spent time in a monastery in Spain, close enough to London to get there. Knowing European history and how much they love their antiquities, I'm sure it's partially still there in 1888, even though it was the twelve hundreds the last time they were there."

"Why would they go back? Were they happy there?" I can't imagine being happy in a monastery. Or in Spain. Or in the twelve hundreds. Or at all really.

"Happy enough, it sounds like. Noah attempted to dry out a bit there though it didn't last, and it sounds like Sonnet enjoyed the company of the monks as a kid. Besides, it would be a good place to hide out when your revenge-bent family members come a-calling."

"Not funny. You know I don't get your jokes. Stay serious and help me figure this out. So you think we should go to Spain? Now?"

"No, in 1888. And it's just an idea. Frankly, I don't like the idea of you making us go anywhere at all, not with what it's been doing to you lately. What did you find around here?"

"Nothing relevant. I'm tired. What about Emme's mother? Do we know anything about her past?"

"Ugh. Didn't ask about her. I suppose that's an avenue we could try, as

well. I wish you'd let go of this, though. Haven't we done enough to them?"

I pushed his feet off me. The same old song and dance. He was always trying to talk me out of my plans, at least the ones involving my family. He just doesn't understand. He left his family. They didn't leave him. It's two entirely different things. They've shaped who we are: he is good at leaving; I am only good at being left.

"I'm sorry. I'm sorry," Luke put his hands up in surrender, like he does when he knows he's pushed me too far. "Forget it. We'll go to Spain. If there's nothing there for us, we'll research Emme's mother. Okay? Forgive? Forget?"

I was feeling too petulant to answer, but I nodded. We pulled an "all-nighter," as Luke called it, in order to stay and pick the old brother's brains one more time, and then we left for Spain, with our forever-predictable night at Bedlam in between. And things started to really unravel.

Chapter 24

I'm ready for the ball, but I'm too engrossed in Rose's tale to feel much like Cinderella. My gown is bunched up at my ankles, as I curl up in the corner of my bed. Sam will be here any moment, but I can't stop reading. I have applied my red lipstick and done what I can with my flyaway hair, and my mask is safely inside my handbag. My old black shawl is shabby, but it matches, and I will take it off once I'm at Mina's anyway. I have no looking glass besides the shiny side of the tin cupboard I keep my biscuits in, so I don't know exactly how nice I look. I hope it's good enough for the ball. I'm torn between the excitement of the ball and being seen in my beautiful dress and wanting to cry the whole thing off and finish the diary. I have only pages left. I could finish it easily in an hour, even with the outrageous handwriting.

And then go back to my normal life? What would I do once Rose was torn from me? The idea of catching her now seems ludicrous, and I wouldn't know what to do with her even if I could track her down. It occurs to me that I am tracking her the same way she is tracking Sonnet, only I, of course, am not plotting any murders. I desperately hope she isn't either. Perhaps her homicidal tendencies are all in her head? (I remember the girl from the side show, and Rose's own mother. Perhaps not.) Then again, I can't trust a single thing she says in this diary of hers; maybe I am fretting for nothing. We had a patient at Bedlam who confessed to dozens of murders and claimed they were all buried in his yard. Scotland Yard dug up every square inch and never found a soul. It was all in his head. That isn't to say we didn't all watch our backs around him though.

I glimpse at my clock: 7:58.

Firmly, I snap the diary shut and stand up. I should meet Sam outside. I may not be marvelous at being a lady, but I really shouldn't let my reputation get too far out of hand. It wouldn't surprise me if he marched up the stairs to claim me, and that really wouldn't do. Marianne has a big mouth.

I'm halfway down the stairs before my resolve runs out. I race back up to grab the journal and tuck it inside my handbag. Maybe the party will be dull as watching paint dry, and I can steal an hour away when everyone else is dancing. Here's hoping.

The Phantom is already here, and I get a little twinge of excitement in the pit of my stomach. I've never really done anything like this: been taken to a sophisticated party with a rich man. Well, the rich part doesn't impress me overly much; it only overwhelms me, but the man part is difficult to wrap my head around. His age isn't much more than mine, and in fact, were he anyone else, I might call him a boy, not a man at all. I think of Mack as nothing but a boy, and they're around the same years. But something about Sam is timeless, that old soul thing again that occurred to me when I first met him.

I see him step out of the car, and the expression on his face is one of appreciation and admiration. "You look stunning," he says, so softly, I nearly have to strain to hear it. His hand reaches out to me then, and I get the wild, crazy thought that he is going to pull me into his arms. I shy away without even thinking about it; it's only reflex. He puts his hand stiffly in his coat, and smiles, but I don't miss the flash of hurt in his eyes. Why did I act like that? I feel stupid. He probably only wanted to take my elbow, escort me around to the passenger side of the car, like a gentleman. Now I'm left to fend for myself, and I nearly slam my dress in the door as I get in.

"It fits perfectly," I say, quietly. I'm feeling shy, and I clear my throat.

"Yes, it does."

"You're frightfully good at estimating women's sizes." Good. My voice is back to a normal squeak, instead of a hardly audible squeak.

"I spend a lot of my free time trying on their clothes." Sam confesses, pulling away from the curb.

I chuckle. "Must be tough to find shoes to fit. Your feet are the size of boats."

"You injure me. I have to tell you now, I'm a terrible dancer. I think you should know I practically maimed the last girl I danced with. Flattened her toes into pancakes. They were never the same. After that, she was the one who couldn't find shoes to fit."

"Thanks for the warning. I'm used to staying one step ahead of Mr. Limpet's wheels, so I bet you won't maim me yet." I'm already picturing his arms around me as we dance, and I feel suddenly warm. "Can I have the window down?"

"Certainly. Aren't you afraid of the wind mussing your hair or blowing your cosmetics off?"

"No." I lean out a bit.

"You're a funny thing, little one," he says.

"I know," I reply. "I've been called worse."

*　*　*

At Mina's, the ball is far more festive, fancy, and crowded than I ever imagined. I'd only ever been to fetes at the hospital or the orphanage, and those always had a point to them: a plea to raise monies or funding, or find homes for children, or reward patrons, etc. This is just a party, a party for party's sake; a party for the rich and bored specifically. I feel as though I stuck out like a sore thumb, even though my gown is every bit as lovely as the other girls'. Mina had swooped out of nowhere and embraced me with excitement. She oohed and ahhed over the black dress, berated me for forgetting to put on my mask immediately, and then scampered off to find me a beverage, even though Sam had already done so. He is wearing his mask—it's a black raven—and I am suddenly grateful for his height and how well I somehow know his build, because I could find him easily enough in the crowd if I needed to. Why would I need to, I chide myself. Oh yes, the den of iniquity I was warned about.

206

"Hullo, Lizzie," a cheerful voice shouts. It's Mack; I can tell even with his silly peacock mask. He and Mina are a matched pair. I wonder what Mrs. Dobson thinks of that. I doubt she approves. Silently, I give Mina a little huzzah! for her spunk. Mack hands me a goblet of liquid. I will need more hands if people keep bringing me drinks. "Having a marvelous time, are you?"

"Sure. Marvelous. I'm not thirsty, thank you." I hand it back rather petulantly. I know it's immature of me, but I just can't seem to get over my dislike of Mack. Work place jealousy, I know, but I can't help it.

"Suit yourself." He drinks it all in one long swallow. With his mask on, he reminds me of a peacock I saw at the zoo once during an orphanage outing or one of those silly bobbing bird statues that tip when you tap their tail feathers. He disappears back into the throng of party goers.

I can't see Sam anymore, and I can't see Mina either, and suddenly I feel very alone in a sea of people in which I don't belong. *Is it possible to drown in people?* I wonder. I feel like I'm going under. It's too stifling hot, and I feel conspicuous in my huge gown, even though it blends in perfectly with everyone else's. I lift my hair off my neck and breathe deeply.

I'm completely surprised when I catch sight of Miss Helmes. It has to be her. No one else has that figure. I'm so taken aback at her fashion—an actually stunning white velvet gown with a swan headdress—that my wits have left with my voice.

"Lizzie," Miss Helmes' voice echoes out of the swan's head. "Lizzie, you look as though you're going to faint. Are you well?"

I manage to recover my wits and even find the muscles with which to turn up the corners of my mouth. "Yes, yes, ma'am," I stammer. "You're looking..." I pause, stumped for an adjective, "quite nice, and plump. I mean, plump like a swan is plump."

"Thank you." If she's insulted, she doesn't show it. Perhaps a rail thin woman finds the word plump to be a compliment? "You are certain you are well? Are you corseted in that thing? Corsets are terrible for women's health. They're very outdated. You should know better."

I span my hands on my waist. "No, no corset. I was just feeling a bit overheated."

"Well, sit down," the swan sighs. "I'll get you something to drink."

Just then, my other drink bearers, Sam and Mina, arrive. "Lizzie, come on! Quit lurking by the door!" Mina pulls my hand and sets a goblet in the other.

"Sorry. I was feeling a bit sick for a minute there, and it didn't help to suddenly have Miss Helmes' bosom heaving up and down at me. It gave me motion sickness. You could have warned me she was coming. Who in the world is working tonight if the whole hospital is here?" I drink my beverage. It's deliciously cold, and I feel instantly better. I help myself to the one Sam brought as well. I may spend half the party in the toilet, emptying my bladder, but at least I don't feel sick anymore.

"Oh, the new staff doesn't need to be babysat anymore. They'll do fine, even without Doc Ford." Mina motions with her gloved hands, waving away any worries.

"Wait. Doc Ford is here, too?" I'm not sure if I'm concerned for the safety of the unmanned hospital, or if I'm insulted that I was far from the only employee Mina had invited.

"It's a party, isn't it? He's the porcine wonder over there."

I squint. "Oh dear, that's a lot of bacon."

Mina giggles, and Sam chuckles. "He is positively roly-poly, isn't he?"

"I'm craving ham," I say, seriously. "Like never before."

"Lizzie! Stop it, you two, you're awful." Mina looks suddenly sorry that she had been laughing a moment before. Her nose wrinkles. "That isn't nice."

"I'm sorry." I put on my best contrite face, though it's completely false. She appears to be mollified until Sam snorts like a pig very softly in my ear, and I lose my composure in laughter.

"You're hopeless," Mina scowls. "And you, sir, are only encouraging her lack of manners. I have to go see to my guests. Try to stay out of trouble, Lizzie!"

"I love hearing your laugh. You don't do it often enough." Sam stays close to my ear, his arm around my waist, and I shiver.

"That's because you spend too much time annoying me instead of making me laugh," I reply, but I'm careful to not turn my head so his breath stays exactly where it was before: on my neck. I don't feel like shying away from him now. What is in this punch?

"Come mingle with me; I want to show you off."

I like the idea of being shown off, of being beautiful enough to show off, so I do what he asks, mingling. I keep seeing a swan's head focused my way, so I am sure to be on my best behavior. When we say hello to Dr. Ford, I have a difficult time keeping from dissolving into schoolgirl giggles. Anything and everything he says can be put through a filter of pig and seems alarmingly hilarious somehow. His pink forehead shines with sweat from his silly costume, and Sam tortures me by making small talk for what seems like an eternity, managing to work mentions of gravy and chops and bacon into every sentence. I am grateful to my mask for concealing at least part of my smiling.

Finally, we dance. The music is loud and rather clashing to the ears; I prefer what we heard at the restaurant with the singing lady who had made me think of Sonnet. That will always be Our Restaurant in my mind, forever and always. I would never confess that to him, of course.

He would think me silly and young.

The way he looks at me, though, he doesn't think me silly and young now. I hadn't bothered with eye makeup—partly because I don't own any and partly because it seemed a pointless thing to do if I'm covered by my masquerade mask anyway—but I had freshly applied my red lipstick. He stares at my mouth in a way that makes me somewhat breathless, or perhaps that's the dancing?

I had learned all sorts of dances in the orphanage, and wherever Sam had learned, they had taught him well.

"You don't dance terribly, you big liar," I say, when we pass by one another. This dance is an old fashioned reel, where we switch partners and wind in and out from one another. I had just been handed off back to Sam by a reindeer that had nearly gored me with his chivalrous bow. What a way to die.

"No? I think you're blinded by love. I really am a terrible dancer."

"Oh?" I laugh. "Love, is it? My, but your head and ego are large. I am surprised you fit in this ballroom."

"I came through the side entrance, so as not to smash it. My big head, I mean. And are you suggesting you aren't wildly in love with me, little one?" His tone is light, but I still blush beneath my mask.

I open my mouth to answer, but nothing comes out, and it's just as well anyway, because I am stolen away by Mack in the next part of the reel.

"You look nice, Lizzie. Did I already say that?" His breath smells of punch and an assortment of food. He is too close to me.

"I'm not."

"Not what?"

"Nice."

"Oh," he chuckles. "Will you put in a good word for me with Mina?"

"About what?" I turn, grateful for space away from his breath, and reluctantly come closer again when he pulls me in.

"About us." He has a forlorn look in a hangdog face. "I am falling for her, you know. I think she is simply too nice to reject me. Do you think that's it?"

"Yes, probably. She's frightfully polite."

"And you're not, which is why I thought I'd speak to you about it. Turn."

"I am turning," I glare. "And I'm polite when I need to be. I think she likes you fine, actually."

"It's you that doesn't. Promenade."

"Well, you don't need me to like you."

"Fair enough. What can I do to win her over?" His mask slips crookedly, and he looks like a child. My heart strings are effectively plucked. Damn.

"Well, stay on her mother's good side, for one thing. Bow. To me, dummy. And, I don't know, be interested in what she is interested in, I suppose."

"You mean, medicine?" He brightens up. "We already have that in common."

"Well, remind her of that then. Find a common goal to share or something. I don't know! I'm hardly the expert on love." Suddenly I feel grumpy.

"Aren't you?" How does one look sly behind a mask? Somehow, Mack accomplishes it. "I thought you and that Connelly chap were...you know?"

"No, I don't know. Promenade me, for crying in the night." I glare again.

"You and that Connelly chap were what?" Sam intervenes and takes my elbow. The music ends and we all bow and curtsy. I hear a yelp from the reindeer's unfortunate partner.

"Nothing, nothing," Mack answers, brightly. "I have to go find Mina. Here's your partner back, chum. Thanks, Lizzie!"

"That Connelly chap missed you. How about a beverage?" Sam takes my arm and guides me towards the refreshments. I see Danvers standing there, looking bored; come to think of it, though, he always looks bored. He'd look bored at a public hanging, I think. Perhaps that's another requirement for butlers, the same way the rich can't be jolly, and the mistresses of Bedlam must be skinny and rude.

"Oh, I couldn't. I'm positively swimming in punch already. I am a bit hungry though." Did he really miss me? Is that just a gentleman's form of attentiveness, to be so flirty? Did he look at all the girls this way, with need in his eyes? He stares at me sometimes as if he wants to devour me whole. The thought should give me more pause than it does. Not for the first time tonight, I am grateful for my mask that hides my flushed face.

"Go sit down. I'll bring you a plate. There's a sticky pudding that's been calling my name. Seriously. If you're quiet, which you never are, you can hear its plaintive cry." Sam gestures to an empty chaise lounge. I had sat on it once during my unfortunate sewing circle with Mina and practiced my chain stitching and top knots. My thread had snarled one too many times for my patience, and I had misplaced at least two needles in that chaise. When I reach it, I sit down gingerly, fearing to locate them once again.

I amuse myself by people watching until Sam returns. When he does, he brings me so much food that my eyes widen at the sight.

"You needed a platter, not a plate," I comment, taking it from him.

"It's mostly for me. You can have that suspicious-looking brown stuff." He wrinkles his nose. He looks adorable. I want to kiss it. I want to smack myself upside the head.

"It's liver mousse, and it's absolutely divine. You don't know what you're missing." We munch in silence for a bit. I watch the dancers twirl about, not far from me. They look so elegant. Had I looked so elegant, I wonder, in the arms of Sam? He would make any girl look glamorous, even an orphan; at least, I hope so.

"That swan keeps staring at me," Sam licks pudding off his fingers. "Have we met, do you think?"

"I do indeed. It's Miss Helmes."

"Ah. The warden of Bedlam. She is around every corner, isn't she? That's a trifle unsettling. Can't you ever get away?"

I laugh. "She does pop up everywhere, it seems. She likes to keep an eye on everyone, I suppose. I'm not sure I could properly escape from her."

"No? We should try."

"And where would we go?" I say, lightly. "How far will your wonderful car go?"

"Oh, it will go forever, I guess, but it won't cross oceans, and I was thinking of islands, deserted ones. Yes, island living would agree with you, I think, with a flower behind your ear." Sam reaches over and tucks my hair behind my ear. I react as though he slapped me.

"What do you mean?" I feel cold and shaky suddenly.

His face undergoes a transformation. I see several different answers in his eyes: confusion, alarm, nonchalance. Of course, he chooses the latter when he speaks.

"What is it? What did I say? You don't like islands? Mountains then or the desert. I don't mind, as long as you say you'll come. Oh, don't pull away. You know I won't hurt you." This time when he reaches for my hair, I stay perfectly still, but it's a struggle. He tucks it behind my ear slowly and then pulls it back out, letting it run through his fingers. Finally, he tugs on it, teasingly.

This has passed from flirting to something else, and I don't know how to handle it. All I could think of for a moment was Rose Gray and Luke, traveling to islands together, alone.

Except of course, they hadn't. Had they?

"Lizzie?" He is very close to me now, and my heart is beating what feels like a hundred beats per minute. It's beating so loudly and so much that I am having trouble breathing, and I think I may faint or burst. "Lizzie, look at me. Do you see me?"

"I see you."

"Keep your eyes open." And then he does what I think I've been wishing for since the day he tipped his hat at me when I scrubbed blood off the wall at Bedlam; he kisses me.

And my whole world shatters in an explosion of light both beautiful and terrifying.

Chapter 25

I am wandering the hallway like a fool. The kiss had unnerved me and
scared me and left me wanting more and wanting less, all at once, and I
had pulled away and murmured some ridiculous excuse. He watched me
go, and I knew without looking back that I had left an expression of pain
on his face. Not only left it there, but I had put it there. Now I'm
somewhat lost, and though I've passed several people (a Mallard duck, a
cat, a jester, and two horses, respectively), I feel completely alone and
vulnerable. I wish Danvers would materialize, the way he always does,
and hand me my shawl. I don't belong here. I feel cold in my gown and
rub my arms. A sparkling Raja with an enormous turban offers me
champagne and looks offended when I walk away without answering. I
bump shoulders with a gorgeous woman in a deep purple dress who
glares at me, but the man she's arm in arm with gives me an approving
once over. Everything and everyone seems to be moving in slow motion,
like I'm drowning again in a sea of people, but this time we're all in a sea
of thick fog. I look over my shoulder and see the man still looking back at
me. The woman in purple jerks him back to her, but not before he lowers
his checkered Harlequin mask and winks at me. He thinks I'm alluring,
beautiful. Sam must think so, too, to have kissed me the way he did.

I should be thrilled, happy, lost in romantic planning. That's what
Marianne would do. Why should she get all the fun? Why can't I allow
myself to fall in love with Sam? Is it just the fear of him leaving me,
because I'm not good enough, not rich enough, not suitable enough? Had
it been the offhand island comment that set off warning bells in my head?
What had he meant by that?

The hallway I am in now is filled with portraits, nestled in between small
windows. I look out at the gardens, silhouetted in the moonlight as I
move along, my fingertips trailing along the glass and the panes, wishing
they were Sam instead. I linger at one window and allow myself to think
back on our kiss. When I turn my downcast eyes up again I see a figure in
the glass. Small, but solid. Clear as a masked woman standing in the night
can be, her gown shimmers in the moonlight, and her hair seems to

almost glow. She is far too close to me for comfort, and I am at first
startled, and then unnerved. We watch one another, almost warily, it
seems. Neither of us will pull our gaze away. We are so close; only a pane
of glass separates us. Then, I feel rather than see her let out a breath, and
the glass fogs over like steam from a locomotive. I know, though, that she
hasn't moved; there isn't enough fogginess to disguise all of her. I still see
her silhouette. I watch her as she watches me, and I as I stand there, my
fingertips still poised on the glass, I see her reach up and pull up her
masquerade mask. I know her even before I see her face clearly. I
remember the photos from the diary, especially the Victorian wedding
photograph. Though the picture was old and not of good quality, I would
know Rose Gray if I saw her, and I am seeing her now.

* * *

I had felt very sick, and also more than a little scared. I had whirled away
from the window and nearly run over the Raja in my desire to leave.
Leave where? To go out to the garden? To find a murderess? Alone? I
thought not. But what else could I do? Would someone believe me? Mina,
perhaps, or Mack or Dr. Ford. Having half the hospital staff here in
Mina's den of iniquity could prove helpful after all.

But could I find her again? She is masked and in public. Though I know
her face, I can hardly rip away every mask from every eligible female. I
had not thought to get a good look at her gown; I only had a dim memory
of the way her light hair shone across the darkness of the fabric. But it
was dark; any gown would look dark—blue, black, brown, gray, purple,
green; they would all look dark. I halt my awkward running at the
doorway of the ballroom. I see Miss Helmes dance by, and Dr. Ford
picking at a plate of food, alone. I see Mack and Mina, their peacock
heads close together in conversation, over by the chaise lounge where I
had left Sam. He is no longer there, and my heart falls. I need to find him.
Together, we might stand a chance of recognizing, and therefore, finding,
Rose. To do what with her, I have no idea. Lock her away again? Sam said
the doctors had been at a loss with her. She had been officially signed out
and freed by Luke, although since he was only posing as a doctor, perhaps
that could be revoked. But could we help her—the hospital, I mean? There

are too many questions swirling in my brain that don't have answers. It's maddening. I remove a full glass of champagne from the hand of a nearby handsome prince and drink it in three long gulps. It burns my nose and makes me gasp for air. I really am drowning; I am sure of it.

"Another?" says the prince, dryly. "I could fetch one for you while I replace my own."

"No, thank you," I whisper, my throat aflame with all the bubbles. I cough. My stomach churns and then settles. I lean against the doorfsecrectsrame. I am completely at a loss as to what to do. Only part of my turmoil is the fact that Rose Gray is here, in Mina's house, tonight. The other part—the more frightening part—is reconciling her presence here in 1931 with the aged photograph. She has not aged at all. She is not a bit older than the photo she claimed was taken in 1888. My mind turns back to something Sam had said the first day I met him. What was it? We had been speaking of the diary. I had said it was old. He had said—what? That it **was** old, and someday I would understand why. It had only seemed a bit odd and eccentric at the time, but now I wonder.

I'm beginning to believe this Lost story isn't just a story, that it isn't just in Rose's sad, messed up, and twisted imagination. I'm also starting to think that Sam has known this all along. If that's the case, I no longer want to look for him. What I want to do is find my handbag and finish the diary that I had tucked inside. If there are any answers to Rose Gray's fantastic life, she might be the only one to provide them for me; since I'm not eager to rummage them out in person just yet, the last things she wrote may be my best option.

Spain was useless and a waste of my energy. With each travel, I was getting worse—I could no longer deny it. That, coupled with my fear of becoming my grandmother and of my dead mother chasing me (though I didn't see her ghost but once in Spain), I was falling apart. Bit by bit, the pieces of my puzzling life were disappearing. I was remembering less and less. When we woke in the old monastery, I didn't know Luke. I saw the terrified look on his face when I stared at him blankly, and it all came back in a rush. Still. It was a premonition of things to come.

Coming back to Bedlam was even worse. It was twentieth century, that much was certain, and that much was good as far as Bedlam goes (no manacles on the floor, no torture or leeches or starvation), but I was sick and weary. I didn't even try to escape or plan a way out the way I usually did. I didn't care that the staff tucked me into bed, and I was meek as a lamb. That scared me more than anything, truly. I was slipping away. I had no energy to be myself even. Luke stayed by me; he didn't disappear the way he usually did. I knew he was worried. They treated him with respect and me with the typical bedside manner I had grown accustomed to: stern lectures about food and behavior with silence in between. I lay in their white sheets but didn't sleep. How could I, when every travel brought me closer to madness? Everyone thinks I was born this way, born crazed and off kilter and mad, but I was always me. Always just Rose Gray.

Was the madness really just beginning?

Slowly, I at least regained my temper, which was encouraging. I pushed a nurse and bit a doctor, and then there was the episode with the sewing scissors. That nurse had quit over it and said I was trying to kill her. Dumb woman. I can aim better than that. Ask the girl with pearl button gloves if you don't believe me. I remember her, though I can no longer picture her face. I remember the strangest things, the unimportant things. For instance, I remember with all the clarity in the world, a dance we held at Bedlam. It was 1816 and they would let anyone who appreciated music out for the night to dance. Luke was with me; I was fifteen years old. I suppose we were wearing the same dirty frocks we always wore, but in my mind I wore the most beautiful red dress. There was music and laughter – the nice kind for the most part, not the lunatic kind. Almost everyone came, and the staff just ignored us. It wasn't uncommon for people on the outside to come and gawk at us patients; in fact, on the second Tuesday of every month it was Visitor's Day. They could come and stare all they liked for an admission price or a donation. I liked to give them a show on the second Tuesdays. Anyway, my dress was red and my heart was merry. There was a handsome boy singing, but he wasn't as handsome as my Luke.

To see Mad Tom of Bedlam (he sang)
Ten thousand miles I've traveled
Mad Maudlin goes on dirty toes
To save her shoes from gravel

It's well that we sing, bonney boys
Bonney, mad boys
Bedlam boys are bonney
For they all go bare, and they live in the air
And they want no drink nor money

I went down to Satan's Kitchen
For to break my fast one morning
And there I got souls piping hot
All on the spits a-turning

These spirits white as lightning
Did on that journey guide me
The sun did shake and the pale moon quake
Whenever they did spy me

It's well that we sing bonney boys
Bonney mad boys
Bedlam boys are bonney
For they all go bare, and they live in the air
And they want no drink nor money

Tonight I'll go a-murdering
The man in the moon to a powder
His staff I'll break and his dog I'll shake
And I'll howl a wee bit louder

To see Mad Tom of Bedlam,
Ten thousand miles I've traveled
Mad Maudlin goes on dirty toes
To save her shoes from gravel

How is it that I could remember every word of that song, and forget the important things? I remember another night of dancing as well – later. I imagined up my same red dress and heard the same song. I hummed it and sang it as I spun in the lantern light. There were terrible pies that tasted bitter and astringent and the inmates threw them at each other since they were no good for eating. I twirled a young man around in his wheelchair and he was delighted with me. He thought I was pretty and he told me pretty things as I danced the rag-time dance, around and around his chair. He clapped for me. I took him for a ride through the halls of Bedlam, but after a while I got bored of him. He kept talking and I didn't want to listen to him anymore so I parked his chair at the top of a staircase and when he got angry because I had put the brake mechanism on and he couldn't retreat and he couldn't go down, I pushed him down. I suppose it wasn't very kind of me, but he was all right in the end. Tumbled like an egg, he did, Humpty Dumpty, but he lived to tell the tale, didn't he?

My temper came back, but my memory was getting worse. I was retreating into myself, the doctors said. Whatever that means. "She's going where no one can hurt her," they whispered to Luke. "Inside her own mind."

I worried that he was conspiring with them. How could he? I didn't want him around anymore if I couldn't trust him. Angry, he told me he was afraid I would travel without him. Was that all I was to him? A ticket around the world, around history? I looked into my husband's eyes, and I didn't know them anymore.

He faded away.

"Write it all down," said the doctor. "Write it all down, and maybe someday it will all make sense. Good therapy, good for the soul and good for your mind."

At first, I resisted, remember? I didn't like making my letters and seeing how slowly they all came together. But I was so bored.

Boredom makes us do strange things. So, I wrote it all down and left it for someone to find. Maybe they'll make sense of me.

Maybe they will love Rose Gray.

It's over. I don't believe there is more for me to find. She was coming undone, she'd said so herself. What had she meant by "Luke had faded away?" From her memory, from her love, or from her life? He had signed her out, let her go; that much I knew. How could he just leave her?

I am prepared now to accept what I have been rejecting before: the Lost had to be real. Maybe their genes had something special; maybe cutting edge medical research would discover it someday. In the meantime, what am I to do with the knowledge?

I tuck the diary back in my handbag but don't move from Mina's bed. This was the only place I had thought to come to read in peace. Nestled above the ruckus of the party, I can only just hear the merry making. I wonder if Sam is looking for me, but I do not know what to say to him, and until I do, I don't want to be near him. I can still feel the scorching burn of his kiss on my mouth, the way he hungrily seemed to need only me, my shy and willing response, but that doesn't mean I trust him.

If he knew of the Lost, could it be he is one of them? Would he go to sleep one night, and I would never see him again? The thought seems ridiculous, and yet, it fits.

Something else doesn't fit though, and that's Luke. I don't think he would have left Rose. He seemed to really love her; completely and utterly. A terrible thought is pushing itself up to the surface, and I don't want it to break free. If I don't allow it to fully form, I can push it back under the waters. It's a thought I want to drown.

Is the boy I know as Sam the man Rose knows as Luke?

Chapter 26

I'm still there, curled up on Mina's enormous bed like a tiny spider in a huge web, when the door opens. At first, my stomach tightens, worried that it could be the masked Rose, come to confront me, but it's only Amy, Mina's little sister.

"What are you doing?" Amy bounces onto the bed, and makes me bounce with her. I steady myself.

"Taking a break from the party. What are you doing?" I slip my bag under my arm where prying little eyes can't see it.

"I can't go to the party." Her lip sticks out in an adorable pout. Amy is five and very precocious. I've only met her one other time—it seems as though Mrs. Dobson hides her away—but I found her to be very smart and quick. Also, she makes me laugh with her antics. "Can I sneak in under your dress?"

"Under my dress? I think not."

"Like Mother Gigogne? From the ballet? It's big enough."

"You should be in bed."

"I know. I know. But it's boring in bed. I want to go to the party. You hardly fill it out. There's plenty of room." The lip sticks even further out.

"I know it's hard to be little—"

"I'm not little!"

"I know it's hard to be littler than everyone else and feel like you're missing all the fun." I keep my voice stern, like I assume a mother would do. "But someday you'll be big and grown up and can go to all the parties. I promise." I yawn and pat her curls encouragingly.

She scowls. "That's not for forever! Tell me what's happening down there." She snuggles in closer.

"Hmm. Well, there **is** a wild pig about!"

"A wild pig?" Amy leans in, in delight. "For real?"

"Yes, I think so. Danvers is trying to trap him with butter, so we can cook him for Christmas. He's very big and will be delicious with onion and gravy."

"Yum! What else?" She leans down on the pillow with me, wide eyed. "Is there anyone kissing my sister?"

"Amy! Of course not. What a thing to say."

"Well, Mummy says I must report back to her if I see anyone kissing my sister, that's all. She's not allowed to get rumpy pumpy with anyone."

I can't help but laugh at her choice of words, but disguise it in a cough. I wish, though, that I had a mother or a sister who cared whether anyone kissed me. I touch my lips, remembering.

"What else, what else? Is the food wonderful? Are the gowns beautiful? Is the dancing perfect?" Her blue eyes are starry and dream filled. I remember being a dream-filled orphan.

"The dancing is exhausting, and I was nearly gored to death by a rabid reindeer. The gowns are nice enough, if you like that sort of thing, and I know you do. The food is superb, but you know that already; Cook makes it for you every night." I poke her in the ribs.

"Yes, but mine is served on dumb plates with dumb drinks and dumb forks. It's all dumb."

"You're being ridiculous. It tastes the same."

"Does not." Amy deepens her scowl in her determination to prove her point.

"Does too! What kind—"

The door opens again, this time in a burst of urgency.

"Amy!" exclaims Mrs. Dobson. She is dressed in a huge gown of blue. "Amy, come here this instant!" I am startled to see the white swan peer over her shoulder—Miss Helmes. The entire party seems to be relocating to Mina's boudoir. I will never understand the habits of the rich.

"I told you," Mrs. Dobson hisses to Miss Helmes. "Amy, come here!" This time she snaps her fingers, no small feat in silk gloves, and Amy scurries to her side.

"I will take care of this, ma'am," the swan responds. "Lizzie, you shouldn't be here. Amy is supposed to be in her bed, and you are supposed to be downstairs." Mrs. Dobson and Amy leave, Mrs. Dobson stomping dramatically, Amy dragging her feet.

"I'm sorry." I frown, but don't get up from the bed. "I had a headache, and Amy found me here."

"Well, Mrs. Dobson doesn't want you..." pause, "associating with Amy. Come downstairs and rejoin the party, please."

"Well, that's slightly insulting," I grouse, but I take my leave of Mina's wonderful bed. I don't forget my handbag. "I'm not that bad of an example for the little thing."

"You know how the wealthy are." Miss Helmes' pat on my shoulder is very nearly sympathetic. She must have had a boatload of champagne to be feeling so magnanimous. "But don't wander off. It's not good form. And your young man was looking for you."

"He isn't my young man."

"Hmm. You might tell him that then. He's very nearly pulled this place apart looking for you. I don't approve of love affairs in the work place, you know." She sniffs.

"Yes, ma'am. I will keep my love affairs to a minimum, ma'am. I am trying to cut down, you know. One love affair a week, I promise. Two maximum and three strictly on holidays."

My sarcasm is wasted, as we are at the bottom of the stairs, and the swan that is Miss Helmes has rejoined the crowd. I am left alone in a sea of people again. Lucky me. I miss Mina's bed more than ever. Mrs. Dobson doesn't want me associating with Amy? Well, I don't want to associate with anyone.

"You scared us, Lizzie!" Mina appears at my side, like a fretful apparition. "Where have you been? Sam has been looking all over for you!"

"I've been," I frown, "Around. No need to send out Scotland Yard, for goodness sake. Suddenly, everyone is concerned about my whereabouts."

"You scared us, is all." Mina's pretty eyes fill up with tears at my rebuke. "I worry about you."

"Well, don't," I respond, fondly, and kiss her cheek. "I'm sorry for being a dreadful party guest. I very nearly took a nap on your lovely bed. I probably mussed your pillow. Forgive me?"

"Oh, you!" Mina returns the kiss affectionately. "You're welcome anytime."

"I doubt it," I think, remembering her mother's reaction to seeing me, but it's a nice enough sentiment, so I don't make a rebuttal. "How goes the tumultuous love match with Mack? He confess his love yet? Because he did to me. Confess his love for you, I mean."

Mina waves away the notion with one sweep of her pretty white hand. "He's just a boy, not like your handsome thing. There Sam is, over there.

Oh, look! He's still looking for you. Lizzie, go put him out of his misery, for goodness sake!" She peers across the ballroom, where I can see Sam pacing. Dancers whirl and twirl in front of him, as if they are going double time, while he moves in slow motion. I don't want to go to him, and yet, I do. My feet seem to move of their own accord and their own volition. I want to make them turn away, go another direction, any direction, but they are on a set course towards Sam.

I push through dancers like they aren't even there, like they're a cobweb I move aside. The reindeer grunts when our bodies hit, but I keep walking. Sam sees me, and his whole demeanor relaxes. He runs his hands through his already mussed hair and stays put, waiting for me to come to him. Irritating thing.

I reach him. We stand, our bodies facing one another, but neither move to touch the other. I want him to... I think.

"You had me concerned." His voice is gruff. He clears his throat.

"Concerned for what?" I counter.

"I couldn't find you." His eyes are clouded, possibly angry. It occurs to me I don't know what he looks like when he's angry. Is this it, then?

"I wasn't far. You don't need to be so controlling of my whereabouts just because you brought me here." Wonderful. I sound about as mature as Amy. I stop myself before I can scowl and put my hands on my hips, or maybe stomp my feet, or throw myself on the floor and kick my legs and flail about. The possibilities are endless when you don't have maturity to hold you back.

"Yes, I do," he snaps.

"And why is that?" This time I do put my hands on my hips, if only to stop their trembling. "Do you worry that I'm not safe here?" Does he know? Does he suspect Rose is here?

"I think you know why." Sam searches my face as if looking for answers, but he's the one with all the answers, isn't he?

"Do I? I don't think I know half of what you know." I reach out then, and pull him away from the crowd, into an alcove. "Tell me about the Lost. Are they real?" I pull him into me, as well. He's so close, I could count every eyelash.

Sam continues to search my face. He's going to consume me whole this way, I think. "Yes," he murmurs. "They're real."

I have so many questions; I don't know where to start. We look at each other, me in dismay, and he in what looks like sadness. After what seems an eternity, I ask the one that means the most. "Are you one of them?"

Another eternity passes. I know, because I have grown up. He tenderly tucks my hair behind my ear again, but in answer, he doesn't answer, not with words. He just bends down and kisses me.

Chapter 27

"I think I saw her. I know I saw her." Better to leave no room for doubt, I think.

"Where?" Sam looks at me, confused. "Here? Now?"

"A bit ago. Outside, on the other side of the window I was standing at." We are outside now, strolling through the paths and walkways of Mina's estate, like a pair of lovers, only we are too distracted by other things to properly play the part. There are others, though, who hide off in dark corners, giggling and toying with each other. I feel slightly jealous. Why are we the ones affected by time travel? I have changed my opinion of the whole thing. Once I thought it would be delightful to never be tied down, to wake up someplace new; now I want Sam anchored here with me forever. At least I think I do. "Over there." I gesture back towards the north side of the mansion.

"Did she know you?"

Strange question. Then again, maybe it isn't. She may have recognized me from my odd night in Bedlam, when she scrawled her name on the wall and pulled the diary out of my hands. I always thought she knew me somehow, but I attributed the feeling to the way she addressed her reader in the diary. "I don't know. She seemed to want me to see her. Do we look for her? Sam, I don't know what to do. This whole thing is too fantastic. I don't even know where to start." I don't really want to talk about Rose. I'm consumed with how long I have with Sam before he sleeps and leaves me forever. "How long?"

"How long what?" he replies, carefully, but I know he knows what I'm referring to: how long before he leaves me.

"Don't waste time being polite."

"I never do. I just..." He runs his fingers through his hair again. He has lost his mask somewhere. "I just don't know how to say everything that should be said."

"You're trying to figure out how much I know, you mean." A bit of bitterness creeps into my voice, unbidden.

He appears taken aback at my honesty. "Yes," he murmurs. "I suppose you could say that."

"What is your name? Don't lie to me, please, Sam. I can't bear that." I also can't bear having kissed a married man, but one unbearable thing at a time, if you please.

"What is a name? It doesn't matter." We had paused in the darkness of a willow tree, but now he moves on again, restless.

"It does matter. It does matter if your name is Luke Dawes!" I catch up and grasp at his elbow. I stare into his beautiful face, his dark, disloyal face. "How could you? How could you?" He won't look at me though, and I find my legs giving out. I sink to the cold ground. "How could you?" I repeat, but it's little more than a whisper.

For a long moment, no one says anything, and just when I think he is going to walk away from me, he folds up his long legs and sits down. Close, but not too close. I think he knows I wouldn't stand for it. "Rose is gone," he says, carefully.

"No, she isn't."

"She is." His tone is firm. "She's been gone for some time. I don't think she's coming back. The girl I loved is," his voice cracks, "gone. I've tried everything I can. Eventually, I'm going to travel. We've been here over a year, and it's been months since I've seen her. She doesn't know me anymore. What am I to do? I can't find her."

"I'm not sure you've tried hard enough." The bitterness is back. I don't look at him; instead, I wind blades of grass through my fingertips and sift dirt. My lovely gown is getting mussed and dirty. I will never wear it again, so it hardly matters. I may even burn it after tonight.

"You'll never know how hard I've tried," he answers, harshly. "It isn't as though I want to move on without her; she's my wife. God! She's my wife."

"You do still love her then?" Now my voice is small, like a tiny child's. What do I want him to say? That he does? That he doesn't? He's damned if he does and damned if he doesn't, and either one leaves me behind.

"I always will. But, Lizzie," Sam—Luke—reaches for my hand. I sternly tell my body to thwart him, to pull away, but it doesn't obey, and my traitorous hand holds his desperately.

"Don't say it."

"Why? It's true. I love you."

I do pull away then. "Don't say that! Just don't. You can't," I answer, flatly. "Not if you still love her."

"I would have said the same thing just a few weeks ago, but something's changed. This wasn't part of my plan."

"What exactly was your plan? Playing bridge and driving cars—" I stop, horrified. "That car is stolen, isn't it?"

"That's the top of your worries right now?" Sam looks amused. I can't think of him as Luke; he'll always be Sam to me. "I'll give it back if you like. I'd like to do something right to please you in all of this."

"Forget the car. I haven't forgotten what Rose spoke about with you. You're a murderer. You met her in Bedlam, and then you helped terrorize her family. How can that be you?" I can't reconcile what I feel for Sam with what I know of Luke. This is ridiculous. Why ever did I allow myself to fall for him, much less come wandering out into the night with him

230

with no protection? Am I the dullest girl in all of history? This man has rubbed shoulders with Jack the Ripper. He has spent time locked up in a mental institution. He steals cars when he's bored. Even Marianne would be out of her element and run away, screaming. Then why am I not moving?

"You can't believe everything Rose says."

"Can't I? I assumed so when I didn't believe the Lost were real. Now I don't know what to believe. I know you're a liar."

"Yes." This is said slowly. He is proceeding with caution. "But if I've lied to you, it's been to protect you. You've become intertwined with Rose's life. She won't let you go now."

The thought is somewhat horrifying, but also not surprising. "Wonderful. You go traveling off to some magical island, and I'll just stay behind and fend off your violent wife. I feel like Jane Eyre. You should have locked her in the attic."

"An attic wouldn't hold her." I can't believe we're joking about this, but a smile curls his mouth. "And you wouldn't believe how difficult it is to find a decent Grace Poole these days. But I have been thinking about an idea."

"What?" I still don't think I should be sitting out here in the dark with him, but my feet are loath to move. How is possible to be so comfortable with a possible murderer? There must be something wrong with me. Is this what love does? Makes you blind and stupid? I was better off without it.

"Nora."

I'm confused, though that's becoming my normal state of mind. "Nora? In Bedlam? What of her? She doesn't know anything. Whatever she does know is locked away inside her mind."

"But if we can get her to remember just enough, just enough to help me travel where I need to go..." he trails off. And looks at me expectantly, as though what he said just made any sense at all.

"Where do you need to go? I don't understand." I shake my head.

"I think," he proceeds carefully. "I think if I can bring back Sonnet and Noah, they could help Rose."

I'm appalled. "For one thing, if you think they'd help, you're as batty as Rose."

"You don't know Sonnet like I do."

"Whatever. She'd be a fool to come anywhere near her sister after she what she did to her." I remember the entry about the locked house, not to mention the murder of her best friend. Not things easily forgivable. "Besides, you couldn't find her. She could be anywhere."

"I know where she is."

I sit up straight and gape at him. "What? How? You didn't tell Rose?"

"No. She was losing all touch with reality. I knew all along where they would end up after 1888, but I didn't think it would help anyone to say. When we, Rose and I, found them the first time, when we found Noah's arrest record, I found something else: an article about a hospital in Africa that named Israel Rhode as a founder and a photo that said, *Not pictured: Noah Gray, Sonnet Gray.*"

"I can't believe you kept that from her all this time. When? Where and when?"

"1889. They hadn't traveled eras yet, just continents. Like we suspected, actually. After Emme's funeral, they just ran. Probably followed Dr. Smythe's footsteps: they were living with him at the time. I don't know how long they stay there, but I know they were there in October of 1889. I know the village even. I think this could work."

"If you can convince them to come back here with you and Nora. And if we can get Nora to remember how to manipulate traveling. She's been here for a long time, hasn't she? Years and years, and she hasn't woken up anywhere new!" I'm skeptical of such a wild idea, and I'm also not convinced he won't travel away and leave me with his wife.

"But if it works, if we come back, I could possibly get Rose back. The sight of Sonnet, of Rose's obsession, could be what brings her back. Something tells me you won't be with me when there's still a chance of finding and helping Rose. And if it doesn't work," he falters. "Then I have to move on."

What an insane mess I've gotten into. I long suddenly for boredom, for changing bedpans, for sewing circles with Mina. My heart is heavy, and my head aches. I want him to kiss me, and yet I regret the ones we already shared. They are filled with poison.

"There's nothing in it for me either way," I reply, bitterly. "I'm in love with a married man, and not just a married man, but one who will disappear forever at any moment. I should go away and never come back. That's what I should do."

"Please don't." He has to know I won't, but he still looks worried. I'd smooth his anxious brow if I didn't still want to slap him silly. "You made a vow to help those who needed your help."

"That's a cheap shot." I almost choke on the bitterness. "And it's not fair."

"I know. She needs help, Lizzie. You're the only one who can help me. I don't have much time. If I travel without her, I'm gone forever. I can't get back the way she can. And she won't look for me because she doesn't know me any longer."

I'm silent for what feels like ages, while I quietly will myself to be somewhere else, anywhere else. If I could travel through time, I'd go anywhere right now and never come back.

"All right," I say, at last. "What do you want me to do?"

* * *

Stay where he could find me again, he'd said. Stay awake. Don't be alone. Don't go home. Stay where there are plenty of people: Bedlam. He'd pay Miss Helmes, he said, so she wouldn't give me any trouble. He'd look for me in Nora's room when he got back.

Which is where we are now, convincing an old woman that she holds special powers.

It's not going well.

"I imagine Carolina was a beautiful baby," Sam is saying conversationally. He is holding her paper thin hands and helping her eat a biscuit, as though it was any other unremarkable tête-à-tête. We've been here for three hours. I want to jump out of my skin. "And remember when she married Noah? He is a nice man."

"He drinks too much," Nora says, then.

I do jump at that, and even Sam allows his eyebrows to shoot up. "You remember?"

"I remember something," she replies, slowly. "Some things I remember now. How do you know my baby? Carolina?"

"I've never met her, Nora, but you're my grandmother." Sam leans forward and I can tell he wants to embrace her out of excitement, but he doesn't. Good call on his part: the insane don't appreciate random acts of affection. Of course, being married to Rose, he probably knows that better than anyone. "Carolina had a little girl, two little girls actually: Rose and Sonnet. I'm Rose's husband, and I need to find Sonnet. If I tell you where and when she is, can you take me there? Bring us back here?"

"Through time, you mean?" Nora looks appalled. "I don't do that anymore. I had forgotten. It's been so long, hasn't it? Look at my hands. Am I very old?" The spider veins and wrinkles and age spots are like a novel written on her hands.

Neither Sam nor I want to answer. Finally, Sam nods. "It's been a long time. But you can help us now. It's very important that I get to Sonnet and bring her here. Will you help? Do you think you can do it?"

It took another hour. Another hour of biting my nails, my stomach churning, Sam being ever patient. For a thieving murderer, as Rose called him, he was long-suffering and calm. I kept jumping at the slightest sounds, which, when you're at Bedlam, is a silly thing to do. The sounds here are endless. Once, Miss Helmes walked by. She saw me sitting there, by the side of Nora's bed, but she didn't say anything. It was a new day, the day after the ball, and she looked a bit worse for wear. So do I, after being up all night. My ball gown feels heavy and cumbersome. I lost my mask. I lost the diary. I suppose it doesn't matter. I tell myself it doesn't matter, though soon it may be the only link to Sam I'll ever have. Small comfort. Here I am, helping the man I love fight for the sanity of his wife. It doesn't get any stranger. I should have my head examined. I wonder if Dr. Ford has any openings later in the week.

Once Nora was convinced and agreed to try, Sam produced a bottle of Nightfall pills from his jacket. He had her swallow three of them with her water. I watched her throat move as they went down. He swallowed four of them himself. Too wired up to sleep, he told me.

What about me? I wanted to say. But I was useless. I could only sit there and watch as Sam tucked Nora back into her bed. She watched me under hooded eyes until they closed.

"How long?" I ask him. He has lain down next to her. It should seem strange to see a young man next to an old lady, holding her hand, but somehow it doesn't. Of course everything in my life is strange lately, so perhaps it's just in comparison.

"Not long." He begins to talk to her of 1889. The sights, the smells, the feel of Africa. He speaks of Sonnet and of Noah. He talks about things like the plains, and sick children, the heat, the desert. He repeats 1889 over and over again, until I personally want to scream. Eventually, he stops murmuring and I know he's asleep.

And all I can do is watch and wait, and hope that Rose isn't nearby, doing the same.

Chapter 28

If I hadn't seen it, I never would have believed it. I *have* seen it, and I don't know that I believe it. One moment they were there, curled up in the hospital bed with one thin blanket between them, Sam's feet sticking out the bottom side, and the next, the bed was empty. I don't know what I was expecting, a flash of light, a puff of smoke, but what happened was hardly noisy or theatrical. They were just gone. An indentation in the bed, and that was all to prove they were ever there to begin with. I whimpered like a kitten and found myself clawing at the blanket. The pillow was still warm. I lay on it for a moment, pressing it to my face, trying to smell him. I didn't even really get to say goodbye.

My life is a train wreck. This is insanity. What am I doing? They had neatly escaped Rose's clutches and left me to fend for myself. I had no promise that they would or even could come back. And if they did? What then? Use Sonnet to lure Rose back, that's what. If we were all lucky, it would bring back Rose's memory, and if we were luckier still it'd only bring back the good parts. If there were any. I'd read her diary; I wasn't feeling hopeful. Rose was as sociopathic as they came. I didn't think she had any good feelings to fall back on. If we weren't lucky, Rose would finish off her sister for good, and she and Sam would retire to their island getaway and leave me to find a good physiologist and maybe a Holy Father to confess my sins to.

There was no happy ending for me. I had to face it. I couldn't travel with Sam, and he couldn't stop himself. Even if Rose was out of the picture, it would do nothing for me. I was going to be alone, and I may as well face it. Maybe I could dedicate my life to finding a cure for the Lost. Wouldn't that be wonderfully ironic?

I smooth my hair with my fingers and braid it the way I used to. Something should feel normal around here. I go down to the laundry and get myself out of my ball gown and into a uniform. I leave the gown crumpled in a corner, and then I change my mind and toss it in the potato bin. I never want to see it again. I make my way down to the kitchen to beg for some tea. I'm still jumpy, and it doesn't help that I've been up all night, but I don't see how I'll ever go to sleep again. If I do, my dreams will be filled with horrible nightmares; I'm sure of it. My cheeks are wet with tears, and I rub them away harshly with my fists. I haven't seen Mina yet, or Mack, but I do see what looks like Dr. Ford's immense frame from a long way away, down one of the long hallways. I have no idea anymore if I'm scheduled to work today, but I figure no one else knows or cares either. I can blend in well enough, though if I don't look busy and scrub something, Miss Helmes will have my head.

The tea is weak and bitter, the way Bedlam's tea always is, and the only food I can find is someone's leftover tray from breakfast. I hope it wasn't full of crushed up medication, because I devour every bite quickly. If I feel dizzy or sleepy, I only have myself to blame. Though, lately, I swear, dizzy is the norm for me. I imagine dizziness and feelings of anxiety are common side effects of too many fantastic, improbable goings-on.

I hadn't even asked when to expect them back, if they came back at all, that is. Would it be immediately? A week? A month? Could Nora steer them through time so effectively that only moments would have passed for me here? I hope so. I hope Sam is back in Nora's room right now.

I know for them it could take time to locate Sonnet and Noah—even if Sam is correct and knows exactly where and when they are—and a lot more time to convince them to come back. It could take weeks maybe, in their time. They know him as Luke—Luke, the violent sidekick to Rose and her delusions. Israel Rhode didn't seem a pushover; how would they convince him? Even Rose was nervous around him, and Luke's history with him was anything but friendly. I'd say they hate one another's guts really.

No, the odds are not in our favor. If I were Sonnet I'd run him out of town. I wouldn't want anything to do with Rose Gray. Then I consider an angle I hadn't thought of before: if Nora and Rose are the only ones who manipulate time, then Sonnet might have use of them after all. Would it be possible to go back and right the wrongs? Would Sonnet wonder the same thing? I'm not well versed on the thought process of changing history, but if anyone could do it, it'd be the Lost. What if Sonnet could go back and catch Carolina before she fell? What if she could save Emme that night in Victorian London, save her from Jack? If I were Sonnet, wouldn't I try?

I hear a creaking sound and nearly jump out of my skin before my mind registers the fact that I know this particular creak. It's Mr. Limpet's wheelchair, and sure enough, he rounds the corner and stops at my feet. He is still under heavy medication, I can tell, though he is no longer being completely sedated. His eyes are heavy and hooded and red rimmed, and he has the ever present bit of spittle at his mouth. He looks up at me in alarm.

"Hello, Mr. Limpet. Lovely day for a stroll, isn't it?" I pat his head like I would a puppy.

"Lizzie? That you?" He squints up at me. "I haven't seen you in too long. I thought she got you."

"Who, Mr. Limpet?"

"That wicked girl. The one who threw the scissors. She's always here." He glares at the walls. "I've been here longer than anyone, and she's always here. Can't get away from that blasted girl."

Now I know he's not insane, or at least not in this regard. Poor man. He knew and was trying to avoid Rose all along. I should have paid better attention to him. I feel terrible.

"I'll keep an eye out for her," I promise. "Don't worry. She won't come after you if you stay out of her way."

"It's not me I'm worried about." Mr. Limpet glares again. He really is in a mood.

"I'll take care of everyone." Of course I will. Keep her away from everyone, especially me, the girl who kissed her husband; if she has a vendetta for anyone, it's me. And then? Well, that's up to Sam and Sonnet. "Go back to your room. I'll see if Miss Helmes can convince Cook to make those honey carrots you like so much."

"Honey carrots aren't gonna keep that girl at bay," he answers, darkly. "She's here. I can feel her. And she's close."

Not a comforting thought, but I force a smile and repeat my offer of honey carrots as I push him back along the corridor the way he had come.

I don't want to admit it, but I can feel her too.

* * *

Sam isn't in Nora's room when I get back. He isn't in the hallway, he isn't in the dining room, and he isn't in Bedlam. I know it's only been a couple of hours, but I'm worried and anxious and every bump and noise makes me jump. Miss Helmes asks me if I am all right and when I say I am, she snaps at me to earn my pay and quit wandering the halls like a cat. I busy myself in the largest, most populated room, and read books to one patient, help feed another. Still, the time slips ever so slowly by. I feel sick.

What if they never came back? What should I do? No one would believe my story, even with Nora gone. They'd assume that she had escaped. What else could they think? No one would even care; she had no family that they knew of. No one had visited her in years. Meanwhile, Rose is somewhere, doing or planning who knows what, or just existing, not knowing who she is. I am the only one who knows her. Well, and Mr. Limpet, but he's hardly helpful. What could he do, fight her off with carrots? No, I am utterly, hopelessly, on my own.

The day has faded into evening. I'm so tired I can't see straight. My head is still aching, but still he doesn't come.

* * *

I have to sleep in Nora's room. There is nothing else for me to do, or if there is, I can't think what it could be. I could go back to my flat, but it's dark out now, and I don't relish the walk. There was a day when I could walk the streets of London carefree. I didn't check behind me. I didn't pay attention to every noise. Those days, I fear, are long gone. The thought of sleeping in Nora's bed, in a lunatic asylum, makes me nervous and anxious in all sorts of ways I can't explain, but unless I want to stay up another night, I'm out of options. I'm going on too little sleep as it is. How do the Lost do it? Force themselves to stay awake, then force themselves to sleep. It's no small wonder they're a little odd. I would be, too.

One thing I can't bring myself to do: don Nora's nightgown. No, there are some boundaries I cannot cross, and wearing an old lady's sleepwear is one of them. I lie down in my uniform, and burrow deep beneath her blankets. It seems peculiar to be in the same spot that Sam and Nora were when they disappeared. Had no one else in the history of man watched a Lost person vanish before? Was I the first? It seemed strange, but I suppose there have been tales of vanishing and disappearance for as long as tales have been around. Have I known other Lost? The thought is intriguing enough to distract me from my real problems: Sam and Rose. I ponder a girl who went missing a few years back at the orphanage, and an old man who used to beg for scraps outside the bakery by my flat until one day he was gone and no one knew where. We assumed the girl had run away, though at the time I thought it strange, and no one had even bothered to look for the old man.

I yawn, and will myself to think of more people I have known who have left me. The list is depressingly long, my parents included. I don't remember them at all. Eventually, I sleep.

*　*　*

I awake to the sound of rustling and scraping. My eyes open; they rest on the doorknob of Nora's door, just barely illuminated by the moon. There is nothing there, and the doorknob does not move, does not turn the way it might in a scary picture or in my overactive imagination. Why then did I wake and my attentions fly there? It's no good willing my bad feelings to go away, so I gingerly make my way out of Nora's blanket (I have always wrapped myself up in covers at night the way a swaddling baby would prefer) and walk swiftly to the door, barefoot. I had wanted to lock myself in as a precaution against Rose, but being a mental hospital, locks are hardly the norm, not on the inside. We don't want our patients locking the staff out and doing God knows what inside. Instead, I had borrowed a chair from the dining area and tipped it beneath the knob, hoping it would do the trick. I move the chair silently aside and place my hand on the knob. I wouldn't mind a trip to the kitchen anyway and maybe a cup of hot tea. Nora's room is freezing. How does she sleep in this temperature? I think perhaps I'll try convincing Miss Helmes to heat the hospital better tomorrow. There's nothing like seeing the place through an inmate's eyes.

The knob doesn't turn, and I realize quickly that I'm locked in. Had it been Miss Helmes? We only lock in the new patients and the violent ones typically, and Nora is neither. She's been here forever, and she's as meek as a lamb. I can't imagine why Miss Helmes would have locked the door, but then again, I have never understood Miss Helmes. She confounds me.

I will my heart to slow down. There's no reason for alarm. After all, being locked inside a safe room when there is possibly a vindictive wife out to get me isn't the worst thing, not if Miss Helmes pocketed the key and didn't leave it resting in the knob on the other side for anyone to turn, that is. I will simply have to wait for Miss Helmes or the morning staff to let me out once the sun rises.

That's when I realize something else. The sound that woke me makes yet another noise, a kind of scratching, a kind of hissing, but it isn't coming from the door. No, it's coming from the other side, closer to the bed, closer to where my head had lain moments before. Confused, I turn slowly and peer into the darkness. The moon illuminates the bed and the figure crouched by the foot. The head down by the knees, small, almost like a child. I know instantly it's too small for Sam, but it could be Nora. Would she have come back without him? Where was Sam?

But it isn't Nora. I know when I look harder. Her yellow hair spills over her shoulders, and I know this is the same girl I had seen in last night's moonlight, framed by the window. I know it's Rose, and I'm afraid.

While I was concerned she could be wandering the halls of Bedlam, frightening Mr. Limpet, pinning someone's hand to the wall with scissors, maybe even following Mina home or searching my flat, she was with me all along. How long had she been near me, hiding by Nora's bed? Had she shut us in together somehow? With a chill, I remember Sonnet, locked in an old, crumbling house, alone. Rose would have cheerily let her starve, if not for Luke intervening.

Luke.

Sam.

Where was he?

My thoughts race, millions of them per second, it feels. I will my breaths to calm, not come out in shuddering gasps like they want to. What does she want from me? Is she here for revenge, a displaced wife, scorned and vengeful, or is she here for help, for shelter? Does she know I've read her diary, that I'm perhaps the person who knows her best?

If she didn't walk in here while I was sleeping, then she must have traveled here, anchored to Bedlam the way she always was and would be. Had she simply woke here then?

My mind is coming up with all sorts of questions, but no answers. I am shut in with a murderess and have no recourse, except my training as a nurse. She is small, but so am I, and she has violent rage on her side. I only have fear. Overpowering her is not something I'm eager to jump to, not without reasoning first. This was the lonely girl who had some love in her heart—Solomon, Luke—and I would not abandon all hope of sanity quite yet. I would find some redemption in her if it killed me. The thought chills.

I only have to keep her calm until Sam and Sonnet and Nora arrive.

That's all.

She lifts her head and gazes at me with such a forlorn expression of grief
and sadness that my heart feels as though it stops. I grow even colder
when she says my name - I am virtually made of ice, I think, and I will
melt away - and just like that, when she begins to speak, slowly and
carefully, I know my life is over and I am going to die.

Chapter 29

"Please let me out!" I scream and throw myself against the door to Nora's room. Outside, in the hallway, there is sweet escape from Rose. I can hear Miss Helmes on the other side, but she does not help me.

Rose stands by the window and watches me, sadly. She has not spoken in moments, not since I began banging on the door. The things she said before I cannot even bear thinking of. I see her sigh, and she turns and faces the window. Her face is reflected there, a mirror image of what I saw on the night of the masquerade ball: a beautiful face with yellow hair, and deep, bottomless blue eyes.

"Miss Helmes! Please! Why are you doing this to me?" I sink to the floor, but I don't give up beating on the door, from my knees.

I hear footfalls in the hallway and hushed voices. They come, and they go. They have for what feels like hours. I swear I heard Mack and Dr. Ford, but they do not help me. Why won't they help me? What madness is this?

"Lizzie?" I hear Mina's sweet voice from the other side of the heavy door, and I feel a rush of relief and thanksgiving.

"Mina! Mina, tell them to let me out. She's here with me! Rose Gray is in here! Don't let her hurt me! I need to get out! Please, Mina, unlock the door!"

Unbelievably, I don't hear the sound of a key turning. I stare hard at the knob, but it does not turn. Has my only friend abandoned me then?

"Lizzie, no one is going to hurt you." Mina's soft voice comes through the crack in the door. I press my ear to it to listen and imagine I can feel her breath. "Calm down. Take a deep breath. No one is in there with you."

I sputter with indignation and unbelief. "How can you not believe me? Mina, let me out!" This last time I shout with all the passion and anger I can muster, which is plenty. I never thought she would—could—do this to me. And for what? What was their gain?

I turn to face Rose, but she still stares out the window. She's quiet as a mouse, blast her, not making a sound to let my friends know that she is here. I hear more footfalls, and these ones are familiar. Sam's.

I want to cry out, but my voice is strained and cracked, and I can't catch my breath. I hear his incredulous rebuke of Miss Helmes, and I want to cry with thanks. He will make them let me out, and then they will all see who they locked me in here with. They'll be so sorry. I will kiss him, and right in front of his wife, too. I won't care. They can get the marriage annulled. He won't stay with her after I tell him what she told me. He wouldn't be so cruel. No one would. Jack the Ripper himself would take pity on me.

"You shouldn't have shut her in here." Sam's voice is full of rage. "Do you have no heart at all? Give me the key!"

There is a moment of silence, and I can see Miss Helmes evaluating her options in my imagination, sure as if I were on the right side of the door. She would be standing, with her bony arms crossed against her large breasts, and she would not give him the satisfaction of hurrying to obey him. I hear her yelp, and can't help smiling. She should have given in quicker.

I turn one last time to face Rose Gray, and she turns too, to look at me. She cocks her head, curiously regarding me. I hear the key turn.

"Goodbye, Lizzie," she says, softly. "I loved you." And unbelievably, as though her strange words weren't odd enough, she begins to blur and grow fainter, not like Sam and Nora when they disappeared, more like a fading, like a photo in a darkroom, in liquid, only in reverse, lighter and lighter until she is gone.

I can breathe again, and everything is clear, and everything is right. All's right with the world.

The door explodes open, and I launch myself headlong into his arms. I am pressed up to his coat, my nose buried in the crook of his neck, his familiar smell invading my space; it feels like home. I feel his mouth on mine, and he pulls away, only for a brief, hard moment; then he cups my head and looks at me.

"Luke." I breathe, and when I pull my gaze away, it's only to stroke the neglected ring on my finger: shimmering gold with a single pearl in the center.

And he smiles. "Rose."

Luke. Not Sam. *Rose.* Not Lizzie. I was finally home.

Chapter 30

Everything had come back so swiftly, all at once. Perfect clarity—no more confusion, no more questions. The vision of Rose had shimmered and left and once it did, Luke's name had passed by my lips. Like a cold wind blowing by, Rose Gray left the room, or rather, Lizzie did.

As a little girl, alone and ostracized by the village and by Old Babba, I used to sit and play with Lizzie. She was the only one who ever tried to understand me. She was a good girl, an orphan like me. She was going to be a doctor, and sometimes when I cut myself playing or experimenting, for sometimes my cuts and scrapes were on purpose, she would bandage them for me. She was the only one who loved me, until I got too big for imaginary friends.

After Spain, I began to unravel. We barely made it back to Bedlam together at all. I was coming apart at the seams, and I no longer remembered Luke at times. He was fading from my memory, blurry around the edges, no sound to his voice, no comfort in his arms. He forbade me from traveling anymore, but it was unnecessary; I didn't recall ever having the capability. With Dr. Ford's prodding, and Luke's too, I painstakingly wrote everything down that I could remember. Now I know Luke placed the first diary where he knew I could find it, and the second at the Bodley, where he hoped I would track it. It was the last hope he had. He would have done anything for me. The last time I knew him as Luke, I begged him to just let me go, help me escape the hospital, give me time and space. Maybe it would all come back to me. I could feel myself slipping away, and the thought of doing that in front of him was more than I could bear. He let me go.

After a while, all I could remember was Lizzie. Luke was always there, of course; he never really left, never really went far, but I didn't notice him. He was a stranger to me, and I was building my life as Lizzie. He arranged the flat for me and convinced Miss Helmes to take me on as a nurse. She knew me as Rose, but as long as I was no longer being violent, she was willing to play along; all in her pursuit of science and medicine, or perhaps the wealth it could bring her. If this kind of therapy worked, she could be rich and infamous in the medical world and much more than just the glorified housekeeper. Mina knew, and being sweet Mina, she had confided in her mother. The reason Mrs. Dobson didn't want me near Amy was far from her distaste of the poor. She was frightened of me.

Mr. Limpet knew me as Rose Gray when my hair was loose. He and I had several interactions over the years, the most memorable for him of course being the stairs. When my hair was braided in two plaits, he only saw me as Lizzie, the helpful nurse, and he didn't fear me. Such a pathetic disguise for anyone but him. Him and I, I suppose.

Danvers, of course, isn't Danvers. That's the housekeeper in Daphne du Maurier's Rebecca. The butler's real name is James; I remember that now. And there was no Miss Temple in the orphanage; Miss Temple was the mistress in Jane Eyre's orphanage. Of course, I had no orphanage to begin with, so does it really matter what I call her?

When I felt myself slipping away and losing my memory, Luke had distanced himself like I asked him to, but he couldn't keep it up indefinitely, not if he wanted a chance of being with me. Eventually, he would travel on without me. If I had no memory of being Lost, I would lose the ability, like my grandmother had. He couldn't risk it; he didn't have time. He had to interfere to save me. And save me he has. In many ways, I think.

The night at the ball, when I had seen Rose in the window—it wasn't a window. It was a mirror on the wall.

Mirror, mirror, on the wall... I remember that story from the library. Grimm's Fairy Tales. Solomon read it to me one dark night, while the thunder crashed outside. I remember the voices he used for each character, and I remember the way my eyes followed along the print with his finger, as I learned to read. I remember the Bodley, and the sideshow. I remember Old Babba and her cackling prophecies: *Goosebumps. Someone has just walked on your grave, little girl, on your grave.* I remember Sonnet and our father. I remember the way my mother's hair blew around her face. I remember my wedding day.

I remember everything.

~ The End ~

Acknowledgements and Notes

I could not write a paragraph, much less a page, without the following
people:

My husband, who thinks I'm Supergirl, even when I get tangled in my
cape

My kids, who don't mind popcorn for lunch (again)

My parents and siblings, even the one who hasn't read the first book yet
(ahem, Dad)

My fan base (quality, not quantity), whether in person or on online. I
couldn't have done this without you and all your shout-outs,
encouragements, eagerness, and drum rolls (and occasional eye rolls)

Libraries everywhere

Finally, Shadows Falling is a work of fiction, but some things are true.
Nathaniel Lee was an English playwright who was incarcerated in
Bedlam, during which time he uttered the infamous quote, "They called
me mad, and I called them mad, and damn them, they outvoted me." This
quote was far too wonderful to pass up – thank you, Nathaniel!

The Roxyettes later became the Rockettes

Mad Tom O' Bedlam is a poem that dates back as far as the 1600s. For the
most mad musical version, check out Charlene Kaye and the Brilliant
Eyes. It's marvelously twisted and catchy and I adore it.

Gretna Green is the site of many secret weddings, and my 13 year old self,
who ate up Regency Romances by the dozen, just had to make mention of
it

Lillian Gish and Mary Pickford were the Jennifer Anistons and Angelina
Jolies of their day

Sylvia Plath was a recipient (or victim) of electric shock therapy

Lobotomies were a common practice and began around the late eighteen hundreds: removing small pieces of bone by drilling in the hope that violent patients would become calmer and passive (some were so calm and passive afterwards, they were dead). Walter Freeman was the most notorious lobotomy doctor, and was famous for performing them with ice picks, sometimes in a factory line session and as quickly as ten minutes each (trying to break his own speed record), and was reputed to have performed them on up to 25 women a day. He was killed by a patient

Bethlem Royal Hospital (Bedlam) was relocated in 1931. The thought of ghosts being at each location is a delicious thought that first came to my mind at the very beginning of Shadows Falling. What if Rose came back to the wrong location? Though this ended up not playing as large a part as I first planned, I still enjoy the idea. They did charge admission to see the "lunatyks" on the second Tuesday of each month, back in the day. They also allowed their patients to hold dances. There are many sources on the history of the hospital, each more disturbing than the last. Truth is stranger than fiction, and never more so than here in Bedlam.

About the author

Melyssa Williams is a mom, sister, daughter, wife, friend, ballet teacher, ex-contemporary dancer, writer, and blogger, who resides in Southern Oregon. She was homeschooled back in the day when it was slightly odd and eccentric, which came in handy when she decided to be a writer. She drinks coffee too often and reads fiction at inopportune times. She has parented inner city teens and wants to sky dive, but that's the extent of her excitement. Other than that, she finds baking bread and sipping wine to be the most thrilling parts of life.

She can be reached at: http://melyssawilliams.com